YOU DON'T
KNOW JACK

YOU DON'T KNOW JACK

ERIN McCARTHY

BRAVA

KENSINGTON PUBLISHING CORP.

http://www.kensingtonbooks.com

BRAVA BOOKS are published by

Kensington Publishing Corp.
850 Third Avenue
New York, NY 10022

All Kensington titles, imprints and distributed lines are available at special quantity discounts for bulk purchases for sales promotion, premiums, fund-raising, educational or institutional use.

Special book excerpts or customized printings can also be created to fit specific needs. For details, write or phone the office of the Kensington Special Sales Manager: Kensington Publishing Corp., 850 Third Avenue, New York, NY 10022. Attn. Special Sales Department. Phone: 1-800-221-2647.

Brava and the logo Reg. U.S. Pat. & TM Off.

ISBN 0-7582-1409-X

First Kensington Trade Paperback Printing: October 2006
10 9 8 7 6 5 4 3 2 1

Printed in the United States of America

YOU DON'T KNOW JACK

Prologue

" Ten bucks says he's not wearing any underwear," Allison whispered in her ear.

Tempted to laugh, Jamie Peters turned to her roommate and shushed her. "Don't disturb his essence, Allison."

Beckwith Tripp, ex-*junkie* and current psychic, was leaning over the coffee table, eyes half closed as he chewed his lower lip, currently sporting *Pucker Up Pink* lipstick. While his vintage Chanel suit did match the lips to a tee, it was a startling contrast to the very obvious male bulge below his waist.

So Beckwith was a little on this side of odd. He had the *gift*. He sensed things and could translate them into remarkably accurate predictions of the future.

Jamie had been ecstatic when she had stumbled across him while working on one of her many post-prison reentry cases as a social worker, and had seen his talent. Beckwith had been straight for four months, had an apartment in the Bronx, and a booming business telling fortunes.

She loved the success of helping someone better his life.

Jamie also loved the thrill of hearing what lay around the corner for her, besides the Village Deli, that is. Hopefully it would involve losing ten pounds—actually twenty—and an unlimited supply of funding for Beechwood, the social services agency where she worked.

Jamie's friend, Allison Parker, a nonbeliever in fortunes, karma, healing crystals, or the power of love, was intent on scoffing at everything out of Beckwith's mouth. She lounged on the sofa next to Jamie, swinging her crossed leg so that her red toenails flashed in her stiletto sandals.

Caroline Davidson, her cool blond hair swept into a twist, sat across their living room, looking nothing short of horrified. Jamie recognized the expression well, since Caroline wore it every time she popped her head into Jamie's bedroom and saw the vibrant and cozy warmth of kitsch that Jamie surrounded herself with.

Mandy Keeling, the fourth resident of their two-bedroom walk-up in Greenwich Village, was on the floor on her knees, across from Beckwith, her brow crinkled in concentration.

Jamie thought Beckwith's prediction for Mandy was interesting, a nice hodgepodge of hope, love, and pastries. It was a bit subject to interpretation, but a nice fortune all the same.

It was Jamie's turn now.

Jamie knew Allison was closed to the possibility of anything unscientific. Not Jamie. She wouldn't hold back. She believed, and she had every intention of letting Beckwith scramble around in the depths of her past, present, and future via her mind, heart, wavelengths, aura—whatever it was called.

Beckwith smiled at her, adjusting his pearl earring.

She grinned back at him. "Are you going to do the cards?"

"Yes, honey, I know you love the cards." Beckwith drawled his words out slowly as he slapped the deck of tarot cards in front of her. "Cut the deck."

Jamie closed her eyes and tried to feel the right place to separate the cards. Nothing. Not an ounce of intuition. She either didn't have Beckwith's sensitivity or she was approaching the whole thing wrong. Either way it was cause for a good sigh. She had spent a good many years of her childhood wishing she were psychic or, even better, a witch.

The only sign she'd ever shown of being a witch was the wart she'd developed on her thumb at age seven.

Beckwith took the split deck and flipped the first card of the new pile over. "This is an accident card."

Now that wasn't a very promising beginning. She wiped her sweaty palms on her long floral skirt. "What kind of accident?" Maybe she should stop using the food processor to make guacamole.

"Oh, nothing major." He waved off her concern. "And I think . . ." He flipped the next card. "Yep. It has to do with meeting this man."

His long pink fingernail tapped the card.

Jamie's heart stopped pumping. Well, not really, but it certainly felt like a malfunction. Accidents involving strange men sounded like the contents of a future police report. "What man?"

"One not like your other men."

"You mean he has a job?" Allison said sarcastically.

Everyone laughed, and Jamie nudged Allison with her knee, but didn't protest. It was sad but true. She had dated a disproportionately large number of unemployed men. But that was just the way she was, and she couldn't help herself. She liked to help people, fix them up, send them on—better off than when they'd met her. It was why she was a social worker.

Still, she defended herself, happy to talk about the irrelevant and avoid a discussion of who the man in the cards was. "Scratch had a job."

Caroline raised a perfectly arched eyebrow. "True, after you got it for him. Now he's a tattoo artist who dumped you the first chance he had and left you with nothing to show for three months of your life."

That wasn't entirely true. Jamie did have a daisy-chain tattoo wrapping around her left ankle compliments of Scratch.

"Tell me about *this* guy, Beckwith." She pressed the tip of her finger to the card before yanking it back. The colorful swirls and rather creepy sticklike figures were starting to weird her out. Maybe the downside to knowing her future was that it might not be good. It might be really horrible and twisted. "Is he going to hurt me?"

Beckwith waved his hand. "Jesus, no. Holy crap. I didn't mean that kind of accident, sugar." He frowned a little. "Damn it, I have to work on my technique or I'll be sending people screaming out of my shop."

No kidding. Jamie sagged in relief. "Well, then who is he?"

Beckwith smiled slyly. He loved moments like this, she knew. He rubbed his five-o'clock shadow and drew out the suspense. "He will touch your soul like no other has," he declared.

Jamie sighed, a flush creeping out over her face in a warm rush. That sounded simply luscious. Touching her soul. In the past no man had ever even seen her soul, let alone had contact with it.

It had been nine months since Scratch had dumped her. Having an affair certainly sounded like a good plan to her. She'd never done that, had a hot and heavy short-term relationship. But passionate, steamy sex to warm up cold winter nights . . . now her skirt was as hot as her face. The man had definitely better show himself soon.

"Dang, I like the sound of that. When will I meet him? Where? What does he look like?"

"Soon. On something moving, some sort of minor accident. And he is tall, light brown hair, carrying . . . food. Or maybe liquid. Something edible, at any rate."

"The market," Mandy said in her clipped British accent. "Pushing the buggy."

"Or he could be a pizza delivery man."

Her three friends launched into a heated discussion about the meaning of Beckwith's words, but Jamie didn't participate, startled by the serious expression on his face.

Beckwith was watching her, his brown eyes probing. "Jamie, this man doesn't need mothering. He doesn't need fixing. He's your destiny, your soul mate."

"What? What do you mean?" Jamie wrapped a finger around one of her many unruly curls and tugged her hair in distraction. That almost sounded like an insult. Like she dated men to fulfill some kind of maternal need.

"You are one of the sweetest women I know, but you date for charity. You're never going to find a man to marry if you don't steer clear of these fucking fixer-uppers you keep going for."

Allison cleared her throat.

Jamie felt a pain somewhere in her chest. She didn't need a man in her life, not permanently anyway. Not to marry. That wasn't in the cards for her, she was positive, no matter what Beckwith saw or said. She'd learned a long time ago that the kind of men who were attracted to her did not stick around to pick out china patterns.

It didn't matter, because her mother had taught her to be self-reliant. Heck, her mother had taught her to live off of no money and nothing more than a plot of land and your own hands. At eighteen Jamie had left her home in rural Kentucky for New York and had been happily independent ever since.

And she got more fulfillment on the job than she had ever expected from helping others. That was her destiny, to continue in the career she loved, no matter what Beckwith or her granny back in Kentucky said about snagging a man.

Marriage wasn't about snagging or trapping or coercing a man into spending his life with her. She didn't want that, never had. "I don't regret dating the men I have. And I'm not looking for a man to marry."

Fanning herself a little, she shifted on the couch and met

Beckwith's knowing gaze. He had a disturbing, penetrating stare that seemed to reach inside her, scrape off the layers, and find the secrets of her heart.

Beckwith took her hand and squeezed. "He won't leave you, baby doll. This one isn't like your daddy."

That shocked her spit dry. She swallowed hard, trying to work up some moisture so she didn't choke. Not many people knew about her father. "My self-esteem is fine, Beckwith. I don't have a daddy complex."

He didn't let go of her hand, but he just shrugged, as if it was unimportant. "This man will make you happy."

"I already *am* happy."

Beckwith grinned. "More happy. Giddy happy. The kind of happy that makes everyone around you gag."

Allison said wryly, "It's working already. I feel sick. I would love a crack at Mr. Right, and all I get is the nineteen-year-old intern at the radio station coming on to me."

The disturbing, raw thoughts of her father dissipated, and Jamie laughed, grateful that Allison could turn anything into sarcastic humor. "Maybe I can pass my destiny on to you when he shows up, Allison."

Beckwith gasped in horror. "Bite your tongue and break your nails! You can't do that."

Allison grinned. "So, Jamie, do you want to go to the grocery with me and see who's squeezing the melons? Maybe you have a major falling-melon accident, suffer amnesia from a conk on the head, and fall in love with your doctor."

There was an image. "Thanks, I'll pass." She didn't want to meet the man of her dreams in the grocery store. In fact, she didn't want to meet him at all. She was just a little bit worried that a soul mate was more than she could handle.

She knew what to do with men who mooched and made promises they couldn't possibly keep. With them, she never made the mistake of falling in love. Mr. Right could be a whole other story, and she was sure it wouldn't have a happy ending.

Mandy shook her head. "I don't think you're going to meet him at the grocery. I think you bump into him at Caro's wedding reception in July, doing the funky chicken. See there? Moving food."

Beckwith ignored the bantering. "Don't turn your back on him, honey. Embrace it. It's meant to be, even if a dishonest act will bring him to you."

Now, that sounded promising. Not. If there was one thing Jamie didn't understand or tolerate, it was lying.

"Sugar, there is no reason to be afraid if you meet him dancing at a wedding or otherwise."

Easy for Beckwith to say. He wasn't the one who had his future staring him straight in the face, making him question what he wanted, and wondering why he had ever asked.

So Jamie merely tilted her head, smiled with a confidence she didn't feel, and said in imitation of the chicken she was, "Baawk, baawk."

Chapter 1

Jack Davidson had become a stalker. Retired from Wall Street at age twenty-nine, stalker at age thirty. That was attractive. He followed Jamie Peters down into the subway, keeping an eye on her ginger hair as she paused in the crowd. She dug in her purse, cell phone to her ear, lips moving rapidly.

He felt like a complete and total idiot following her, the music to *Mission Impossible* tripping across his brain. Spying wasn't exactly his area of expertise, given that he was an ex-stockbroker and day trader. Numbers he could follow, but people were a whole different skill set, and he was pretty sure he looked ridiculous and obvious. Not to mention he didn't normally even breathe without planning it in a spreadsheet first.

But staying out of Jamie's business wasn't an option. Not if she was caught up in something illegal without her knowledge. Or with her knowledge, which would be worse. Even though he'd never actually met her, she was his sister Caroline's good friend, roommate, forthcoming bridesmaid. He was concerned for her safety. It was the right thing to do. Motive good and pure.

That didn't make him feel any less of a jackass, though.

And it was starting to occur to him that maybe he had

too much time on his hands since retiring, if discovering illegal day trading activity in a social services agency got him
this excited.

Deciding to switch it up a bit, he got on the train first, so
maybe she would think it was a coincidence that he'd been
following her for three blocks. The bag of food in his hand
was a decent alibi, too. Hell, he'd needed some kind of
reason to be hanging around outside her office for two
hours.

His cousin Steve had warned him this was a stupid idea,
and Jack was inclined to agree with him now as he held on
to a pole with one hand and turned to face out. The doors
were about to close, and Jamie wasn't even on the train yet.
She was still digging in her suitcase of a purse. Christ, she
was going to miss it altogether. Maybe he should get back
off.

Or maybe he should go home and rearrange his DVDs al-
phabetically, which was probably a smarter use of his time.

But after depositing her phone back in her purse, Jamie
suddenly realized the doors were closing, and she went into
action, skidding through sideways, bracelets jangling and
hair bouncing. She was about to collide with a rather hard
looking ex-hippie type in dirty jeans, tattoos up and down
his arms.

Jack quickly shifted in between them and took the impact
of Jamie slamming into his chest.

His pasta box burst inside the brown bag, leaking oil.

Oh, yeah. This had been a stupid idea.

Because when she looked up at him, horror stamped on
her face, Jack felt like someone had grabbed his nuts and
given them a good twist.

Surprise, surprise. Jamie Peters was *gorgeous*.

Jamie shifted her large duffel bag that served as part
purse, part file folder for her cases and waited for the train

as she tried to decipher what Beckwith was saying. He had called her on her cell, sounding frantic, and in three minutes solid the only thing she'd managed to understand was that it wasn't a life-threatening emergency.

"Why do I need to check my make-up, Beck?" It was the end of the workday in July. The little make-up she'd started the day with had probably slid off hours ago.

"Because it's now! Or like really soon, anyway. I was at the handbag sale at Saks—got the cutest little Kate Spade—anyway, it just hit me, right there, at the counter. You're going to meet him today."

"Him?" Jamie repeated, this call finally starting to make sense. She had a pretty good idea of where Beckwith was going with this. The tarot card prediction. Intrigued—no, make that freaked out—she stopped trying to shove her subway swipe card in her bag.

"It's been five months since your prediction, and so far, nothing." Thank goodness. The problem with believing in Beckwith's psychic ability was now that he had predicted something she'd really rather he hadn't, she was stuck waiting for it to happen.

Why couldn't she be a total skeptic like Allison?

At first Jamie had been seriously on the lookout for Mr. Right, the dishonest dream man. She had walked cautiously past the melons in the grocery store and had scrutinized the deliveryman carefully when she'd ordered a veggie pizza twice. She'd even taken to using the stairs at work instead of the elevator like she normally did since movement had been integral in Beckwith's prediction.

Nothing. No scary accidents with men fated to make her happy. But Jamie was optimistic by nature. It served her well in social work. She had figured the man Beckwith had described would show up eventually, which did not thrill her in the least.

Not only was it a little unnerving to imagine accidents

around every corner, but she was absolutely certain she had no clue how to handle a man whose personal assets added up to more than his T-shirt collection and a carton of Marlboro Reds. Since the thought of both breaking her leg and meeting a man who wore a suit or something crazy like that gave her cold sweats, she had pushed the prediction to a back corner of her mind.

It was going to happen sooner or later, she was convinced, but if that time was *now*, why couldn't she be looking cuter? As it was, she probably resembled a Brillo pad with eyes.

"There's no time frame on destiny," Beckwith said with great dignity.

Nor was destiny something she sat around and thought about on a regular basis. It certainly hadn't been in her thoughts that day at all. And at the moment she just wanted to get home and pull a pint of ice cream out of the freezer and inhale it. Then she could meet the man of her dreams. After she'd gained five pounds from the mint chocolate chip. Shoot, that would make a bad situation worse. If her fated soul mate saw her and ran screaming, she would be humiliated on top of everything else. Maybe she should skip the ice cream and have a salad with low-cal dressing.

"I'm on my way home, you know. And I wasn't planning to do anything tonight but paint my toenails, so I don't see how I could meet anyone. Maybe the handbags interfered with your radar. Maybe I see him tomorrow." That would be better anyway.

Digging through her purse to put her swipe card away, she sensed movement and realized everyone around her was surging forward.

Dang it. The train was here, and she would be last one on. There was nothing worse than folding yourself into a full subway car and sharing your personal space with approximately thirty people of various age and odor.

"Gotta go, Beckwith! I'll call you later, sweetie."

Running as fast as wedge sandals would allow her, she launched herself through the doors as they began to close and grabbed for the nearest available surface to hold on to.

Not fast enough. The car moved again with a frantic lurch, and Jamie went stumbling forward, her handbag clipping the woman in the seat to her right.

"Watch it," the woman said.

But Jamie couldn't apologize. She couldn't speak.

Because the man she had collided with in her forward motion was *him*.

Him of the tarot cards. Him of the light brown hair, the minor accident . . . She looked at his chest. And the food.

Now crushed against him in a brown bag that was leaking some kind of oily sauce from multiple directions.

"Oh," she said. Beckwith had been so completely right. It was disarming, unsettling, weird, not as bad as she'd thought. It even felt a little . . . wonderful.

His hand was on her arm, gripping it firmly to keep her steady.

It was a strong hand. A warm hand.

Oh, my. Jamie stared up at him and smiled in spite of herself. "I'm sorry," she ventured, not exactly sure what she should say to the man of her destiny.

He smiled back, showing white teeth in a somewhat crooked grin. "I'll be alright, but I don't think my shirt will ever recover."

When he shifted the bag of food, she saw that he was now wearing a red sauce on his white T-shirt. Her hand came up without thought to brush it, but he shook his head. "It's without hope. Don't bother."

"Aaaah. I'm such a klutz. I'll pay you for the shirt."

The train came to a stop, and Jamie was pushed and jostled as four or five people moved around her to get off. She was pressed up against him, a blush starting to creep up her face.

They were close enough that if she were to tilt her head up, they could kiss.

He had a strong jaw and smelled like soap and tomatoes.

The need to fan herself was overwhelming. Either the air-conditioning was on the fritz, or she was experiencing an explosive burst of lustful heat. Chances were it was the latter.

He shrugged, the movement drawing her attention to his broad shoulder. She fought the urge to squeeze his biceps. Beckwith hadn't warned her about the sexy factor. This guy was built like a race horse. No, that didn't sound right. He was . . . was . . . *lickable*.

Before Beckwith had spouted off about marriage, her original thought had been that she was destined for a rather fun affair, her first strictly steamy relationship. Looking at super sexy in front of her, she thought he was probably capable of fun with a capital *F*.

Hopefully unaware of her lecherous thoughts, he said, "Don't worry about it. I mourn my ruined dinner more than my ruined shirt."

"Italian?" she guessed, thinking of the tomato scent.

A stale, hot pocket of air fluttered over her as he nodded. "Spaghetti and meatballs. With garlic bread."

Of course. A traditionalist. No trendy pesto for this guy. He probably didn't even own a suit, given how comfortable he looked in his jeans. And his eyes were blue, swimming with amusement and perhaps hunger. For his pasta.

"I'm so sorry about your dinner. I'd offer to take you out to replace it, but you could be weird or something." Weird? Oh, geez, why had she said that? Jamie wanted to groan. Followed by a mental kick in her sundress-covered behind.

It was intelligent and important for a single woman to be cautious, but heck, she could have phrased that differently.

But he only grinned. "No weirder than anyone else in New York."

Staring up at that cute grin, Jamie knew she couldn't let this moment pass. He had to be the man in Beckwith's prediction, and she couldn't let him get off this subway without making plans to see him again, in a safe, public place. Even if she had to drag one of her roommates with her for security, she was not going to let this guy get off this train and turn her life into a romantic tragedy.

This wasn't about marriage. Beckwith had said soul mate, and that phrase had the word mate in it, which was really a polite way to say sex. Maybe that's what this really was. They would date. Sleep together. Then he would move on like all the other guys, and she would whistle as she walked away, heart intact and body happy for a while.

Not that she'd ever engaged in a wild, steamy affair before. Men didn't see her that way, and she was more inclined to pack a man's lunch than to grope him. She was modest to a fault when it came to her body, and maybe this was what fate had in mind for her. Sensual liberation. Just looking at him made her feel pretty darn liberated.

Dang, that sounded like a good plan. For once, to just let it all go, to be the sexy one, to have a man look at her and want, want, want.

"That's true, there are plenty of weirdos running around. And I do feel just terrible." Then she added in a breathless rush before she lost her nerve, "So how about dinner, then?"

He studied her for a second, his blue eyes darting down to her chest and back up again. She wished she had worn one of those body-clinging dresses that Allison favored, but instead she was covered in one of her standard loose-fitting, draping, no-waist dresses.

When the silence drew out, a sudden horrifying thought

popped into her head. "Unless you're married, or dating someone or something. That's fine. I just thought that I could, you know, make it up to you, because of what happened when I tripped. I wasn't implying anything . . ."

Shut up, shut up, shut up, she told herself. Babbling was never a good thing.

"What's your name?" His hand was still gripping her arm, only it loosened and relaxed, until he was stroking her skin.

A shiver ran through her. "Jamie. Jamie The Klutz."

He grinned again, little lines forming in the corners of his very close, very moist, very kissable lips. "Well, Jamie The Klutz, I'm Jack. Jack the unmarried and unattached."

Stroke, stroke on her arm.

She struggled to control herself.

It would be very embarrassing if she fainted on the subway. Her dress would probably slide up, and everyone would see her underwear, which was unbleached cotton. Environmentally responsible, but majorly unsexy.

"And I would like to go out to dinner with you, Jamie The Klutz. Tomorrow? Neutral territory?"

"Sure. But what's neutral?"

"Times Square. If I'm weirder than you thought, then you can ditch me in the crowd of tourists."

She laughed. As if. He would probably need a fire hose to get her off of him. "That sounds good."

"Seven? Mama Luigi's on Forty-fourth? They have a patio, so if you need to escape you can leap over the fence to get away from me."

"Okay."

He looked around her. "This is my stop."

"Okay." Nothing brilliant, witty, or original came to mind to say, so she smiled again as he let go of her and stepped off the train.

"See you tomorrow." He waved, clutching his leaky pasta bag and grinning at her.

Jamie gulped as the doors closed, then turned in search of a seat to sink into. She needed it before she collapsed in a heap of tangled legs to rival Jack's spaghetti.

She had met him.

The One.

Chapter 2

Jack watched the door close in fascinated silence.

What the hell had just happened?

He sucked at this spy thing. The point of following someone was to stay incognito, which he hadn't exactly done. Garlic was more subtle than he was.

But he hadn't wanted her to crash into Free Love, the aging hippie.

He had thought to save her discomfort and embarrassment. Now he was standing on the platform with a giant red stain on his shirt, staring at Jamie The Klutz as she smiled shyly at him.

It was a smile that went straight to his groin.

Damn, she was hot.

She glowed.

It was true. There was a rosy, peach color to her everywhere, from the rich auburn of her curly hair to the blush of her cheeks, to the riotous flowers on her dress.

She was just . . . peachy.

Which made him hungry. And made him want to see what she looked like naked. See where else she might be peaches and cream.

He came close to groaning out loud at the thought.

The door had long since closed, the train pulled away, and he was still standing there, like the horny idiot that he was. He checked his watch. Only twenty-five and a half hours until he saw her again. He could survive.

Maybe.

As long as he didn't think about her chest, hiding behind that loose floral dress, but glorious nonetheless. It brought to mind all sorts of metaphors about flowers and fruit, with words like ripe, budding, and juicy rising up and tormenting him.

He took the stairs to the street two at a time and ordered his hormones to lie down and play dead. It didn't work. His sister owed him an explanation. Never once when talking about her roommate had she mentioned Jamie was a sexual goddess with breasts that could stop traffic, war, and obliterate the need for Jack to hang on to the Victoria's Secret catalog that had been accidentally delivered to his apartment.

Ten lust-filled minutes later he stepped into his grandfather's room at the nursing home and found him sitting in his recliner, watching a game show. "Hey, Pops, how are you?"

"Stuck in this hell hole, but other than that, no complaints."

"Come on, Pops." Though Jack could sympathize with his grandfather. Living in a nursing home must be an anticlimactic ending to life. It was a rehabilitative facility, but Jack got the impression Pops felt this was the beginning of the end. One stay led to another until you never went home. "It's nice here. It doesn't smell or anything."

"Hah. You haven't been here on taco day." Pops turned and studied him. "What's all over your shirt?"

"Your dinner." He'd bought it for his grandfather in the first place, being more of a pesto sauce, lean chicken kind of guy. But he wasn't sure how appealing it was going to be now that it had bounced around the inside of the bag. "Spaghetti. It got shoved against me by this woman on the subway."

Pops narrowed his eyes as his gaze dropped. "You've got a hard-on, Jack."

Though shocked at his grandfather's words, Jack took a quick glance down. "Jesus, you're right." Just the thought of Jamie leaning against him was having an immediate and painful reaction. Or maybe he had been like this from the very first second she had collided with him.

"Spaghetti always does that to me, too." Pops reached for the bag. "Give me the food, don't just stand there."

"It wasn't the spaghetti." Not by a long shot. "The woman who fell against me, well, she was . . . Pops, there was something . . . she had . . ." He couldn't find any words to describe Jamie and her soft skin without sounding like a jackass.

Wait. Too late.

"That good, huh?" Pops took the bag and started ripping it open. No sign of his stroke there. Pops tore with fury, his left hand a little limp, but the right one compensating.

Jack shifted painfully. "Oh, yeah."

He suddenly realized that Pops was lifting noodles out of the exploded plastic carrying container with his fingers. "What are you doing? That fell all over the inside of the bag."

"So? Didn't fall on the ground, did it?" Grabbing another handful, Pops jammed the noodles in his mouth.

"Well, at least let me get you a fork." Jack looked around the room, forgetting there was no kitchen in Pops's one-room accommodation.

"They don't let us have utensils in our rooms. Might stab someone or ourselves with them, you know." Pops shook his head. "Treat us all like we're whacko."

"I'll go ask someone for a fork." Jack pictured the look on his mother's face if she saw Pops eating with his fingers. "Good thing Mom's not here."

Pops snorted. "Don't know how I raised such a snooty daughter. Nose always in the air. Yet she doesn't have a pot to pee in that I didn't give her. It's not like your father's ever amounted to much."

Jack's father was a partner in a prestigious law firm. He was more than successful, but Pops liked to rib him. To a man like Will Hathaway, anyone who wasn't self-made like he was didn't deserve the same level of respect. Pops had started out playing stickball in Brooklyn, and he made sure everyone knew it.

It was part of why he was so proud that Jack had made his own fortune, independent of the family trust.

"And you're the one who's rich," Pops added with a grin.

Jack folded his arms and grumbled. "I'm not rich, Pops. I'm comfortable." Actually, he was rich. But sometimes that embarrassed him. He'd never set out to be successful for the reward of wealth. He had been aggressive because he loved the challenge, the thrill, winning the game—the money just happened to come along with it.

Pops was unrepentant. "You're sitting on a cool ten mil, ain't you? That makes you mighty comfortable in my book. Most people would call it rich."

Taking a seat on the bed, Jack stretched his arms over his head and tried to ignore the wet sauce stain sticking against his skin. "I guess you're right. It's just that being considered rich makes me *un*comfortable sometimes. Maybe I should just give it all to Mom. That would make her happy."

"Over my dead body." Pops slurped a noodle up, sending tomato sauce spraying over his blue striped shirt and his chin. "You made that money legally and it's yours. Not your mother's. Besides, you bought her that fancy car. That's more than enough."

Jack flopped back on the bed and checked out the ceiling. When he had first made the money a few years back, day trading, taking advantage of the market and its ups and downs, he had been ecstatic. He could retire from Wall Street, dabble a little here and there and increase his net worth without killing himself with fourteen-hour workdays.

That was the plus side.

What he hadn't counted on was the negative side.

The fake, fawning people who played ass-kissing games, yet would stab him in the back the minute he turned around. It was a cold, hard world for even the single-digit millionaire, and it had been a long time since Jack could trust that any woman was interested in him and not his money.

Until today.

Jamie didn't know he had anything more than the shirt on his back. And he intended to keep it that way.

Jamie wanted to see him, Jack. Joe Ordinary who rode the subway like everyone else and carried spaghetti in a brown paper bag.

Jamie who looked normal. Like a regular girl from small town, USA, with a slight twang that still lingered in her voice.

Hair that just spilled all over the place, untamed by a hairstylist named Ricardo.

And she didn't watch what she said. She just said it, without weighing whether she would sound déclassé or grasping or uninformed.

He doubted Jamie had ever suffered through a cocktail party in her life.

He had suffered through enough for the both of them.

"Don't worry, Pops. I'm just blowing smoke."

"So, you seeing the girl again? The one who gave you the hard-on just thinking about her?" Pops set the bag down on the end table next to his recliner. "Toss me a hand towel."

Jack got up and retrieved the towel from the small bathroom. "Yes, I'm seeing her tomorrow night."

Pops grinned, his bushy white eyebrows moving up and down under the few remaining wisps of hair on his head. "Moving fast. Just like I used to back in my day. No grass ever grew under these feet when it came to the ladies."

Jack handed him the towel. "I don't doubt it, Pops. But this is complicated. She's Caroline's roommate."

"So?"

"So she doesn't know who I am. I acted like it was an accident that we met."

"You mean it wasn't an accident? What are ya, stalking her or something? Don't be a loser, Jack." Pops wiped his mouth and gave him a look of disdain. "You should've just called her up and asked her out for Chrissake. If I were younger, I'da had her six ways to Sunday by now."

Crossing his arms over his chest, Jack glared at his grandfather. "I wasn't stalking her." Not really. Much. Shit.

"The thing is, Jamie is a social worker and her agency requested funding from the Hathaway Foundation. Since I investigate financials for all organizations asking the foundation for money, I spotted something not exactly legal in the records for the agency Jamie works for. And by the way, I wouldn't be in this awkward position if I hadn't agreed to take over your cake retirement job while you're rehabbing. I mean, we're both supposed to be retired, and here we are both working. It makes no sense."

"Retirement is for schmucks. And if it's a cake job, what the hell are you complaining for?"

Because it made him feel better. He actually hated retirement. He had been slowly and surely going insane until Pops had the stroke and Jack had taken over his job at the charitable foundation Pops had created a decade earlier. It was easy work, only twenty-five hours a week, and Jack got to feel as though he was contributing to the good of society.

But he was still bored, which was ironic. He'd left the corporate grind behind to take some time to smell the roses, and he'd found out his nose didn't work.

"I'm complaining because now I know Jamie Peters could be implicated in illegal day trading, and calling the feds on the woman I think I want to have sex with for the rest of my life is not cool."

Pops cracked a laugh. "Har. Guess not. But listen, Jack-o, this could actually work to your advantage. You go in there and clean it up for her. She'll be grateful. More willing to go down on you."

Jack shouldn't be shocked at anything that came out of his grandfather's mouth, yet he still found himself gaping. "Pops! Christ. You don't have to be crude."

Unrepentant, Pops just shrugged. "What? It's the truth."

Pacing the small room, Jack tried to think the whole situation through, and not visualize Jamie Peters going down on him. "The problem is, if I tell Jamie who I am, she's going to freeze me out. I mean, I rejected her funding request. And she's not going to believe me that someone within her organization is defrauding them. Or if she is willing to believe it, she's not going to let me poke in their business. She'll just take it to her boss or to the perpetrator."

"I'm with you. But what's your other option?"

Jack wasn't sure. But he didn't want the look in Jamie's eyes to change when she found out who he was. When she realized he had money, both personally and professionally, and had denied it to her project.

But more importantly he was worried about her safety. "The thing is, whoever is dipping into the till is not going to like being found out. I'm worried if I just tell Jamie, she'll confront the most likely suspect and wind up hurt. Criminals panic when they've been backed into a corner."

"You think someone's going to kill her for a little cash?" Pops raised an eyebrow.

"Maybe not kill her. Or rape her or hit her, though those are possibilities. But more likely they could fire her, or pin it on her." Which was why Jack had been following her in the first place. He had wanted to make sure Jamie wasn't involved.

Two minutes in her company and he was convinced she wasn't.

"You're screwed, kid." Shaking his head, Pops adjusted in his chair. "You either tell her who you are and risk her running into trouble, or you keep it a secret and have her pissed at you when she finds out. And you know as well as I do there's really no choice."

That's precisely what Jack was concluding.

"You always protect a woman, even if it leaves you out in the cold."

"I know. I don't like it, but I'm not going to risk Jamie getting in over her head." Lying wasn't something he wanted to do, but he'd deal with it.

"So you've got two weeks to find your culprit and wrap this up, because if she's Caro's roommate, she's going to be at your sister's wedding, and it's going to be hard to keep your identity a secret when you're sitting at the goddamn bridal table."

Jack grimaced. "I'd totally forgotten about the wedding. Maybe I was hoping Caroline and Brad would suddenly decide to elope."

The thought of enduring that family affair was painful to begin with, despite the fact that he adored his sister. Too much like a dinner party, but with people you didn't like.

Half of his family thought he needed a stint in the psych ward for walking away from a thriving career. They tended to speak slowly to him and give him gifts like soothing scented candles and spa gift certificates.

Then the other half would spend the evening giving him their latest hard luck stories and why they needed a little bit of cash to tide them over. He usually gave it to them, feeling it would be selfish not to help if they really needed it, but the trouble was most of them didn't need it.

And it ruined all family gatherings for him. Leaving him depressed and isolated.

But he would endure it, and with a smile for his sister's sake. In two weeks.

Tomorrow night he was seeing Jamie and had every intention of tasting those plump pink lips of hers. Tomorrow night he wouldn't be Jonathon Davidson, millionaire. He would be just Jack.

A glance at the clock confirmed that time had ceased to move forward.

Only twenty-five more hours to go.

A call from Allison saved Jamie from having to eat ice cream for dinner.

"Meet me at Dorsal. I'll be there in ten minutes."

Jamie looked down at her wrinkled dress and weighed the embarrassment of looking like a poster child for Calgon in public versus eating mahimahi and sipping a lemon drop.

Food won. Besides, she really needed to talk to someone about Jack on the subway, and she was only a block from Dorsal. To change, she'd have to go right past the restaurant to their apartment. "Alright, I'll be there. Are Mandy and Caroline coming?"

"No. Since Mandy got knocked up, married, and moved out, she's always busy. And Caroline's off doing something bridal. If I ever get married, I'm eloping to the Caribbean like Mandy did."

"I thought you said no man was worth saddling yourself to for life, or for the time it takes to get a divorce." Jamie worried about Allison sometimes. She was such a strong, intelligent woman, yet she bristled around men and wouldn't let any of them get close to her.

"You're right. Good, I'll never have to worry about having an obnoxious wedding."

"Oh, come on. Caroline's not being obnoxious." Though Jamie had to admit, she seemed stressed out.

"Are you kidding?" Allison snorted. "She tried on her wedding dress and burst into tears. Not a good thing." The sarcasm left Allison's voice. "I'm actually kind of worried about her."

That was serious. Allison wasn't known to get concerned

without just cause. Pausing outside the restaurant, Jamie pushed her curls out of her face. "Okay, I'm here. I'll get a table and order drinks. What do you want, Ali?"

"A real job, fame and fortune, and the respect of men everywhere."

Jamie laughed. "I meant short term."

"Oh, you mean to drink? I don't care. Order me something that sounds perverted."

He shouldn't be watching her. He should go home, though home was an exaggeration for what he had. He could go to the shelter, if there was room. Go to Wendy's apartment, though she'd been spitting mad at him the week before when she'd tossed him out.

The shelter was probably a better choice, even if it smelled like overcooked cabbage. Worse than prison.

But first he'd found himself following Jamie again, and he needed to stop that. He wasn't planning on talking to her or anything, though, so what was the harm in just watching her? She never noticed him, even when she glanced around her like she did now as she talked on her phone in front of a restaurant.

She was too trusting, too nice. Unaware of all the dangers that lurked around her.

Nice girl like that was going to get hurt if she wasn't careful.

When Allison breezed in the door fifteen minutes later, Jamie was sitting with what the bartender swore were two Screaming Orgasms in front of her. She was almost certain they'd given her the wrong drink just to mess with her, because these were a vibrant pink color, lapping against swizel sticks. Jamie kept thinking if she dropped an egg in each, she'd have a pair of beautifully colored Easter eggs.

"How was your day?" Allison asked as she dropped into the chair across from Jamie.

"Mixed. The Hathaway Foundation rejected my request for funding." She was extremely disappointed that her pet project, Urban Gardens, an extension of her works programs, had been rejected by their major source of funding. Without the Hathaway Foundation's funding, she didn't have a prayer of continuing on with the project that had kids of incarcerated adults caring for their own gardens.

The board, including Caroline's brother, Jonathon Davidson, had rejected the proposal without even allowing her to plead her case in person. Now she was stuck scrambling for money anew.

"Jerks."

That's kind of the way Jamie felt. She didn't understand the corporate mentality and probably never would. The men who made funding decisions that could make or break serious social programs like the one Jamie worked for sat around in their posh offices and decided who was worthy of their crumbs.

"We used a grant writer and everything. They have our financial records, so they know we're a responsible organization. I mean, we have an eighty-six percent success rate with our reentry program. We help men fresh out of prison find jobs and become productive adults. How could they find fault with that?" Jamie sipped her drink and sighed. She'd really wanted to expand their program to include the families of those men, but it was going to be tough now. There just wasn't any money left in the budget.

"A lot of people might think those men should stay in prison. Or that why waste resources on men who will just commit another crime and wind up right back in jail?"

Jamie wasn't naïve. She knew some men could never be rehabilitated, could usually pick them out at the first introduction. But that didn't mean every man was a lost cause. "Well, they would be wrong. Including Caroline's brother, Jonathon, who was the final no for my project."

Allison kept eyeballing her drink, but she'd yet to take a

sip. "Don't take it personally, sweetie. Jonathon is a businessman, but he's a nice guy. If he thought it was an unsound financial investment, he would say no. Not because the program's not worthy."

Jamie wanted to believe that of her roommate's brother. Of any person. But she couldn't help but picture a bunch of stiff, well-dressed Scrooges taking sick delight in saying no.

"And nobody works at a charitable foundation without having some sense of decency."

Allison was right. Jamie was ashamed at her attitude. She had no more right to judge Jonathon Davidson than he did her clients.

"You're right. I'm just disappointed." Jamie shivered a little in the air-conditioning, wishing she'd brought a sweater. "But the weird thing that happened today was that I met a guy on the subway. The guy from Beckwith's prediction."

That thought caused more than a shiver. Her whole body underwent an earthquake shake. Jack had been so . . . delicious.

Allison didn't look impressed. "Beckwith couldn't predict his way out of a paper bag. You shouldn't be talking to strange men with that crap in your head."

"It was too freaky to be nonsense. The height, the hair color, the moving accident, the food, it was all accurate." And then there was the look in his eyes. Admiration. As though he thought she was attractive, despite no make-up, frizzy hair, and lack of Manhattan polish.

Jamie would reserve judgment on what kind of man Jack was until after they'd had some time to talk, but right now she was feeling strangely optimistic. So maybe Beck might have exaggerated the longevity of this relationship and was clearly wrong about the whole dishonesty thing—after all, what was dishonest about colliding on the subway? But Jamie still thought she and Jack might have a good old time, even without the whole happily ever after thing.

Beckwith did have the gift, she was sure of it.

"Just look at Beckwith's prediction for Mandy, Allison. Back five months ago, he said she was going to find a man who made her melt, and that there were buns in her future. Now she's married to Damien and having a baby. He was completely right."

"What do melting buns have to do with marrying your boss and getting pregnant?"

It did seem like kind of a stretch when Allison put it like that. But that didn't mean it wasn't true.

"Jamie, please tell me you're not meeting this guy."

"Okay."

"Okay what?"

Jamie sipped her drink and tried to look innocent. "I won't tell you that I'm meeting this guy."

Allison made a sound of total exasperation. "Would you be going out with this guy if Beckwith hadn't told you about meeting a man while moving? Don't let that sway you to do something you wouldn't normally do. Something stupid."

But Jamie knew what she was doing.

She had a date with her sexual destiny.

Jack might turn out to be a total jerk-off, but she'd never know unless she met him. And if she had an orgasm or two along the way, she wasn't going to complain.

Chapter 3

Jamie stood outside Mama Luigi's and rubbed the crystal in her hand. "Okay, this is it. I hope he showed up." She closed her eyes and took a deep breath, which wasn't a good idea in her clinging tank top.

In a moment of impulse she had put on a melon-colored sleeveless shell, which strained to contain her healthy chest. To make it even worse, there was a flower in the middle of the shirt, and Jamie felt like the petals were serving as directionals to her nipples. She couldn't begin to imagine why she had thought wearing it was a good idea.

But she had been motivated by the need to feel attractive, to gain Jack's attention. Allison, resigned to the date, had wanted her to wear an elegant skirt and one-shoulder blouse, but she knew she needed to meet Jack wearing her own clothes, so he would fall in lust with the real her.

She suspected the only thing falling tonight would be her breasts, right out of this shirt. Of course, that would serve her purpose of securing Jack's attention, though it wasn't a sure bet that he'd enjoy the view.

Slipping her crystal into her tiny handbag shaped like an alligator, she fluffed her hair and licked her lips. Jeans had seemed appropriate since Allison had told her the restaurant was casual, but now she wondered if it was too late to go home and change.

It was. It would take her an hour to go home and change and come back.

"Don't let me regret this," she whispered, and pulled open the door.

He was the first person she saw.

Jack was standing in the waiting area, staring right at the door. Jamie thanked her crystal from the bottom of her melting heart. He was hot, hot, hot.

His short hair was clean cut, not so short as to look military, but not long enough to be trendy. It was the kind of brown that started to lighten and streak in the summer, and now that it was July it looked like caramel. He smiled and started toward her.

Which was a good thing since her legs were incapable of carrying her anymore. She might always have to be sitting down when she saw Jack since she felt in danger of collapsing whenever he was around her.

He was wearing jeans. That hugged in the right places.

And one of those nondescript guy shirts that buttoned up the front, was machine washable, and cost one-fifth what a woman's shirt did, but still managed to convey style. The navy color caused the blue of his eyes to deepen until they were the shade of a stormy summer sky.

He was just as gorgeous as she remembered. It hadn't been a trick of the fluorescent subway lighting or the power of suggestion.

"Hi, Jamie. I'm glad you came." He touched her hand briefly.

"Hi, Jack." She felt herself grinning like the Greenwich Village idiot.

"They have a table ready for us." He gestured to the dining room.

"Great." Concentrating on moving forward in a normal person fashion, Jamie wasn't ready for Jack's hand to slide across the small of her back as he guided her.

Only a swift lockdown on her jaw kept her from yelping out loud like a nipped puppy.

The table was in the corner of the semidarkened dining room. It was a casual atmosphere, with stucco walls and rich vibrant paintings in red and mustard yellow. A large planter hid the view of the table next to theirs.

Jack held out her chair, and Jamie sat down in confusion. Men she dated didn't pull back chairs. Of course, her dates usually had no money to take her out to dinner either.

"Would you like some wine?" Jack leaned against the back of his wrought-iron chair, looking relaxed and comfortable.

In stark contrast, Jamie was thankful she'd worn the sleeveless shirt since anything else would now be sporting massive pit stains, due to the copious sweating she was doing. Maybe Jack was out of her league. He looked a little too . . . normal. Conservative. Nary a tattoo anywhere that she could see.

"Sure, I'll have a glass."

"Red or white?"

She cared not one bit, since she had every intention of guzzling it down in three seconds to steady her nerves. "Red."

Jack fingered the menu, but didn't open it. "So, tell me, Jamie The Klutz, where are you from? I can't place your accent."

Setting her alligator handbag—shaped like a grinning alligator, not actually made from alligator, because that would be cruel—down on the floor, she smiled at her napkin in relief. She could do small talk. It was just looking at him that was a problem.

"I'm from La Grange, Kentucky. I've been in New York eight years. And I thought my accent was gone."

"It comes and goes. It increases when you're nervous."

That got her attention. How could he have noticed that already? How embarrassing. She looked at him, but he was just sitting there, with a casual half smile on his face. "What makes you say that?"

"I noticed it right away yesterday afternoon. You started out with more Kentucky in your voice, then it just faded away as we talked."

"And now?" Stupid question.

"I'm expecting you to say y'all in a minute or two." His smile disappeared, his serious gaze turned sensual. "Why are you nervous?"

Fighting the urge to fan herself with her menu, Jamie knew that she could never be anything but honest with Jack. If this—it, destiny, fate, whatever it was—was even going to have a lick of a chance, she needed to tell the plain truth.

"Because . . . I'm attracted to you." Lord, she could not believe she had said that out loud. Allison would croak.

But Jack said, "The feeling's mutual." And the burn in his eye confirmed it.

The question was, what exactly were they going to do about it?

She wasn't sure she wanted to know yet.

"How's your shirt?" she managed to force out, determined to behave like a normal woman and not grab him and make love to him on the table the way she suddenly wanted to.

"It's in the garbage." He shrugged with a grin.

"That bad?"

"Yes, but you'll be happy to know, despite sloshing around the inside of the bag, my grandfather thought the spaghetti was great. He ate it all."

"It was your grandfather's dinner?" She struggled not to show exactly how much it pleased her to hear that a man would take food to his grandfather.

"Yep. I bring him dinner in his nursing home every Thursday. He hates eating in their cafeteria."

Jack spoke casually, like it was no big deal for a man to give up his Thursday after work every week to visit his grandfather and bring him a meal. And maybe it wasn't a big deal to Jack, maybe he expected that anyone with half a heart would do the same.

But Jamie had seen too much in her line of work not to appreciate the enormity of such a gesture. The world was filled with selfish, cruel people who constantly overshadowed the many others who were living out their lives as good, caring people.

It confirmed what she had sensed the minute she had looked up into Jack's eyes on the subway.

He was different. Special. Maybe there was more to Beckwith's fortune than she had thought. Maybe Jack wouldn't just touch her body and all its one thousand parts, but her soul, too. Maybe there was such a thing as Mr. Right and she had crashed into him.

She felt a cheesy grin spread across her face. Lordy, she was in trouble.

Jamie smiled at him in a way that made Jack's insides twist like taffy. She looked so soft and warm and lush. Between yesterday's floral dress and the clinging sleeveless shirt she was wearing now, he suspected he would never be able to look at another flower again without thinking of Jamie's breasts.

That wouldn't be a bad thing.

Jamie's breasts were a gift to man. A total sexual feast for the eyes.

And his eyes were directly connected to his dick, which was enjoying the view. Jack coughed and tried to focus on her words.

While he was entertaining fantasies of licking her nipples, she was talking about his grandfather.

"That's so nice of you. I'm sure he likes the company."

Her green eyes had gone round, her shoulders dropping

down into a more relaxed position. He was really having trouble concentrating on their conversation. All he could think about was her, all curvy and sweet, and how he had the sudden overwhelming urge to take her home and keep her there.

Forget Hathaway and illegal day trading. The only thing that seemed important was getting to know Jamie Peters. All of her. Of course, he couldn't forget anything about the funding request. Because he knew who she was, but she didn't have the same advantage.

Jack should tell her the truth. Let her come around to it on her own through conversation. Like it was an accident that they'd met. Like he wasn't a total freak weirdo who had followed her. He would just act surprised when she mentioned who her roommate was.

"Pops is a real character. He's seen it all, and he gives good advice. Taught me all I know, really."

Jamie nodded. "I have a granny like that back in Kentucky. She's never been more than fifty miles from her house, but she knows everything."

As the waiter brought their wine and took their orders, he wondered why Jamie didn't look out of place in Manhattan. She should, with her country voice that came and went and her doe-eyed innocent looks. But she also looked earthy and new age, and that certainly blended with New York.

She did not look like the kind of woman who would be friends with his sister. Caroline was meticulous, driven, polished, a little uptight. She had Darien, Connecticut, written all over her, whereas Jamie screamed twenty-first century hippie.

Jack wasn't sure what was written all over him. Right now probably something like undersexed workaholic looking for woman to share friendship, possibly more. A lot more.

"So, ah, what do you do, Jamie?" Lead her around to it. Yeah, he was slick.

"I'm a social worker."

Well, that just got him nowhere. Which was a good thing, because rationally, he knew he couldn't tell her about the potential fraud. But the corner he was backed into wasn't feeling very comfortable. "Wow, that's tough work."

She shook her head. "No, it's not. It's wonderful. The pay is lousy of course, but what I do has a real impact on people's lives. That matters to me."

He could see that it did. Sincerity shone in her eyes. His heart turned over like an engine roaring to life. This was a new feeling, a strange, exciting, vulnerable sort of feeling.

When he'd broken up with his last girlfriend, Meredith, after hearing her tell a friend Jack's best quality was his money, he hadn't thought he would ever feel eagerness for a new relationship. But it was there, and it wasn't as terrifying and horrible as he had expected.

It actually felt a lot like when he'd first start investigating a possible business venture. Like it could be lucrative or a disaster, but in the beginning there was cautious optimism, excitement.

"Do you work with children, or teens?"

"Everyone." She waved her hand in an all-encompassing gesture. "We try to salvage families if we can. I work with teen mothers a lot, helping them learn how to raise their children. They love their kids, they're just lacking in basic skills."

Her voice grew animated as she talked, and he nodded to show his interest. "I can understand that."

She went on. "We had this mother, she was only fifteen, and her baby was born with colic. The baby cried all the time, and the mother was really on the edge. She didn't know what to do with the baby, and she hadn't bonded with her."

Jamie took a sip of her wine. "After all, it's kind of hard

to fall instantly in love with a creature that does nothing but squall at you no matter what you do. We were afraid she was going to eventually lose it—shake the baby, or leave her home alone or something."

"So what did you do?" Jack watched her run her finger around the rim of her wineglass, her thin, creamy fingers long and unfettered by fake nails or polish.

"We sent her and the baby to baby massage classes. They taught her how to touch and rub the baby to soothe her and ease her crying. After a month of those classes, the baby had stopped crying, and that mother was glowing with love for her baby."

She stopped and gave him a rueful grin. "I'm running on and on, aren't I?"

"No," he protested immediately. He didn't want her to stop talking. "We're having a conversation. You're talking and I'm listening."

Jack leaned forward and said, "I want to hear what you have to say. And I had no idea that social work was so creative. We, the general public, have this idea that all you do is take kids away from parents who abuse them, then stick them with foster families that are equally as bad."

"It's so much more complicated than that."

"I can see that it is."

Sitting on the board of directors for the Hathaway Foundation and writing a check was nowhere near as difficult as what Jamie was doing.

She was in the trenches.

This sweet, smiling woman who looked like she wouldn't swat a fly no doubt saw all manner of horrific things in her job. Obviously there was a layer of toughness to her to deal with that day in, day out. Yet he couldn't find it. Not yet anyway. There was nothing but warmth and compassion.

"Right now I'm working mostly with a reentry employment program. We train ex-prisoners to fill out job applications, make a résumé, how to handle tough interview questions about their conviction, and guide them to jobs that can utilize their skills."

"You work with prisoners?" That alarmed him a little.

"Ex-prisoners. It's an important program because a lot of these men only have a window of a few weeks to get their lives back on track before passing bad checks starts to seem like a good idea. We support them so they won't commit a crime out of desperation."

Jack wasn't sure desperation was what lead men to commit crimes. He thought it was probably greed. He'd seen plenty of that in the corporate world. "So you teach them how to get a job?" The thought of Jamie, who looked like a poster for naïve white girl, working with prisoners made him a little nervous. A lot nervous.

"Yes. And sometimes we let them work around the office, answer the phones, do data entry, to practice their office and people skills."

There was his potential thief. And it was worse than he'd thought. This could be a criminal straight out of prison who wouldn't hesitate to use violence if confronted. Jack did not like the way this sounded at all.

"What do you do, Jack?"

He froze with his wineglass at his lips. "Uh." Truth or evasion?

There was her safety.

And there was his comfort in not having to wear the mantle of millionaire for one night.

If Jamie could like him, just the way he was with no knowledge of his money, then expanding on the truth later wouldn't matter in the least. Probably.

"I'm between careers right now. My last job was very stressful, and I'm looking for something that will allow me to actually have a life outside the office."

The minute the words were out of his mouth, he wanted

to groan aloud at his idiocy. What woman wanted to date a man who was unemployed?

In striving to hide his wealth, he had made himself out to be a loafer. That was sexy. Not.

But Jamie only nodded. "It's important to be happy with what you're doing. No one should be a slave to the workplace."

"Exactly." He beamed at her. That was exactly why he had walked away from the firm after cashing in his stocks. He had felt as though he lived and breathed nothing but work every minute of every day. He had felt strangled and old at twenty-nine. Restless. Ready for the next challenge.

Most people had considered him nothing short of crazy for quitting his high-paying job, but Jamie seemed to understand. She didn't care about his money, or lack thereof.

God, she was damn near perfect.

He was almost perfect. The thought hit Jamie like her latest rent increase had, leaving her feeling stunned and incapable of speech.

Of course, no one was perfect. After all, he had admitted to liking action movies as they had talked over their dinners. And horror of all horrors, he didn't see the charm in her favorite flick, *Gone With The Wind*.

But everything else seemed to yell and scream and shout that this man was perfect for her.

He was kind, considerate, he listened to her talk, and he had insisted on paying for dinner, despite the fact that he had admitted he was between jobs. She felt extremely guilty that her calamari and wine had cost forty-five dollars. Had she known he intended to pay, she would have ordered a salad and water.

But he hadn't blinked at the bill, had paid it with cash while telling her about playing Little League as a kid. Unless he was doing something illegal, he had obviously planned to quit his job with a hunk of money set aside.

Now as they walked down Broadway, his hand rested across the small of her back, guiding her, protecting her from the crowd. It felt right. Tingling.

There was nothing awkward or uncomfortable about being with Jack.

Jamie breathed in the scents of fried food and exhaust fumes that permeated the summer air and sighed with contentment. Tourists were rushing along to catch shows at various theaters, and the crowd surged across the intersection, daring the taxis to hit them as they ignored the Don't Walk sign.

It felt as though they, too, were careening forward with the speed of a cab, eye on a future fare.

"I never come to Times Square," she said.

"Most New Yorkers don't." Jack stopped walking in front of a store and looked down at her, his blue eyes dark. "It's a tourist trap."

His words were absent, spoken in a whisper, but his eyes were focused and intense, bearing down on her. He was leaning, bending, right there on the sidewalk while they were jostled by people on either side of them.

"Jack?" Jamie fought to steady her breathing. This was it. Right here, right now, he was going to kiss her.

And she had no ability to stop him. She wanted it. Bad. In a way that made her tilt her head back, slide her mouth open, and wait.

"I'm going to kiss you," he said, his hands gripping her back as his mouth came closer and closer to hers.

"Okay . . ." Any other words were cut off by his lips on hers, brushing with a lightness that made her tremble.

Then he increased the pressure, and her thoughts scattered like marbles. Excitement. Desire. Confusion. All colliding in a powerful burst of emotion, so that she threw her arms around his neck and kissed him back.

Their lips slid together, hot and moist and anxious, while Jack's hands guided her hips against his, grinding them together.

Oh, yes. This was it. This was kismet.

This felt like everything she'd been waiting for, a surging of heat and excitement, as his tongue dipped into her mouth. He tasted like wine, smelled like aftershave, his chin chafing hers. There was no goof, no incorrect tiltage of head or nose, no awkwardness. There was only hot, thrusting tongue and more emotion, more tenderness, more questing than she could have ever expected on a first date.

They stood there, mouth against mouth, locked in passion, striving, reaching, yearning fully for that connection, that magic, that fantastical moment of anticipation, of understanding that this was special, this was going farther.

Until someone bumped Jack's back, sending them stumbling backward. Jamie connected with the glass window of a kitschy T-shirt and souvenir shop, her head giving a resounding smack.

It didn't hurt, but Jack pulled her quickly forward, his voice full of alarm. "Are you okay? Let me see."

He dug around through her thick curls searching for damage while she tried to shake off the sexual haze she had been drowning in.

Jack had taken her to red-hot and raring to go in a heartbeat. She hadn't reacted that intensely since . . . ever.

"I'm okay," she said with a breathless laugh, enjoying the feel of his fingers gliding across her head. "I think my hair protected me."

Jack dropped his hands. "Good."

A man nudged past them and said in annoyance, "Get a room and get out of my way."

Jamie looked at Jack in shock and giggled. Jack's lip twitched.

"I'm sorry," he said with a grin that clearly showed he *wasn't* sorry.

"Sorry for kissing me?" If he said yes, she was going to collapse on the sidewalk in a puddle of disappointment.

"No."

Before she could turn a triumphant cartwheel, he spoke in a sexy, low voice that made her rethink her stance on collapsing.

He said, "I'm not sorry for kissing you. I'm sorry I got interrupted."

Oh, mama.

She was still against the window, and he was in front of her, large and damn good looking, very much a man. His leg was tucked between hers, and his broad chest was inches from her own.

He hesitated. "Do you . . . do you want to go somewhere *private?*"

The word came out on a ragged groan that set Jamie's heart thumping like Indian drums. Of course she did. That was a no-brainer.

But whether she should was another story altogether.

She thought for exactly one-point-one seconds. "Okay."

Maybe it was insane, maybe she would regret it, but right here, right now, with the thousands of neon lights flashing behind his head, Jamie wanted Jack in a way that she had never felt.

There was a knowledge deep down inside that come whatever of Beckwith's prediction, this much was true. That she was meant to meet Jack, and that she would share a powerful connection with him.

That he would touch her soul.

In a sense, he already had.

He'd made her rethink her future, made her think that not everything was concrete, that she needed to be open to all possibilities.

That she needed to be open to Jack. Literally.

Dang, she felt herself blushing on the sidewalk. She was a total hussy and couldn't even regret it.

"Thank you," Jack muttered, straightening up in relief. "Yours or mine?"

Jamie felt a little faint and wondered if she had knocked her head harder than she had thought. She wasn't an impulsive woman, yet here she was going home with a man after three hours of conversation. "I have two roommates."

"Oh, hell, that won't work." He lifted her hand and kissed her knuckles, the feel of his lips on her skin sending a rush of heat to her abdomen.

"My place, then." He smiled and tugged her off of the wall.

She couldn't think of a single thing to say, just let him draw her against him. Even as his body felt hard and comforting and arousing, doubts crept in. She swallowed, fear rising up into her throat. She didn't do this. She didn't go home with men she had just met.

She didn't have casual sex, didn't have a wild bone in her body.

Jack's face grew puzzled. "Do you know, Jamie The Klutz, that I have the strangest feeling that I've been waiting to meet you? That you were supposed to collide into me and my spaghetti."

Before she could respond, he shook his head and grinned. "Damn, that sounds crazy."

A group of preteens was walking by, jostling each other. The one closest to Jamie lost his balance and dumped half of his soft drink on their entwined hands. Jamie jumped at the sudden cold liquid splashing her.

"Sorry," the kid mumbled, his friends laughing.

Jack took his shirttail and wiped her hand dry, dipping between her fingers with the fabric. "Maybe I am crazy and that was meant to be a cold shower of sorts."

"I don't think you're crazy." Jamie touched his bottom

lip with her finger, heart pounding. "I know exactly what you mean."

Fear disappeared.

For while Jamie didn't believe in casual sex, she believed in fate.

"Let's go, Jack."

And his response was to turn around, raise his hand, and yell, "Taxi!"

Chapter 4

Jack didn't know what the hell was the matter with him. He had just dragged Jamie off to his apartment in some caveman imitation. Or worse. Like a horny teenager.

But he hadn't been able to stop himself. They had spent three hours in the restaurant, talking and laughing, and just enjoying each other's company. They had a lot in common and more still not in common, but it didn't matter. Being with her just felt *right*.

And his attraction had grown steadily every second, until he had been walking side by side with her, his hand on her smooth back, when the urge to kiss her had been overwhelming.

He hadn't even told her his last name, for God's sake.

Yet they were stepping out of the cab in front of his building in TriBeCa, and he was going to see this compulsion through to the end. He had been suffering through a twenty-four-hour hard-on because of this woman, and if the way she jumped out of the cab was any indication, she had been suffering something similar.

She looked around her in amazement, her eyes landing on the doorman. "This is your building?"

Damn. He was supposed to be unemployed, not living in a pricey apartment in a trendy neighborhood. "It's a friend's apartment. He's out of town, so I'm staying here to watch the place for him."

Jack fought the urge to wince. He ran his fingers through his hair and started to question his keeping the truth from Jamie. It wouldn't matter. She wouldn't care what was or wasn't in his bank account, and he wouldn't have to tell these ridiculous lies.

She was rational enough to know not to confront a criminal.

He opened his mouth to tell her the truth.

Then she said with a laugh, "Oh, good! You had me worried there for a second. I don't know if I could date someone who lives in a place like this."

He clamped his mouth shut again. He nodded to the doorman and ushered her inside the building. "Why not?"

She gave a mock shudder, gesturing to the art deco lobby. "It's a little pretentious."

Oh, hell. He gave a weak smile and slapped the elevator up button. It just figured. Jamie gave the opposite reaction to every other woman he'd ever met. Most women's eyes lit up in possessive greed when they first saw his apartment. Jamie was disgusted by the opulence.

And he had never once thought of the lobby as being pretentious, but now that she had planted the seed in his mind, it took root, making him uncomfortable. "The apartment's not so bad," he assured her.

His sister was always complaining that he needed to hire a decorator. She thought his apartment needed a theme to pull it together. One besides black plastic electronics equipment, that is.

Jamie clutched that silly little purse of hers that looked like an alligator and licked her lips. She looked as nervous as he felt. Maybe it was time to slow this down before she thought through the ramifications of going home with a guy she didn't really know. Jack knew who Jamie was, but she didn't know him. Had no reason to trust him. And given that look on her face, she was realizing that.

"Hey, Jamie, why don't we go grab some coffee before we head up?" He took her hand and squeezed it in reassurance. She smiled at him, that soft tilting up of her lips that showed her teeth and lit up her eyes.

"You really are a nice guy, aren't you?" she asked. "I don't mean to be a tease . . ."

"Are you kidding? In my book, there's no such thing as a tease. A woman is allowed to say no at any time, for any reason. No questions asked, no arguing." Jack pulled her away from the elevators. He already felt like an asshole for not telling her who he was; he wasn't about to coax her into a sexual relationship she wasn't ready for.

"I'm not saying no," she said, green eyes very glassy and bright. "Just . . . not yet."

He wanted to groan, but instead gestured to the grouping of four chairs to the left of the mail slots. "Let's just sit for a minute."

The chairs were really damn uncomfortable—minimalist, armless jobs with stuffing that felt more akin to steel. It was like perching on a big bar of red soap, but at the moment, he couldn't care less. Jamie was licking her lips again, and she tucked her feet under her legs on the chair.

"Our names both start with *J-a*," she said, distracting his attention from her lips. "Is Jack your real name?"

He didn't care what his name was, but he thought it was cute the quirky things Jamie said sometimes. "My real name is Jonathon." He couldn't force another lie past his mouth. "Is Jamie a nickname, too?"

"No." She shook her head. "Jamie Lynn, that's me."

Jamie Lynn. It fit.

As he studied the upturn of her nose, the wild auburn curls, he wondered which name was the real him. Was he Jonathon or was he Jack? Jonathon at work. Jonathon with his parents.

He was Jack with Pops. And definitely Jack with Jamie.

"Well, Jamie Lynn." He tried to remove the flatness of his Connecticut-raised voice and inject some Kentucky into it. "That's a mighty fine name."

She giggled. "I don't like southern boys."

He lost the accent. "I'm all New York, honey. But I bet you broke a bunch of good ole boy hearts when you left Kentucky."

Rolling her eyes, she smiled. "If I broke Dale's heart, it recovered quickly. Two months after high school graduation he married Trudy Wythbodden, who some girls used to call Trudy Wide Bottom. He wanted me to stay in La Grange and get married, but I had to leave, had to see a bit of the world for myself. I wasn't trying to escape Kentucky—I loved growing up there—but I don't know, I just needed some independence."

"I never thought about going anywhere else. I grew up forty miles from Manhattan, and I guess it seemed stupid to go anywhere else, especially since I wanted to get into finance. But maybe it would have been smart to explore a little more. Maybe I wouldn't have found myself so tired and burned out."

Certain that there was more to life than making money. Winning.

Something he had never admitted to himself was that he had suddenly looked in the mirror and wondered if he was destined to grow old alone, a miser counting his coins.

It had scared the shit out of him, and then some.

But what was even scarier was that a year later he was no closer to content, despite ditching the career. When was he going to be done? Ready to stand still.

In his head he practically heard the screech of subway brakes. Now. He was ready now.

"Maybe this is your time to explore," Jamie said.

"Aren't I too old to do that? I'm thirty, for God's sake. Isn't there like a statute of limitations on finding yourself?"

Jack grinned. "Bet old what's-his-name isn't interested in backpacking Europe or taking up yoga."

"Yeah, but he wasn't worth the spit for the shine, which he proved by falling into Trudy's arms about a minute after I left." Jamie fiddled with her necklace, a twisted rope, kind of a knot with green stones in it. "But most people are like paintings . . . they take forever to create, and every time you look at them, you discover something you didn't see before."

Very true. Jack was noticing that the green in Jamie's necklace perfectly matched her eyes.

And she had freckles. Right across the bridge of her nose. Freaking adorable, every inch of her.

Eight hours later, the end table next to them was littered with paper coffee cups, their rims going soft, the liquid contents cold, the aroma stale. Jamie's legs were stiff, her neck tired, her voice scratchy, and her butt numb from the ridiculous scoop chair she'd been sitting in all night.

Yet, she wasn't the least bit interested in leaving. She had spent the whole night in the lobby talking to Jack, who was funny and kind and extremely smart.

She was going to have to name her first-born child after Beckwith.

Okay, so maybe it wouldn't go *that* far, but it wasn't like she could name her first orgasm or anything, and she was sure that was coming soon, pun intended. The point was, she was falling for Jack. She wanted him more than Derby pie, and that mile-high gooey chocolate dessert was never to be underestimated.

Admittedly, she was a tumbler, falling for various guys and their hard-luck stories, but inevitably, her legs got caught up in the skirt of half-truths, and she fell on her face. For the most part, she'd never minded, because she had never fallen in love.

It was possible she'd done just that in one night.

Or at least taken a serious turn in that direction.

That was the only explanation for the way she felt—sort of inflated and overaware, her skin prickling everywhere, her throat tight, breath anxious. Excitement and pleasure rushed through her, and an irrepressible giddiness made her feet tap rapidly, her heart race.

At some point she was going to have to leave and go home, but for now she didn't want this night, this moment, this feeling, to end.

Jamie tucked her legs over the back of the chair and leaned backward, observing Jack upside down. No one else was stirring in the lobby at six in the morning on a Saturday. "So, what's your one big regret in life, Jack?"

His eyebrow went down, or actually up. "Besides that perm in the seventh grade?"

She laughed, holding her hands over her stomach so her shirt wouldn't ride up. "Fashion faux pas don't count."

"I don't have a one big regret," he said thoughtfully. "More like a series of little regrets. You know, like when you were six and you went along with the kids when they picked on the kid who was overweight. Or when I blew off this girl in high school who asked me to the prom. The time I forgot my sister's birthday. Stuff like that."

Even though the blood was rushing to her head, Jamie stayed upside down. It was an interesting perspective, watching Jack lean closer to her, his hands resting on his spread legs. He had a nice strong jaw.

Jamie's necklace fell over her mouth, and she let the stones slip between her lips, then bit. She was a chewer. Pen caps, sweatshirt strings, fingernails, her hair.

"I know exactly what you mean," she said around the necklace.

His arm came toward her, and his finger brushed across her lip, pulling back the obstruction. "Say that again? I couldn't understand you."

"Sorry. Bad habit. I'm always sticking things in my mouth. I've always been very oral."

He started laughing, and she suddenly realized how that had sounded. Oh, Lord. She blushed. Especially since he'd moved in closer and she was about an inch from his chest, his fingers still tracing over her mouth, her hair brushing down over his waist.

"That's not what I meant."

"What? I didn't say anything," he protested, a grin still on his upside-down face.

She needed to right herself before her eyes bulged or she did something crazy like lick his chest. Smiling herself, she tried to sit back up, but she was stuck in the chair, Jack too close for her to swing her legs back around.

"Geez, I'm stuck." Her back was kind of spasming now, too, protesting the awkward position. But she wasn't even sure she cared. She just felt too darn good to worry about spinal damage.

Besides, Jack already had it under control. With a few gentle pushes and pulls with those impressive biceps, he had her right side up and facing his chest. A pile of curls tumbled over her face, blocking her view, and she slapped at them impatiently. She put her hand on Jack's waist and gripped the fabric of his shirt.

For balance, of course.

"Why don't we go horseback riding later today?" Jack said, playing with her corkscrew hair lying on her shoulder. "I'm sure I'll embarrass myself, but you said you miss riding . . ."

Well, that was sweet. Jamie's hand curled into his shirt tighter as she fought the urge to sigh. "That would be fun."

"Great. I guess we should grab a few hours of sleep first, and we can meet back up later. Let's see if we can find you a cab."

Neither one of them moved. Jack was still leaning toward

her in his chair and he was staring at her lips. Jamie was aware that she was pressed against his thighs, and that she didn't want to go anywhere.

Ever.

Sleeping in her twin bed with purple cotton sheets held no appeal, not even when she'd been up all night.

Her nipples hardened. Her inner thighs went moist. Her breathing slowed, and her mouth drifted open. That one taste of Jack in Times Square had been so long ago. Hours and hours and hours ago.

Just not enough, not when he was so, so close. She wanted another taste. And then some. She wanted to make love to this amazing man, sooner than later.

"I could just crash at your place for a few hours," she said quickly, before she lost her boldness and went shy on him. "Save on cab fare."

His eyes went dark, a stormy blue stained with desire. "That's a good idea. I do have a spare bedroom."

Her mouth dropped in laughter at his teasing. But she knew he was joking. She gave him a flirtatious smile. "How thoughtful."

"Or there's a king-size bed we could share . . . so we don't have to make two beds later. Save us time."

He was moving closer, face so near hers she went cross-eyed trying to look at him. "Well, that's very practical of you."

Before the words were even completely out, his mouth was over hers, kissing her with all the fervor and passion that she felt. Oh, yeah. Bring it home, honey.

This was a kiss. This was Fourth of July fireworks, this was a tall iced tea on a hot summer day, this was hitting the lottery.

Everything she'd ever wanted, wrapped up into one sultry tongue tango.

Good Lord in heaven, he knew what he was doing.

But he pulled back suddenly, and she whimpered. His eyes burned, his breath hot and hard.

"I have to tell you something."

"What?" That didn't sound good. That sounded like a preface to an I'm Married speech.

"My last name . . . I never told you my last name."

"Is that all?" Jamie gave a shaky laugh. "You scared me there for a second." Just briefly, Beckwith's prediction about dishonesty had risen in her head, like a big pin ready to pop her balloon.

"Sorry, it's just that you should—"

Jamie cut him off with another quick kiss. She wanted to hear what his last name was. But later. After they'd gotten naked and she wasn't as likely to be adversely affected by the news that his name was something like Jack Daniels or Jack Grosse or Jack Yacks. Or something completely unpronounceable with twenty-seven letters, most of which were consonants.

She wasn't vain, and while a regrettable name like Jonathon Huffheimer wasn't cause for celebration, it would never stop her from dating someone. But later. "It doesn't matter. Not yet. Tell me later. I don't want to talk right now. I want to go upstairs."

Before she lost the sassiness she seemed to have borrowed from Allison. Flattening her hands on his chest, she said, "I'm so sleepy I can barely keep my eyes open."

But it was his eyes that closed, not hers, and his hand pressed hard into her shoulder. His lips moved as though he was counting to ten.

Then he opened his eyes and said in a husky, urgent voice, "Then we should definitely get you right to my bed."

What a gentleman. Always thinking of her needs.

"How sweet of you."

Chapter 5

Sweet. Yeah, that was him.

Hell, he was thirty seconds away from taking her in the elevator.

Jack wondered if Jamie really understood the enormity of her appeal. She was an amazing mix of sultry and innocent, seductive and selfless. She was the sweet one. But she was also so damn sexy with her curvy hips, slow smiles, and rich, honest laugh.

He tried to tell himself he should wait—take her out a few more times before they took it to this level—but she had seemed so damn willing. She'd even gotten impatient with his attempted confession. He hadn't intended to tell her he knew who she was, but wanted her to figure it out on her own just by hearing his last name. But she hadn't wanted to hear even that, and all thoughts of waiting had flown out his mental window.

Why torture himself when she was perfectly willing to sleep with him?

Any idiot should be able to figure that out.

Gorgeous woman agrees to second date and hot morning sex. What do you do?

He didn't need his high SAT score to answer that question.

Grab a condom and go for it.

They were barely onto the elevator and he was licking her bottom lip, pulling it into his mouth to suck gently.

He groaned.

She groaned.

His hands were itching to land on her breasts, but he forced himself to take it slow.

If ransacking her hair, grinding against her, and sliding his tongue into her mouth could be considered taking it slow.

It took a Herculean effort to pull back.

Then he wasn't sure why he bothered. Jamie looked so frickin' perky and ready, primed for him. She was breathing hard, her eyes wide, curls tumbling all over the place. Her breasts rose and fell, the flower on her shirt straining forward, its petals twining around her very obvious nipples.

"You are so beautiful," he panted, like a thirsty Collie.

Without warning, or any instruction from her, his hand shot out and stroked her. Right at the tip. Of the petal.

The sound she made was a cross between a whimper and a squeak. He took it as a good thing.

"Jamie," he said, trying to find some way to express himself beyond his obvious drooling in her presence. Without confessing that he had the sudden bizarre and almost frightening feeling that in the past eighteen hours he had lost his mind, his heart, his sanity.

That it was just possible he could fall in love with her. In the next five minutes.

Her lips parted. Her little pink tongue slipped out and moistened them, rolling around the plump flesh in a way that left Jack thinking there was a much better place she could put that.

Damn. Shoving her against the elevator wall so he could grind his hard cock against her thighs, he buried his hands in her glorious hair. He pushed his kiss on her, a greedy, selfish kiss, tongue hot and moist and anxious inside her. Part of him knew he was being rough, but that rationale was drowned under desperate lust, under fierce need to take what Jamie had offered so sweetly.

Before she changed her mind. Before he came to his senses and realized he could hurt her by not telling her the truth.

That thought had him crushing her against him, consuming her mouth, wanting to keep her close. He was shocked at himself, at the irrational intensity of his feelings, at the complete impulsiveness of his actions, not a usual personality trait.

But he was also a risk taker. As a businessman, he weighed the odds, took chances, rotated millions of dollars at the risk of losing it all, and he was good at that. He had killer instincts. And his instincts here told him, Take her, take her, take her, you'll never regret it.

Her fingers had risen to grip the front of his shirt, but she jerked back when the elevator opened, breaking the kiss. "I can't breathe, Jack." Her lips were wet and glistening, her big green eyes wide, dark.

"Breathing's overrated," he told her, but he did let go of her, clench his fists, rein in his control. Counted to ten mentally. Pictured Jamie walking out if he didn't ease up.

But damn, it was hard when she was so near, so perfect, so ripe.

"After you. Third door on the right."

She gave him a closed-lip smile over her shoulder, and with one of the hall lights blown, half her face was left in a dusky haze. Beautiful wasn't enough to describe her, sensual an understatement. She was more than he had words for, lovelier than he could ever express.

It only took sixty seconds to open his door, usher her in, and slam it closed. Then he was on her, cupping her face with both his hands and kissing her with everything in him.

She gave a soft moan before lifting her arms to his shoulders, nails digging in. He moved in closer and closer, edging her feet apart with his legs, control shot to hell, the taste of her so tantalizing that he felt drunk with desire.

He kissed her deep, hard, again and again, their mouths slapping together.

Then her tongue slid along his lip in a sexy little lick, shocking him. Go, Jamie. He felt that show of aggression from her gave him the right to touch her breast in return.

So he fulfilled his two-day-long fantasy by spreading his fingers over the whole of her luscious breast and cupping it. It felt better than it looked.

It didn't seem like that was possible, but it did.

Her head fell back, offering an inviting view of her long, creamy neck.

His hand still happy and full, Jack bent his head so that he could suck on her neck, pressing kisses everywhere, his tongue trailing along her clavicle. She shuddered beneath him, and he felt his own control further evaporating.

Control? Hell, he'd lost that about the minute Jamie had collided with him on the train. He had the control of a three-year-old faced with a table full of candy and no parental supervision. None. Not a single freaking bit.

"Am I being too rough? I'm sorry. It's just . . . been a while. I'll slow down."

Jamie's hand reached up, cupped his cheek, stroked over his flesh. A nervous smile played over her lips, cherry red from his kisses. "I don't want you to slow down. It makes me feel sexy."

Her cheeks stained pink.

"You are sexy," he said, brushing his thumbs over her nipples. "The sexiest woman I've ever met." He pointed to his mouth. "I'm drooling right now as we speak."

She laughed, but avoided his eyes, her fingers playing with a button in the middle of his shirt. "Men usually tend to, well, see me as nurturing. Not sexy."

Maternal images did not flood his brain when he looked at Jamie. The exact opposite in fact. "Not this man." There was no need to force conviction into his voice. It was ringing with it.

Forcing himself to abandon her breasts, he gathered her to him in a reassuring embrace. Okay, so his hands wandered a little and wound up on her ass, squeezing and stroking. He was lost to all decency at this point.

"Tell me what you like, Jamie," he whispered in her ear. "Tell me what you want so I can do it over and over again."

She shivered in his arms, her breath coming in quick, staccato bursts. When she answered, it was a small, throaty whisper. "I want to feel desirable. I want it *raw*."

Holy crap. Jack about bit his tongue off. Blood rushed past his ears. When he managed to speak, his tongue was thick, words hoarse. "Raw, I can do."

It was a dangerous place to go, but she had nicked the last thread of his resistance. He wanted raw, too. He wanted to dive into hard, numbing pleasure and take Jamie with him. Fast and furious, slick and slap.

So he reached forward, twisted his fingers into her neckline and ripped the front of her tank top, right through that damn flower that had been taunting him all night.

Maybe it wasn't smart to give Jack permission to do what he wanted with her.

He already had her ruined shirt and unhooked bra on the floor. Another two seconds and he'd probably have her dangling on a chandelier. His mouth hovered over her nipple.

Not that she cared much at the moment.

"I love your breasts," he murmured against her flesh. "I've wanted my mouth on them since the first second I saw you."

Jamie swallowed hard. Every inch of her was hot, itchy, aching to be touched. She was still reeling from her confession and wasn't sure how to react. Since men had never really gone wild for her, she wasn't sure how to do wild in return.

Not that he was giving her time to do much more than moan.

His lips brushed back and forth over her nipple in a maddening tease. Then he brought his teeth down on her, lightly, but enough to make her jump. And dang if it didn't turn her on. Liquid pooled between her legs, and a shiver rolled through her body in a delicious wave of excitement.

Jack hovered over her other breast, and Jamie felt his breath tease over her flesh, felt her nipple pucker under his scrutiny, felt herself edge closer to him. There was a slight pause of hovering anticipation, then he sort of *attacked* her, sucking and licking, nipping and pulling while Jamie's breasts tingled and ached.

"Oh, mercy," she whispered, groping blindly for the wall, furniture, anything that could hold her up because her legs were doing the noodle number again.

"No. No mercy," he said, voice hoarse. And as if to prove his point, his finger slid along the seam of her jeans, pressing into her tender flesh, working front to back, front to back, while he pursed his lips and blew a hot stream over her wet nipples.

Well, she'd asked for it. She'd always wondered what it would be like to have a man go at her like a shark with bait, like he had to have her now, damn it, and nothing could stop him. She had never drawn that kind of lust from men—they'd always treated her gently, protectively, which was all fine and good for the most part. She wanted men to respect her, but it would be nice to know she made a man lose all control once in a while.

This was losing control.

Her eyelids sank closed, her teeth dug into her bottom lip as she enjoyed the scrape and slide of Jack's fingers over her body, wishing her jeans would suddenly evaporate. Skin tingling, nipples taut and aching, Jamie felt each lick and stroke over every inch of her body. Her head swam, lust and lack of sleep making her dizzy.

Jack's mouth lifted from her breast. "We need to get to a bed. Now."

She nodded, then realized he probably couldn't see her since he was back to doing a little lick-suck thing with his tongue over her nipple. "Yes. Okay. Now. Definitely. Ooh, yes, that feels good."

He stopped, damn it. Standing, he wiped his hand over his shiny lips and said, "Take my shirt off."

Now that he mentioned it, he was really overdressed next to her. She was wearing jeans and sandals and nothing on top.

Fingers shaking a little, she reached out and touched the top button. "Okay." Then jumped when his thumb pinched her nipple and his tongue slid into her ear. Her shoulders went slack, her jeans suddenly way too hot. My, oh my, the man knew how to work his tongue.

She got the first button on his shirt undone, but the second proved to be made of sterner stuff. It slipped and caught and eluded her while she tried to work it over and over, Jack plucking her like a harp in a very distracting way.

Oh, yeah, she was hot stuff. A real sex goddess. She couldn't even get him halfway out of his shirt. She was reduced to prying at it, clawing and pulling to try and remove it.

"Rip it," he said, nipping at her earlobe.

Rip it? There was a thought. A wild girl would go for it.

But the only thing wild about her was her hair. Jamie gripped the shirt, hesitating like she did when it was time to remove the eyebrow wax strip.

"Rip it. Get me naked, Jamie." Jack stepped back a foot. "Do it, damn it. I'm dying."

He did look like he was in danger of agonizing death. Compassion forced her into action. Not to mention she really did want to see him without a shirt. She gripped the fabric tightly dead center and just pulled it apart in both directions, buttons flying off.

Dang, look at her. Arms out, legs spread, yanking Jack's shirt open, her breasts bouncing with the movement.

She felt kind of sassy. As she pushed his shirt down over his hard, muscular shoulders, she told him, "I'll sew all your buttons back on, don't worry."

He stood very still, eyes half closed as she ran her curious fingers over his chest, tracing the lines and brushing over the dusting of hair.

"You'd do that for me?"

Letting his shirt drop to the floor, Jamie brushed her lips over his clavicle. "Sure thing." She couldn't ruin something without at least trying to fix it.

"Will you let me take your jeans off?"

"Yes." Her heart started to beat a little faster.

"Will you let me take your panties off?" Jack's finger traced along the crotch of her jeans.

"Yes." She shivered at the light, teasing touch.

"Will you let me put my tongue inside you?"

Somehow she didn't think he meant in her mouth. The area he did mean was hot and moist in anticipation. Jamie nodded, afraid she'd squeak if she tried to speak.

His expression was puzzled, his eyes dark, voice quiet. While one hand stroked between her thighs, almost absently, as though he'd forgotten what he was doing, the other tugged a curl down to her breast, let it spring back up.

"Do you feel it, Jamie? This connection between us. Am I crazy? Should we stop here?"

And suffer the consequences of unsatisfied lust? No, thank you.

"I feel it, too," she said, afraid if she didn't reassure him, he'd have second thoughts. "That's why I'm here with you, not wearing a top. I don't sleep with men I've just met, Jack, but I feel that connection with you. And I'm willing to listen to it." She was absolutely convinced she wouldn't regret it.

"I've never believed in fate, or love at first sight, or anything that couldn't be planned or quantified first. I'm not an impulsive man." He shook his head, a wry grin on his face. "Until now. Until you, Jamie Lynn."

He was playing with her nipple, rolling and touching and twisting, while his other hand continued its exploration of the inside of her thighs.

"Well, for a man without a lot of experience, you're doing a darn good job."

He laughed and let go of her, which was a huge disappointment. All that touching was torture, but only in the best way.

"I feel like you don't judge me . . . I feel a freedom with you that I can never have in my career or with my family. Like I can make an ass out of myself and you wouldn't care."

"I wouldn't care," she said, touched that he could understand that about her. Pleased that he felt like he could be himself with her.

"I just want to have fun with you."

No arguments from her. "I think I can work that into my schedule."

"Good." Turning his bare back to her, Jack said, "Hop on my back and I'll give you a pony ride to the bedroom."

Lord, was he serious? Jump on his back topless? She wasn't sure she was that much fun. And his voice didn't sound goofy, it sounded suggestive and . . . kinky. Jamie didn't have a lot of personal contact with kinky. She wasn't sure it was in her genetic coding.

Neither was coordination, she decided, when she went for it in an act of courage and leaped up on him. Her breasts slammed into his back, her hands grabbing at his shoulders, but the gravity of her big butt pulled her straight back down to the floor until she was just draped across his back like wet cotton.

"I think I'm too heavy for this." Damn that Ben & Jerry's. An embarrassed giggle escaped her as she realized her nipples were poking his firm, warm flesh.

"Try again," he said over his naked shoulder.

"Are you crazy?"

"I think so."

Which made her laugh. If he was going to be a nut, no reason she shouldn't have fun. Anymore she felt like she was either counseling men or trying very hard to impress them. With Jack, she could just be herself and to hell with the rest. Tomorrow she was canceling all her subscriptions to women's magazines with their advice columns on how to be sharp, sophisticated, elegant, and multiorgasmic.

Jack liked Jamie Lynn the way she was. And she had a feeling the multiorgasmic thing was a sure deal.

"Okay, I'll give it a shot." This time when she jumped up, he caught her legs and backside with his arms and jerked her up for better balance.

She let her legs dangle but kept them close to his waist. It was an impressive show of strength to keep her up there like that, and her mind shifted to the fact that her thighs were spread wide, wrapped all around him, her breasts brushing over his bare back in a little tease of touch. She hoped the bedroom wasn't any farther than the swing of a cat, because she was ready and then some.

Jack must have felt the same urgency, because he started down the hall, pausing only to pretend to tip her backward once.

A shriek came out before she could stop it, and he laughed. Jamie took a gander at the living room and kitchen as they went past, and shivered. It was a big apartment, lots of light from the floor-to-ceiling windows. The sun was coming up and peeking through, sending streaks across the ebony wood floor.

But it was kind of austere, empty. There was no color, no warmth.

The master bedroom was small, but featured a big platform bed and a plasma TV hung like a painting over the dresser.

Jack paused in front of the bed, hands tightening on her thighs. "This is the end of the ride."

Jamie slid off of his back before he could toss her on the bed like a sack of potatoes with breasts. She stuck her hands in her back pockets and tipped a little on her sandals, chewing her lip. Lots of white in this room. White walls, white sheets, white mirror, white sheets, white overstuffed chair, white sheets on a big, white bed.

Her gaze kept floating over to that bed. There wasn't much else to look at. Just that big ol' bed, all neat and tidy and waiting for someone to use it. Looking lonely, ready to be rumpled.

She suddenly realized Jack was staring at her. He stood about two feet in front of her, eyes running over the length of her. Under normal circumstances, meaning in front of any guy but Jack, that would have embarrassed the hell out of Jamie. After all, she was topless, wearing tight fitting jeans and platform sandals. A far cry from her usual tactics of cover-and-hide clothing.

But with Jack, she felt desirable. So much so that she tilted her head a little, ran her fingers through her hair, moved her one hip forward to show herself off to her best advantage.

"Wow," he said, hands up as if he were framing a picture. "You are so incredibly beautiful."

It was impossible not to blush when he said something like that. "You're not so bad yourself."

He unsnapped the button on his jeans and winked. "It gets better."

Oh, she could only imagine.

"And seeing you standing there like that has reminded me I'm supposed to be giving you raw, not comic relief."

"Taking your pants off is comedy?"

He stopped unzipping and laughed. "No, that's not what I meant. I was talking about the piggyback ride."

Then he yanked his jeans off and came toward her in his boxer briefs, the laughter replaced by a cocky grin. "I'll show you that taking my pants off is no laughing matter."

Jamie chanced a glance south, but there was no time to see anything before he took her forearms and tumbled her onto the white duvet cover. Suddenly she was looking at the ceiling.

Whoa. Very efficient.

He kissed her with an intensity that had her breathing hard and easing her legs apart, wanting closer contact with him. His erection was along her thigh, thick and enticing, while his tongue moved with determined thrusts. The duvet was soft beneath her, the room cool and crisp from the air-conditioning.

Jamie held on to his smooth back, loving the way he felt, the way he touched her with determination, reverence, desire.

Jack pulled back. "These have got to go." His finger moved around on the button of her jeans, brushing between the waistband and her skin until she thought she might scream with impatience.

"Good idea."

The button came unsnapped, the zipper went down, and Jack's hand slipped inside, gliding over her and coming to rest precisely where she had hoped he would. She fought the urge to squirm, but couldn't contain a groan when his thumb started to move up and down, stroking through the lace of her panties.

Her eyes rolled back, and she gave a heartfelt moan of encouragement.

Jack removed his hand and yanked hard on her jeans, obviously intending to pull them down and off.

They didn't move an inch.

She opened her eyes and found Jack over top of her, frowning, as he tried to make the jeans budge. He was pulling so hard that she was bouncing up and down on the bed. A giggle escaped her mouth.

"I thought they were a little tight when I put them on."

He stopped tugging and smiled at her, the same smile that was responsible for her pants being pulled off in the first place.

"I'll get them."

Jack stuck his fingers on either side of the waistband and yanked. They gave as far as her hip bones, then resisted again.

She bit her lip and giggled once more. "I can do it."

"No, no, I've got them." He gave a few more futile tugs.

"Jack, I think I'm going to have to sit up and do it." That was better than the alternative, which was sticking her butt up in the air and shoving for all she was worth.

This was what she got for trying to be sexy.

Jack looked like he wanted to keep at it until he succeeded, but he lifted his hands. "Okay, you do it."

By the time Jamie was up on the bed on her knees, Jack had sat down and eased his boxer briefs off. She paused with her hands on her waistband and gaped at him.

Mercy.

She had never seen anything like that before.

Maybe the men she had been dating were short on more than cash.

Trying not to drool, Jamie started working her jeans down, wiggling and rocking back and forth.

Jack groaned. "You have no idea what you look like, do you?"

Startled, she stopped with her pants at the knees. She had

been so busy gawking at him, she hadn't thought about how all that movement would look from his point of view. "Sorry."

"Don't be sorry." He clenched his fists. "I've just had a fantasy come true."

While she finished the job, and hastily undid her sandals and let them fall to the floor, Jack opened the dresser drawer and came back with a condom.

"Next time, just leave the shoes on," he said, bending over to give her a kiss.

Jamie was just reacting to it, sighing with pleasure, when he was already pulling back. She was sitting on the edge of the bed, and he dropped to his knees on the rug, between her legs, face level with her breasts. She shivered, from cold, from anticipation, from embarrassment, she wasn't sure. There was a definite blush crawling up her neck, flooding her face with heat and making her shift a little uneasily.

It was seven in the morning and she was naked with an equally naked man between her legs. Not her usual Saturday wake-up routine. Trying not to hunch her shoulders over, she touched his shoulders to have something to do with her hands as he stared at her, inspected every visible inch of her body. Feeling exposed, yet desperately excited, she let him see her, study her, knowing that there would be only one first time between them.

Let him draw it out as long as he wanted.

Chapter 6

Hands on her knees, Jack finished off the few inches between them and flicked his tongue across Jamie's nipple. He honestly felt speechless when faced with the grandeur of her breasts. Works of art. Tantalizing toys. They were both, and he could not believe his luck that he got to hang out with them. Touch them.

Mouth around her nipple, he closed his eyes. Taste them. Oh, hell yeah, he was one lucky guy. The nipple beaded in his mouth, firmed and ripened for him as he rolled his tongue over the taut surface. Jamie's fingers dug farther into his shoulders, her hair brushing over his face, getting between him and her flesh until he twitched it to the side.

Her skin was pale, translucent, with a dusting of freckles across her chest and shoulders. She had a lush, curvy shape, and when his hand brushed down over her stomach, it curved slightly out instead of in. He liked the way she felt, soft and feminine, like he could pet and touch and stroke and never find one spot on her body that was like his, would never find anything hard and inflexible about Jamie.

As he sucked her nipple, licked the underswell of her breast, and moved to the other, Jack wedged closer between her legs, forcing her thighs apart, until his ribs came in contact with her soft down hair brushing over him. She made a sound in the back of her throat, a quick inhalation of air, that had his body throbbing in anticipation.

Yet he wasn't ready, wasn't done tasting and teasing, and as he continued to suck and pull on her dusky rose nipple, he ran his thumbs along the outside of her naked thighs. Down around to the tip of her backside, dangling over the edge of his bed. He stroked over her cheeks, skirting forward, back, forward again, avoiding the juncture of her thighs, desire thick in his mouth.

Her legs started to shift restlessly, her nails sinking even farther into the muscle in his back. Both their breathing quickened, and her head went left and right, tipped back when he glanced up at her. The creamy expanse of her neck, the sight of her teeth buried in her bottom lip, sent a jolt through him, and he let his own teeth sink into her nipple. Jamie moaned, and Jack squeezed her ass, gripping it hard as he fought the urge to stand up and plunge into her.

He wanted more than that. He wanted her body, yes, here and now, but he wanted her, too. All of her. He wanted her open and desperate, aggressive and as turned on as he was. He wanted her eyes to roll back in her head, and he wanted her to stay all damn day in his bed, naked, hot, and willing.

With that in mind, hands still on her ass, he abandoned her breasts, leaving them shiny and wet and Jamie whimpering. He squatted down farther, lifted her thighs a little, and checked out her sex. He'd never dated a redhead before, and the fiery contrast of reddish gold curls against her milky white skin was sexy as hell. There was a coffee-and-cream color beauty mark on her right inner thigh, and when he licked it, sucked it, the flesh around it turned red in the shape of his mouth.

A little shiver went through her, and she shifted, trying to move back onto the bed, away from him. Jack held her tight, abandoning his intention to spread her folds with his fingers and take a nice, long look. He didn't want her bolting, or going shy. So still maintaining a firm grip on her tight ass, he bent over and buried his tongue in her curls, exploring a little until he found the tight bud of her clit.

Jamie went still, hot little pants escaping her mouth. "Oh, oh, oh," she said in a half whisper.

Jack sucked, the scent of her arousal filling his nostrils and making him hard enough to penetrate steel. When his tongue ventured farther south, he found she was slick, sweet and wet, her folds swollen with want. And when he licked up and down that swollen flesh, she went wetter still. Losing the edge of his control, he dipped his tongue into her hard and fast.

Oh, man, he was dying. He was fucking gone. He'd give up his ten million and then some to have Jamie like this, permanently, saying his name with soft, heated, anguished cries of ecstasy.

Her legs surrounded him, and when she dropped back onto the bed, clutching at the sheets, Jack pressed forward, farther into her. The position spread her even more, and he pulled back to take a look, his thumbs pressing her apart.

"Jack." She tried to bring her knees together, though she stayed slack on the bed.

"Shh." He blew on her clit, cool air over her hot flesh. "I'm almost done."

"Doing what?" Her foot kicked his forearm as she shifted uneasily.

"Appreciating you." He wanted to stretch the moment out, make this day, this minute last, make Jamie understand that he wanted more. That he saw how far she was from Meredith and how much he respected that.

If Jack did any more appreciating, Jamie was going to flip right off the bed. As it was, she felt like a single flick of his tongue might send her sliding into an orgasm. She was so aroused, so close to the edge, so flustered with all the touching and sucking and licking, that it was only now occurring to her that she'd yet to lay a finger on anything other than his shoulders.

Yet he didn't seem to mind. He hadn't been waving it in her face, or doing that arrogant head push toward his crotch thing that Jamie just couldn't stand. Jack seemed perfectly content to just look at her, to just pleasure her for now.

She was feeling pretty damn pleasured. But a small, insecure part of her couldn't help but ask, "Do you appreciate me in a social worker kind of way?" She wasn't even sure what she meant by that, and it surely wasn't fair to ask him what amounted to a trick question when they were naked.

But Jack just brushed a kiss over her clitoris, causing her to shiver, and the deep ache in her body to spike.

"I appreciate you as a woman, Jamie Lynn. With all your facets and quirks and exquisite dimensions."

Oh, good God. No man had ever said anything quite like that to her before. Her heart did a trapeze artist flip in her chest. Three somersaults and a free fall.

Before she could think of anything to say in return, Jack kissed her belly, kissed the bottom of her ribs, kissed the tip of each breast.

"I need a condom," he said softly, pushing up onto his feet and moving to the dresser where he had dropped the foil wrapper on top.

Modesty urged her to close her legs, but the need to see desire on his face warred and won. She liked seeing his eyes rake over her, like she was a juicy treat, worth licking his lips for.

He didn't disappoint. When he turned, his blue eyes went dark as he rolled the condom on. He made a low growling sound as he studied her. Jamie stared right back, watching his fist palm his penis as the condom sheathed it. He held tighter and longer than was necessary, and she spread her legs farther and wider than the situation called for.

"Come here, Jack," she said in a husky whisper that pleased the hell out of her. Dang if she didn't sound sultry.

He crossed the tiny room in two big steps, leaned over her, and gave her a hard kiss that stole her breath.

"I can't wait, Jamie Lynn." Already the tip of his erection was aligned with her, teasing and pressing.

Fighting to keep her eyes open, she wrapped her arms around his back, wanting him closer. "I don't want you to wait."

"Good."

Then without warning he was inside her, and the ability to speak left her. Thoughts fled as he filled her, big and hard, covering her body with his everywhere, overwhelming her.

She didn't even have the breath to groan, but just closed her eyes and swallowed hard as his solid flesh pulsed inside her, sliding along her sensitive and aching body.

"Damn," he said through gritted teeth.

Forcing her eyes back open, she saw his arms were bulging, his jaw clenched with the strain of holding back. While he held perfectly still, she wiggled. She was so close to climax, on the edge from all that tongue touching he'd done, that she couldn't lie immobile. She wanted more.

"Jack." Lifting her heels, she wrapped them around his waist, raised her hips to encourage him to push deeper. "More," she moaned.

The corner of his lip turned up, and he moved inside her with breathtaking slowness.

"Ahhh," she said, as her skin tingled and the heat inside built quickly. "More."

"More," he agreed, and picked up the pace, slamming into her hard and fast.

Yep, that was good. That was it. There was no holding back, no wish to, nothing but freedom and pleasure, and the promise that this was only the beginning.

As if he could read her thoughts, Jack said fiercely, "This is just getting started, Jamie. Remember that."

She wasn't sure if he meant making love, this morning together, or the future, but she didn't care. All that mattered was right then and there she was with Jack, he was hers, and she was feeling like she never had before.

His chest pressed against her with each thrust, and she squeezed her legs around him, so close to skittering off the edge that she could only lie still and gasp, her eyes half closed, waiting for it to rip over her.

"Look at me," Jack commanded.

She forced herself to focus on his face, a thin sheen of sweat glistening over his forehead, his breath hot and fast on her cheek. Reflected in his eyes was the same wonder, passion, and exhilaration that she knew was in hers. "Jack?"

"Jamie." Jack crashed to a halt, his erection throbbing inside her. After a quick pause, he pulled back and said, "Come with me."

She tried to answer, tried to force a yes past her lips, but he took her breath away when he pushed deep inside her with a move that she felt all the way to her toes. Her inner muscles contracted in a happy dance, and nothing came out of her mouth but a deep moan as she gave up and let herself be dragged away.

Their eyes held as they climaxed together, and Jamie saw clearly that it was true. Beckwith had been right about at least one thing. As they locked gazes and gave each other that ultimate pleasure, Jack's blue eyes sank into hers, and he touched her soul.

Not to mention her G-spot. He was hitting that dead on.

And no man had ever touched either of those private places.

Two hours later, Jack told himself to take it slow this time.

If shoving his tongue down her throat and gripping her breasts like they'd float off without his hands acting as gravity could be considered taking it slow.

With a hell of a lot of effort, he pulled back.

He shouldn't want her again like this so soon—should give the poor girl a break. He had told himself they would eat an early brunch together, then he'd take her home, let her sleep for a few hours. Catch a few winks himself.

But that was all before Jamie had sat down diagonally from him at the table and proceeded to eat Chinese noodles in the most erotic manner he'd ever seen in his life. All that sucking and tugging and licking had him shifting in his chair, barely tasting his own food.

And when she had closed her eyes in ecstasy over a spoonful of Ben & Jerry's Phish Food ice cream, he had lost it.

He'd attacked her again.

Jamie was breathing hard, her eyes wide, curls tumbling all over the place as she held her spoon slackly and stared up at him. She was wearing his T-shirt, which hung loose everywhere except her chest, her breasts straining against the cotton. The red cashmere blanket from his bed was cuddled around her legs.

She looked like such a nice girl, but the way she licked that spoon screamed naughty, naughty things to him.

"If you wanted a taste of my ice cream, all you had to do was ask," she said, eyes wide in mock innocence.

"Very funny."

Her chest jiggled as she laughed. Since his hand had barely moved back an inch, he was able to reach out and enjoy the movement. Give her nipple a little pinch.

The sound she made was a cross between a whimper and a squeak. He took it as a good thing.

"Jamie," he said, trying to find some way to express himself beyond his obvious drooling in her presence. "I want you again."

Okay, that was a stupid thing to say. Like she couldn't figure out where he was going with the tongue diving. But his brain was like mud. And he didn't know any poetry, which seemed appropriate to the occasion.

Yet despite his lame attempts at seduction, she did the most amazing thing.

She stood up, blanket around her waist, ice cream abandoned, and said, "Take me again. Please."

Oh, yeah. Jack stood up, sending his own chair crashing to the floor. He leaned forward and kissed her hard, trying to stay in control. It didn't work. Control no longer existed in his vocabulary. Just scratched right out. Gone. Especially when she kissed him back, her fingers moving over the front of his shorts.

As she found his cock and gave him a squeeze, he reflected that this felt so damn right. That this could be something damn special. That maybe Jamie was exactly the kind of woman who could help him make sense out of his life, give him a quiet place to rest where he wasn't competing with someone or something, where he wasn't bored and restless.

"Share your ice cream with me," he murmured, nipping at her ear.

"I'd be happy to. I have plenty," she whispered.

Jack wasn't talking about dessert, and he didn't think Jamie was either. He knew he was going to take her again, right here in this chair. Knew he was going to carry her to his bed and keep her there all day. Knew that if she was agreeable, he'd have her back in his bed that night for another round of naked hide-and-seek.

The base of her palm was moving up and down on him as he kissed her neck. She smelled so good, tasted so delicious that he wanted to lap her up. They were way too far apart, the corner of the table preventing full body contact.

Jack stepped around the table, holding a hand out for her. "Come here." He was well aware that he had burst out of his boxers and was reaching for the sky. An urgent desperation had him stalking her when she didn't immediately come forward.

He was probably acting like an ass, but blame it on the noodles. All that slurping and sucking and licking. His reaction was only natural.

One of the things he appreciated about Jamie was her exuberance, her cheerfulness. She displayed those wonderful qualities by giving him a nervous, but excited smile and peeling her panties down her legs. As she dropped them on her chair with a half turn, Jack got a blissful shot of Jamie's backside, before she straightened back up.

"Thought those might get in the way of the taking."

"Smart woman," he managed to spit out in a growl before he erased the space between them and slammed her body against his.

Jamie barely had a second to enjoy the shocked arousal on Jack's face before he had her pressed against him, his one hand cupping her backside, the other caressing across her bottom lip.

Then he pushed a finger into her mouth at the same time he used his other hand to slip two fingers inside her. He moved them all with the same rhythm, a hot push, mimicking sex, her cheeks sucking in automatically, tongue flickering over his flesh. It was invasive, erotic, the press of his index finger into her mouth. There was no taste, just hard flesh pressing into hot moisture, an echo of what was happening between her legs.

Plunge and stroke, here and there, until Jamie moved her head, shifted her hips, wiggling in ecstasy, wanting more, wanting away, wanting fingers gone and Jack's cock to replace them. In her mouth and between her legs.

She couldn't breathe, couldn't think, was desperate . . . then he touched her sensitive nipple with a nice long lave with his tongue. She broke, biting down on his finger reflexively as she came with a hard spasm.

Jack made a little hiss—that sounded like approval—so Jamie clamped down and held on with her teeth as she rode the shuddering crest to its end. It was quick, but powerful, intense, ripping all the way through her until it reached its trembling conclusion. Hands relaxing at her sides, she pulled her head back and released his finger, sagging in satisfaction. Her heart was thumping like a drum again, loud and furious.

"Well, now, that was . . . oh!" Jamie gasped when Jack pulled her forward and swiveled her around. Given that she was still punch-drunk from an orgasm, she had no sense of space and balance and went tumbling in the direction he urged her.

She caught herself on the slipcovered chair she'd just been sitting in eating her Chinese food. While her breasts bounced toward her chin, and her butt automatically shot up in the air as she gripped the seat, she saw where he was going with this.

It was confirmed when Jack gripped her thighs and yanked them apart.

Hello. This couldn't possibly work. Or maybe it could, but she wasn't mentally prepared for this. It was a bit too exposed for her taste, a bit too Kama Sutra for Jamie Lynn. Was she supposed to lock her knees or bend them? No, that was completely weird . . .

Panicking, she heard the rustle as he dispensed with his boxers, and Jamie struggled to right herself out of this particular angle. Stuck for the moment, since he'd come up behind her and blocked her in, she glanced over her shoulder. He was rolling on a condom. Where had that come from? Geez Louise, she wasn't good at this spontaneous, raw thing.

"Um, Jack?" She licked her lips and gave a tentative hip wiggle to encourage him to release her. "I'm not so sure that this—"

His answer was to grab her thighs and plunge inside her

with his hard erection. Jamie held on to the chair and gasped in pleasure, enjoying the full fit of him, the tingling aftershocks of her still swollen folds.

"Yes, Jamie?"

"Nothing . . . I was just going to suggest this might not work."

He pulled back, pushed in.

"But it clearly does."

And it felt shockingly good. He was sliding along her flesh, coaxing sensation the whole way, her body rippling with pleasure. There wasn't anything pretty about this position—at least she couldn't imagine what he was seeing was pretty. There was nothing elegant or gentle about this urgent late morning mating, but it was that very rawness that made it so intimate. Jamie saw and felt vulnerability in Jack's strong pushes, the way he gripped her thighs so hard her flesh pinched. She felt the same vulnerability, the same feeling of walking on uneven ground. She didn't understand her body's reaction to him, didn't understand the emotions that were swirling around inside her.

Nothing, with any man before, had ever been anything like this.

Maybe that was the power of sex for sex's sake. It allowed a pure selfish enjoyment.

But Jamie knew this wasn't just sex. Not for her anyway. She had meant it when she said she didn't go around sleeping with men she'd just met.

Which didn't explain exactly how she'd come to be bent over a kitchen chair with her legs spread and Jack deep inside of her.

Thoughts skittering here, there, and everywhere, she dug her nails into the cotton slipcover and kicked her doubts to the curb. She wanted to enjoy this, just *feel* it.

He didn't make any sound as he moved, but Jamie couldn't prevent small moans from slipping out of her mouth. The hot friction sent jolts through her, and the elemental need between them, all niceties stripped away, was just as big of a turn-on as his actual actions.

Jack came with a silent shudder, pausing before one last convulsive shove.

"Yes," she whispered, as he poured himself into her, letting go, giving it all to her. She felt powerful in that moment, a woman who shattered a man.

It was raw, and she was taking it. Jamie clenched her inner muscles and held on for the ride.

Chapter 7

Jack nearly bit his tongue off. Here he was, recklessly ripping off an orgasm three minutes into sex, and she had done that girl thing. That mysterious thing where she sort of squeezed herself around his cock and pumped more pleasure than he ever could have thought possible from him.

Teeth clenched so tight he nearly cracked a filling, Jack was scrambling to regain control of himself even before the last rippling shudder tore through him.

"Damn." He sucked in a breath. "Damn. Shit. Damn, damn, damn."

Jamie was hanging on to that chair for dear life, her hair tumbling down her back. Her tight, lush ass rose before him, his cock buried between her thighs, T-shirt bunched around her waist. It was a hot, hot shot, but he wasn't sure that totally explained the way he'd gone at her.

And he wasn't finished yet.

But her back was probably going to snap any second now.

With rubbery arms, he shifted out of her, then hauled her upright, kissing the backside of her shoulder.

"Mmm," she said, wiggling her hips against him.

Jack closed his eyes, caught his breath. Swallowed hard. "Keep doing that and we'll be starting all over again."

"Really?" she asked, with a wicked little laugh.

Jamie sounded so intrigued Jack felt a little kick of renewed lust, a little jump from his unit. He wouldn't have thought it possible, but hell, Jamie did all kinds of amazing things to his libido.

"Turn around, please. I want to see you." He turned her at the waist, yanked off her shirt, and when her breasts and her face came into his view, Jack touched her hair, tucked it behind an ear. She was smiling at him, looking satisfied and naughty, and he was shocked by what he felt for her. The frightening deep, dark depth of emotion.

"Wrap your legs around me. Please." He wanted her closer, right against him, in his arms.

Without hesitation, she lifted her legs and wrapped them around him, pressing her wet mound against his belly, full breasts against his chest. Jack closed his eyes for a split second as he held her.

Longing nearly shattered him. She felt . . . perfect in his arms. A soft, warm woman. His woman.

Jamie's hair tickled his shoulder as she ran her lips over his jaw. Goose bumps rose on her skin, and she gave a light shiver.

With a soft laugh, she explained, "Air-conditioning. It makes me cold."

Personally, he felt like a five-alarm fire had nothing on him, but he didn't want her uncomfortable.

"Let's go to the couch." He swiped the red blanket from the chair before walking awkwardly to the sofa, dropping Jamie down onto it.

She reached for the blanket, arranged it over her.

Unrolling the condom, Jack walked to his windows and yanked down his shades. It was before lunch on a Saturday, but who knew what people could see through these windows, depending on which way the sun hit. He dropped the condom in the wastebasket next to his desk. When he turned back, he saw Jamie had tightened the blanket over her so it clung to her curves like linen on a mummy.

Much better than a lumpy draping of the blanket that would hide all of her. Lust kicked him in the gut, surprise, surprise. "You did that on purpose, didn't you?"

"What?" she asked in an innocent little tone that didn't fool him. "Are you accusing me of something?"

The twang turned up in her voice, and it hardened him even further. Jack went on his knees next to the couch and cupped the outline of her mound with his hand. She gave a startled little sound, laced with approval.

He said, "You covered it up, but in a way that would still show everything to me. I appreciate your thoughtfulness." Then he jerked the blanket off of her feet and ankles. Shoved it up toward her chin. "Don't want you to get cold, cutie."

She should have looked vulnerable, lying there on her back, visibly naked from the thighs down, blanket shoved up to her chin as though she needed protection. She didn't. In fact, he had the sense she was the strongest woman he'd ever known, true to her convictions, sure of who she was.

He was waiting for her to say this was enough, that it was time for her to go home, time to put a little distance between them. But she didn't, and he was pushing, shoving, letting them careen forward into an intimacy he wanted, craved, couldn't imagine retreating from. As long as she smiled and let him, he was going to go forward. He wanted Jamie fiercely, possessively, permanently.

"I am a little cold," she said.

"Is it time to stop, Jamie?" No, he was the one who felt vulnerable, on his knees next to her, wanting her so bad he was shaking, his erection the size of the Empire State Building.

But she shook her head. "No. I'm not ready to stop."

He didn't deserve her or that response, but he wasn't going to question it. He was going to have her again before she changed her mind. "Jamie, beautiful Jamie. I am a lucky man."

Jack bent to her ankle and traced the line of it with his finger. He liked the peachy color of her flesh, the way the lamp warmed her skin to the honey gold of a ripe piece of fruit. He kissed her calf, traced his hand over both of her legs, sent the blanket a little higher.

Her smell was different, welcome, the scent of a woman. Nothing in his apartment, his office, even came close to the purity of the lilac aroma that wafted around Jamie, intermingling with the sweet pungency of her arousal. He licked her leg, holding her against the couch when she jerked beneath him.

Leaning forward, he went higher, kissing the sides of her knee, sucking the puckered flesh there. He was so frighteningly aware that Jamie Peters was the kind of woman a man could love, and that he felt a paradoxical, desperate need to settle down with a life partner, like his sister was about to, and fill his apartment with companionship.

And the horrible irony was that he hadn't been completely honest with her. If he told her now, he wasn't sure what she would do.

It was frustrating, infuriating, a completely new feeling to not have confidence in what he was doing, to have backed himself into this ugly little corner, and he found himself shoving that stupid blanket up higher, baring more of Jamie before him. Her curls were dusky auburn, like the hair on her head, and her thighs had drifted apart.

He didn't want to let her go, didn't want to see disappointment on her face when she found out he controlled Beechwood's funding. That he had lied about this apartment.

If there was a stupid fuck-up award, he would definitely qualify for it. Motivated by the need to keep her pleased, needing to hold her close, he bent over her. Teasingly, he kissed, petted, sucked, loved, all around her thighs and hipbones, avoiding the part of her that wiggled in invitation, growing wetter and wetter even as he watched. Moisture gleamed off her curls, and her fingers scratched a rhythmic clawing on the surface of the sofa.

He couldn't hear her breathing or moans, and a glance up showed the blanket had gone past her mouth. Her pert nose was visible, and her eyes were clamped shut, head tilted back. Jack ran the palm of his hand over her in a circular motion, letting his thumb drop down over her clitoris.

Then even with the blanket muffling it, he heard the moan that came from her.

His thumb sank down along her folds, first left, then right, stroking the swollen flesh, making his throat constrict and his blood pound. She squirmed.

The silence tripped around him, his focus on her, and her alone.

Jack bent over. Replaced his thumb with his tongue.

Jamie was expecting Jack's touch. She knew, even as she fought to breathe under the blanket, that he was heading there. But she didn't expect the sweetness, the gentle play of his tongue over her clitoris, over her slick sex. She ached all the more for the way he took time with her, slowly coaxing her to intense, riveting pleasure.

She couldn't see a damn thing as he pushed the blanket even farther up to give him room to palm her breast. Cashmere pill balls brushed her lips, and she turned her head left and right, blind in the darkness. But she didn't care enough to struggle with it, especially when she realized he was doing it on purpose.

It should make her uncomfortable, but it didn't. She trusted him in a way that she really shouldn't. But deep down in her gut, she knew he was motivated by a desire to arouse her, to get her screaming hot.

So she wasn't going to complain. Especially not when his tongue was flicking into her, wrenching desire spiraling all throughout her body, coiling tighter and tighter. She clamped her eyes closed, let the feeling of the cashmere over her shoulders further arouse her sensitive skin, let him push into her over and over while she let go.

Mind empty, body straining, Jamie embraced an orgasm, reaching out to grab on to something. She clutched the blanket, wrapped it around her fingers as she arched up into Jack's touch, waves of pleasure washing over her. In the dark, hidden, she let herself call out as loudly as she wanted, and luxuriated in the way he held on to her, wouldn't release his hold on her long after she'd stopped shuddering.

"You can stop," she whispered, her leg twitching as she settled back onto the couch. "You can let go."

The blanket was jerked out of her hands, off her face, by Jack, even as he continued to press kisses on her clitoris. She blinked in the sudden bright light, then looked down at him, still kneeling, short caramel-colored hair bent over her.

His kisses were moving north, and he plucked lazily at her nipples. His gaze rolled over her, before he gave a little smile that was part smirk.

"You know, I don't really want to let go. Ever."

Well, then.

He must have read her mind. Because while giving him an out seemed like the polite thing to do, she didn't really want him to let go either. Ever.

Chapter 8

At what had to be right smack in the middle of Saturday afternoon, Jamie stared at the ceiling above Jack's bed, tired but wide awake, and sighed with contentment.

Wow. Double wow with a cherry on top.

Never in her life had she imagined sex could be so *hot*. She wasn't feeling like anybody's mother after all of that.

Jack had been the most incredible, thoughtful, sexy lover she could have imagined. And the things they had done.

Who knew they were possible? She was pretty sure they had invented a new position or two during the course of their bedroom adventures.

She had the satisfied ache between her thighs to prove it.

He had called her beautiful.

The sun was pouring through the window and dancing across her face. There was no way she could fall back asleep. Her mind was whirring a million miles a minute.

Jack was on his stomach, mouth open, his arm thrown across her chest protectively. She couldn't resist stroking his hair just a little, curling a strand around her finger as she studied his smooth back.

She wanted to wake him up, but he looked so tired, so deep in sleep, that she knew she couldn't do it. They'd been up for more than twenty-four hours, and had expended quite a bit of energy before they'd finally collapsed in sleep around noon. Maybe she should just leave him in bed and take a shower or fix some coffee.

With that in mind, Jamie slid out from under his arm, pulled Jack's shirt off the floor, and slipped it on.

Checking to make sure he wasn't awake to catch her being a fool, she buried her head in the collar and breathed deeply. It smelled like him. Woodsy and masculine.

In the strong summer daylight, she looked around as she walked down the hall to the kitchen, intent on starting some coffee.

It was a big apartment, filled with expensive, though haphazard furniture. It had the feel of a man, with lots of electronic toys and little in the way of color. She wondered what it would look like if it were Jack's apartment. A lot homier than this, she imagined.

Lack of color worried her. It was like a metaphor for an empty life. Her own side of her room was stuffed with flea market finds like lava lamps, throw rugs, and fuzzy daisy wall hangings. The dominant colors were purple and orange.

Allison gave her a hard time about it, since she leaned toward the beige family in her decorating, but Jamie liked warm, happy colors with soft fabric.

The kitchen in the apartment didn't look like it was used very often. After poking around, she found the coffee, and the French press coffeemaker. It took her a minute to figure it out, and while the water was boiling she wandered into the living room. Even though she'd spent some time in there on the couch, she hadn't been looking at anything but the cashmere blanket and the ceiling. Now she took the room in without distractions.

There were pictures on the console table behind the sofa. She was a little curious to see who Jack's friend was who could afford this pricey address.

It was a pleasant surprise to see Jack in the first picture

she picked up. He was with two other guys, one of whom must be the apartment friend. They were on the beach, and Jack looked a few years younger than he did now. Probably college age. He had told her last night he was thirty.

He even looked cute in an eight-year-old photograph, tanned and windswept, showing off that chest she had explored and licked so thoroughly that morning. Jamie put the picture back and grinned to herself. Yep. She was definitely gone if she was cooing over old photos of him.

Absently she grabbed the next frame. Then did a double take. Jack was in this picture, too. Only it was Jack and a couple in their fifties, their arms around Jack while he stood in a graduation gown, holding a diploma.

Wait a flipping minute.

Why would Jack's graduation picture be sitting in an apartment that wasn't his?

And why did that woman look so familiar?

Curiosity compelled her to grab the next picture. Only she barely managed to keep from dropping this one on the floor in surprise.

Bigger than a surprise. More like breath-robbing shock. Jack was in that picture, too.

But that meant nothing compared to the fact that the woman standing next to him looked way more than familiar.

It was Caroline, Jamie's roommate.

And her arm was slung around Jack and vice versa in a friendly way.

Jamie gasped and looked back at the graduation photo. No wonder that woman had looked familiar to her. She was Mrs. Davidson, Caroline's mom, who Jamie had met when they had gone for a fitting for her bridesmaid's dress for Caroline's wedding.

Which meant that Jack must be Caroline's older brother.

Oh, my word. Aside from the fact it was a strange coincidence she had met Caroline's brother by accident on the subway, there was even more shocking news regarding Jack.

If he was Caroline's brother, then he was also Jonathon Davidson, who just happened to be a millionaire.

The filthy rich Wall Street whiz who had retired a year ago. Mrs. Davidson had told her all about him while Jamie had been getting stuck with the seamstress's pins.

She dropped the frame in her hand as if it were a bomb.

Which in a way it was.

Because if Jack was Jonathon Davidson, then chances were this was his apartment after all.

Meaning he had lied to her.

And she had slept with her friend's brother.

Who was so completely not her type it was unreal.

The phone rang, causing her to jump and look toward the bedroom, feeling guilty and embarrassed. Like an idiot. A complete fool. She had fallen for Beckwith's promise of a perfect man and had flung herself off a cliff without checking to see what was down below.

Sitting on the console table next to her, the phone continued to ring, and she couldn't help but notice the caller ID with its little digital clock that read 4:02 P.M. The caller was Hathaway, Stephen.

It was a name that meant nothing, other than that Hathaway was also the name of the foundation Jonathon worked for, and she couldn't help but wonder who would be calling Jack on a Saturday afternoon. Friend? Relative? Not that it was any of her business.

Really. Since she didn't know any of his business at all. Since he was in fact a total stranger that she had only eaten dinner with, talked to all night, then engaged in multiple sex acts with.

The built-in answering machine clinked on after the fourth ring, and Jamie cleared her throat. Too bad she didn't actually drink coffee. She could go into the kitchen, pour a cup, and pretend not to listen to Jack's personal call. He may not have any ethics or scruples and could lie about his apartment without guilt or compunction, but she was an honest person.

Which didn't explain why she was rooted to the rug like a stubborn weed.

A man's voice spoke. "Jonathon, it's Steve. Why the frick is your cell turned off? Listen, I've got to talk to you about that whole Beechwood business. I talked to legal and you can't sit back on this, you have to call in the feds. So instead of following Caro's roommate like the bored millionaire loser that you are, you need to tell her what we found. Call me back so I know you're on this. *Ciao*."

Jamie didn't know who Steve was, or what Beechwood and the feds had to do with each other, but she did strongly suspect that the gist of that message was that Jack had known she was Jamie Peters, Caroline's roommate.

And geez Louise, did that hurt. It was also humiliating.

Beckwith's words rang in her ears, loud and clear. A dishonest act will bring you the man of your dreams. She had slept with a complete and total liar. She had allowed herself to be sweet-talked right out of her pants like some dumb girl straight off the farm.

Embarrassment sent her into the bedroom to retrieve her discarded jeans and pull them on, retreating to the living room without looking at Jack. Jamie was shocked at her own behavior in hindsight.

Dinner. She'd invited him for dinner, and here she was struggling back into her jeans and bra twenty-four hours later. Knowing her tank top was ruined, she pulled Jack's black T-shirt back on over her bra and knotted the corner of it so it wasn't as huge and baggy.

Her pants were wrinkled to hell and back, and she could only see one sandal. Crawling around frantically on her knees looking for it, Jamie cursed her own stupidity. Coming home with Jack had been one of her less brilliant ideas, and she was just mortified. She had fallen for all of it—the connection, the interest, the caring in his eyes. Maybe Allison was right. She was too trusting. Naïve.

Dating fixer-upper men had always been her specialty. She had thought Jack was different. And yet here she was searching for discarded clothing and praying he wouldn't wake up before she got the hell out of there. She didn't think she could face him. Not after the way she had shared a part of herself, her thoughts, her heart, her soul, with him, and he'd just been looking to get lucky.

Her sandal was jammed under the couch, and she tugged it out. A quick peek in her wallet confirmed she had forty bucks, which meant she could grab a cab instead of the subway, thank goodness for small favors. Remembering the boiling water, she went into the kitchen and turned it off. Hesitated. Then found herself pouring it into the French press and pushing the plunger down.

This was what her problem was. She was taking the time to make coffee for a man who had lied to her. God, she needed counseling. Pressing the pot back farther on the counter, she wiped her hands and retreated out of the kitchen.

On tiptoes, she went back down the hall and took a last peek at Jack.

Maybe she was overreacting. Yes, there was reason to feel uncomfortable. He had seen her naked. He was now in a fairly exclusive club of Men Who Had Done Her. But that wasn't a reason to panic. They were adults. She had known what she was doing both the night before and that morning.

Which didn't make it any less stupid now.

But she was a fair person. Maybe he had a good reason for withholding his identity from her. Besides being a jerk, that is.

Maybe she should wake him up, and they could have a rational discussion about what had happened, who he was, and what his concerns over the funding at Beechwood were.

Jack rolled over in bed, his mouth closed, breathing silently.

He was tangled up in the sheet, and he looked absolutely gorgeous. Sweet.

The lying rat. Who had such a talented tongue in more ways than one.

She had to remind herself to hold on to her anger. It wouldn't be a good thing to start feeling sympathy for him. To start remembering what it had felt like with his you-know-what buried deep inside her . . .

Shit, she was caving. Which was not a good thing.

Wiping her hands on her jeans, she crept into the bedroom and stood in front of Jack's closet.

No.

Jonathon Davidson's closet.

Clenching her teeth, she opened it slowly so it wouldn't creak.

Casual clothes hung in front of her. Jeans, sweaters, button-up shirts. Relief assailed her. Then she turned a little and peered toward the back of the closet.

There they were. At least a dozen suits were hanging. Expensive. She checked the label. It meant nothing to her, but it sounded Italian and pretentious.

Shiny black and brown shoes lined up underneath them, and a tie rack contained an array of silk ties.

She stumbled back, covering her mouth with her hand, tears stinging her eyes.

Her worst nightmare.

She had slept with a Suit.

And had enjoyed every single luscious minute of it.

Chapter 9

Jamie rushed past the doorman as fast as she could in the stupid platform sandals, unable to look the man in the eye. She felt like a bad morning-after cliché—rumpled and regretful.

She had thought Jack was the kind of man she could spend the rest of her life with. Had wanted to believe so much that he found her sexy and appealing and wanted the same thing.

It really sucked that she could have been so wrong. That she could have felt that hopeful, that desperate, that ridiculous, when Jack couldn't possibly be that man. The Jack she had talked to all night and had slept with wasn't even real. She didn't know the secrets of Jack's heart and mind.

Yet she still very much wanted him to be The One.

Which wasn't at all cool.

Patting her hair down, she dialed on her cell phone and tried not to panic.

After four rings, Allison said, "Jamie?"

"Help!" she wailed into the phone.

So much for not panicking.

"Are you okay? Where the hell have you been all freaking night? I was about ready to call the cops. I told you it was a bad idea to go out with a total stranger."

Knowing Allison was right didn't make her feel any better. "I'm fine. Don't call the cops. I'm on my way home."

Jamie was walking unnecessarily fast, which was ridiculous because Jack wasn't going to come flying out of his building and chase down the street after her. She forced herself to slow down. "I need some advice. Things are . . . complicated."

"Uh-oh. That sounds like sex to me. You had sex with him, didn't you?"

If closing her eyes wouldn't result in death by taxi cab, Jamie would have stopped in the middle of the street and done just that. She needed an emergency yoga session. She needed to find her center.

It seemed to have stayed behind in Jack Davidson's bed. No one had ever found her center quite so successfully as he had.

"I did have sex with Jack . . . who just happens to be Caroline's brother."

"What? Jonathon? The goofy guy Jack you met on the subway is *Jonathon?* Good-looking, Darien High School class president, financial wizard, millionaire Jonathon? How is that possible?"

That was the question of the day. "I have no idea. But Jack is Jonathon and I had sex with him by accident." Jamie winced as she glanced around. Where the hell was she? She never came to this neighborhood. Too professional. Expensive.

"An accident? How the hell could having sex with him be an accident?"

Jamie rubbed her temples, the air hot and muggy. "It . . ." God, she didn't even have any words to explain herself. "Well . . ."

"So, what, the wind blew your clothes off, and then you tripped and fell on his penis?"

The image was so ludicrous she almost laughed.

"An accident is something you have no control over, like

sneezing when you're driving and you rear-end someone. Sex isn't an accident, Jamie, admit it."

"You're right." Jamie stopped in front of a bagel shop. "I wanted to have sex with Jack. We went to dinner, we got talking and talking, all night, and I thought . . . it seemed . . . he was so . . . it was like it was just so right." And she had been so wrong.

Jamie propped the phone on her shoulder and wiped her hands on her shirt. Jack's shirt. "Oh, dang it. Caro's going to croak."

"Well, you're not going to tell her, are you?" The horror in Allison's voice showed her opinion on telling the truth. "It's not like you're going to do it again, right?"

Obviously not, since she'd just turned tail and run. "No, of course not."

"Not that it would be a bad thing, I guess. I mean, Jonathon, Caroline's brother, is much better than Jack, the stranger on the subway. Jonathon has some serious cash, Jams."

That's what she was afraid of.

"You could do a lot worse. And obviously you were compatible."

And then some. But everything was different now, skewed and twisted. "We are not compatible in any way. This is Caroline's brother, for God's sake. Mr. Corporate. And I'm Jamie, the social worker, from Kentucky. We might as well be from different planets."

"Don't go quoting that women-are-from-Saturn, men-are-from-Pluto garbage on me."

"I don't think that's how it went."

"Whatever."

Jamie rubbed her temples and fought confusion. She didn't know what she was doing, she just knew what she'd done, which was make an ass out of herself. "I'm not seeing Jack ever again, and I'm certainly not having sex with him."

"So then why tell Caroline? What she doesn't know won't gross her out."

That just wasn't the way Jamie worked. "But I can't lie about it. It will become like this huge, burdensome secret, and if it ever eventually came out, then it would be like a thousand times worse because of the lying."

"If Caroline finds out in five years that you had sex with her brother once I don't really think she's going to give a crap. She'll be too busy changing diapers by then."

Jamie wanted to be changing diapers in five years, too. She sighed and stuck her hand up to flag a cab that was approaching.

"If you tell her now, it will just weird her out, and she's getting married in exactly two weeks. If you have to tell her, at least wait until after the wedding."

"I can do that, I guess." The last thing in the world Jamie wanted was to add to the stress Caroline was feeling in the final countdown to her wedding.

She got in the cab. "Sixth and Greenwich, please." Slamming the door, she shifted the phone. "But I am begging you to run interference for me at the wedding . . . I don't think I can look Jack in the eye without blushing."

"That good?" Allison asked with scandalized glee.

Oh, yeah. That good. Just the memory made her inner thighs feel zapped by lightning.

With a whisper, Jamie said, "Over a chair, Allison. That's all I'm going to say."

"No way." Allison gave a delighted laugh. "Why don't accidents like that ever happen to me?"

Jack came out of sleep slowly. He turned a few times, tangled himself up in the sheet, yawned, and forced his eyes open, anticipating the sight of Jamie asleep, naked, beside him.

He was disappointed to find the bed empty, despite a

quick glance at the clock showing it was only five o'clock. So much for waking Jamie up with a kiss and a strategically placed hand.

The smell of coffee floated into the bedroom and urged him to sit up in bed. Jamie had been up long enough to make coffee already, and he was wasting time sleeping. Time they could be together.

As he ran a hand through his hair, he noticed the closet door was open. He must have left it open last night in his haste to get to his dinner with Jamie.

He hoped she didn't have plans for the next few days. He had every intention of spending every minute with her, especially since tonight he had to go to Brad's bachelor party and wouldn't be able to see Jamie. A bachelor party lost hands down to a night with Jamie, but he couldn't exactly get out of it. Brad was marrying his sister Caroline the week after next, and it wouldn't be forgivable if Jack missed tonight's party.

But that left the rest of today and hopefully tomorrow. And forever and a day after that. As he stood up and pulled on a pair of boxers and shorts, he wondered if it was possible to fall in love in twenty-four hours. Love was about the only word he could think of to explain how he was feeling.

The perfect rightness of Jamie in his arms, in his bed, in his heart.

It was crazy, but true.

He felt a little like he'd been run over by a semi-truck crashing through the Lincoln Tunnel.

Jack started down the hall toward the kitchen, popping into the bathroom to make sure Jamie wasn't in there taking a shower or something. He could offer assistance if she was, but the bathroom was empty.

He had the sneaking suspicion the semi-truck feeling wasn't going to go away. It was Jamie. She was amazing. Sweet, shy, yet so giving, so generous with herself.

She was everything he was looking for in a woman.

Jack glanced in the living room and finally stopped in the kitchen, bewildered.

What Jamie was, was gone.

What the hell?

Jack looked around again, as if expecting her to suddenly pop up from behind the stove.

How could she have left? It wasn't possible.

A frantic search of the living room showed that her bra and her purse were gone, and her jeans and shoes were missing from the bedroom. The only thing he found was her torn flower shirt, kicked under his coffee table.

Clutching the fabric in bewilderment, he looked for a note left in the kitchen or on his nightstand, but couldn't find any.

Finally, he stopped in his living room and stood staring at the door in disbelief, the shirt pressed against his chest. She had left. Without a word. Without a note.

After the most incredible dinner, night, morning of his life, she had disappeared. Not a *call me*, a *see ya*, a *thanks for the memories*, a *you suck in bed* . . . nothing.

All she had left him was a pot of coffee, still warm.

"You did what?" Beckwith shrieked at her, causing other diners to glance their way.

Jamie winced and picked at her bagel. "I left." Normally she loved big Sunday breakfasts, but this time she didn't have any appetite. That was a serious first, noteworthy in the Jamie Peters record book. Disinterest in food. Maybe she was getting sick.

Maybe she was just an idiot. For more than one reason. But she felt compelled to defend herself. "I told you, he lied to me. I don't like people lying to me. It shatters all trust. And he's rich, Beckwith. Rich people make me uncomfortable."

"Oh, for God's sake," was Beckwith's opinion on the subject. He fussed with the back of his diamond solitaire ear-ring. He had gone for the Connecticut brunch look. Silk blouse, light make-up, designer slacks, pointy-toed pumps.

"I told you a dishonest act was going to bring him to you. You should have been mentally prepared for a lie. I'm sure he had a good reason."

"And every man I work with had a good reason for committing the crime he did. I don't want excuses. I want someone who can take responsibility and tell the truth." It was still so darn hard to reconcile the tender and sexy lover Jack with the millionaire Jonathon. She didn't understand why he had lied to her and didn't think the reason was really going to be anything she wanted to hear.

Beckwith waved his hand as if all of that were unimportant. "I practically spoon fed you true love, and you just walk away? Without getting his number or last name?" Spearing a grape, he pointed it at her. "You panicked and ran scared. Being rich is never a bad thing in my book, honey."

He shook his head mournfully. "True love. It was so damn beautiful. There were all kinds of little happy auras all over your cards, and you just spit on it and throw it away. I'm Jamie, I'm too good for love, don't need it, I'm a Bolshevik hippie going to give away all my money because money is bad . . ."

That cut through her melancholy and made her laugh. "Okay, now you're being flat-out crazy. And I didn't get his last name because I didn't need to. I saw the pictures. He's Caroline's brother. That was his apartment." She shuddered just thinking about the horror, the humiliation. "That place was like an exercise in isolation. It screamed workaholic."

"And you're not a workaholic?"

"No!" Jamie sat back in shock, abandoning her bagel altogether. "Of course not."

"Please. You work ten, twelve hours a day for peanuts. You let cases call you at home, on the weekend. You open yourself up both financially and emotionally. You're having brunch with me, an ex-con cross-dressing psychic, for God's sake. You, my darling, are a workaholic."

They were dining alfresco on a little patio outside the bagel shop. A breeze kicked up and sent her hair tumbling across her eyes. Swiping at it, Jamie tried to convince herself Beckwith's words were just flat-out wrong. "I'm dedicated. Committed to my career."

Her voice didn't sound as convincing and firm as she would have liked it to.

Apparently Beckwith agreed. "So is Jack. The only difference between the two of you is he's a Republican."

"That's a pretty big difference." Peasant skirts and designer suits didn't go together.

"This isn't about politics. It's about love." He brought his right hand up and formed an *L* with his fingers, showing off his French manicure. "The big *L*. Destiny. The One."

Jamie had found herself waffling all morning, wondering if she had done the right thing in leaving. It wasn't like her to run away from a situation. She liked to talk through things, resolve with communication. But nothing was going to change the fact that Jack/Jonathon had lied to her and she felt like a humongous fool.

Beckwith's words reminded her just how much.

"Beck, it's exactly that kind of talk that got me into this in the first place. If I hadn't been so sure that Jack was The One, I wouldn't have gone home with him. I wouldn't have slept with him, and I wouldn't find myself in the very embarrassing situation I am in. I let my fortune, my vision of the future, cloud my judgment, and that makes me feel as naïve as people say I am."

She had always prided herself on being compassionate but intelligent, willing to take a chance on people without being gullible and blind. This made her feel like a joke. Like the goofy girl from Kentucky that everyone humored. Usually she didn't care what people thought of her. She was confident, knew who she was, liked herself.

But she had opened up to Jack, told him personal feelings, hopes, dreams, and it hurt like hell to think he might not have been sincere. Especially since she had been just fine without a man until he'd come along. This was what she got for thinking Jamie Peters could have a wild, sexual fling. She couldn't kiss a man without wanting to knit him a scarf.

Beckwith didn't answer for a minute, chewing a bite of his omelet, gaze drifting over to the street. Then he pinned her with a hard stare. "All I know is you can't fuck with fate. If you do, it will just bitch-slap you back."

Then she was even. Because she pretty much felt like she'd been slapped already.

Chapter 10

"You're really going to call her?" Steve crossed his arms and gave him a look of disapproval.

"Yes, I'm going to call her." Jack spun around in his desk chair and reached for the phone. Wandering around his apartment Sunday feeling sorry for himself—not to mention getting shit-faced drunk Saturday at the bachelor party— had not made for a rousing end to his weekend. He had impatiently waited for Monday so he could get to the office and call Jamie at work, where she'd be less tempted to say nasty things to him when he tried to apologize.

He'd heard Steve's message on his machine, coming in at four P.M. on Saturday. Jack didn't know if Jamie had heard the call or not, but it certainly would explain her leaving without saying a word.

Somehow he had to find a way to fix things, to make sure she understood his intentions were good, if a bit screwed up. He couldn't stand the thought that this was it. That there was no future for them.

"Jack, if a woman leaves your apartment without a word after you've had sex, she is giving you a very clear message—leave me alone."

Jack steepled his fingers together and stared at his cousin. "How do you know we had sex?"

Steve rolled his eyes and adjusted his red tie. "Because I'm not an idiot. Look, just let it go. You had fun, it's done."

"No." The very thought appalled him. The last thing in the world he wanted to do was let go of the perfect woman without some kind of discussion, explanation, second chance. Everything was fixable. Failure was not an option.

He picked up the phone and dialed.

Steve shook his head. "Oh, man, this is so embarrassing. I'm embarrassed watching you embarrass yourself."

Jack just glared at him and waited for someone to pick up his call.

"Beechwood Social Services, how may I help you?"

"Could I speak to Jamie Peters, please."

"One moment."

Drumming his fingers on his desk, Jack fidgeted in his chair and glanced around his office, decorated in modern industrial by his grandfather. He liked this job, even if there was no challenge for him. Yet he felt the pull to go back, the restlessness, the need to do something different again.

But first he had to fix things with Jamie before he worried about career boredom. He put the phone on his shoulder and gave Steve a pointed look. "Do you mind?"

"No."

"Get out."

"No. I'm staying to save you from yourself."

"All you're doing is annoying me. Go away—" Jack shut up when he heard Jamie say hello.

"Jamie? This is Jack." He turned to the window, away from Steve, pleased just to hear her voice again.

"Jack or Jonathon Davidson?" she asked tightly.

Uh-oh. "Well, both, actually. I answer to both Jack and Jonathon. Jack's just my nickname like I told you. You can call me whatever you want." Then before she could delve any further into that, he said, "So, are you busy tonight? Let me make you dinner."

"In *your* apartment?"

She definitely knew who he was. No question about it. "Yeah, uh, listen, we need to talk. I want to clear a few things up. Maybe we could meet for lunch. I'll come to your office." He was fumbling, caught off-guard by the coldness in her voice, and by the realization that he *had* lied to her and it was going to be hard to explain that away.

But he was damn sure going to try.

"I don't think that's a good idea. Good-bye, Jack."

She hung up on him. Jack jerked the phone back and stared at it. She had hung up on him. Never could he have imagined that Jamie, his sweet Jamie, would hang up on him. He really was up shit creek without a paddle.

Steve rubbed his hand over his chin. "Cut your losses, man. I'm serious. You're setting yourself up for total humiliation."

"No." Jack wasn't going to give up that easily. He called Beechwood right back. "Jamie Peters, please."

"One moment."

"Jack, I'm not interested," Jamie said as a greeting.

"How did you even know it was me?" he asked, relieved that she had picked up, even if she sounded annoyed.

"We have caller ID," Jamie said testily.

"We need to talk. I need to explain about the apartment, need you to understand that I wasn't trying to be deceitful. I just get so used to women wanting to date me for my money that I'm cautious not to reveal too much until I know a woman better."

Steve was still in front of his desk, and now he was very dramatically playing an imaginary violin. Jack picked up a paper clip and winged it at him. *Get out*, he mouthed to his incredibly nosy cousin.

Jamie snorted. "By the third time I'd say you knew me pretty well."

Ouch. "Jamie . . . I'm sorry. I should have told you it's

my apartment, you're absolutely right. I could tell by the end of dinner that you weren't a money hungry kind of person. But you looked so freaked out when you saw my building . . . you said you wouldn't date anyone who lived there." Jesus, this was not helping. Jack rubbed his eyebrows. "You know, I really don't want to do this over the phone. Can I take you to lunch, dinner, coffee?"

"No, thank you. Good-bye, Jack."

The dial tone hit his ear again. "Damn it!"

He punched the redial button. "Beechwood Social Services, how may I help you?"

"Jamie Peters."

"One moment."

Jack was starting to think the receptionist was a recording. She had virtually no expression in her voice, aside from polite boredom.

A second later Jamie picked up. "Stop calling here," she whispered fiercely.

"Then let me see you." Aware that he was starting to sound like a stubborn five-year-old, he changed tones. Let his voice drop. "I miss you, Jamie. My bed was so damn lonely without you last night."

She gave a heartfelt sigh. "Don't . . ."

He could sense her hesitation, her desire to believe him, to return to where they'd been Saturday afternoon. "Just hear me out, gorgeous. Give me a chance to explain. You said everyone deserves a second chance."

"Jack . . ."

"I'll cry," he teased.

She gave a soft laugh. "Right."

"I'm serious. Please just let me see you."

There was a long pause. Then she said, "Fine. I'll meet you for coffee. Just coffee. Nothing else."

"Great. I'll be there in twenty minutes." Jack pumped his fist in the air and whirled his chair around. "See you then. Bye, Jamie."

He hung up before she had a chance to change her mind. Steve lounged against the doorframe, his coffee mug in his hand.

"You're insane."

"Probably. But I also think I'm in love and that's worth going a little crazy over."

Steve lifted an eyebrow. "You'd better take a peace offering."

Jack stood up. "Good plan. Flowers? No, not for Jamie. What do I give a woman like Jamie?" Jewelry wasn't right either. "How do I show her I'm sorry, I'm sincere, I respect her?"

"The way you've described her, she sounds like a bleeding heart. So you could give money to her favorite charity."

Just when he thought Steve served no purpose other than to annoy him, his cousin pulled something brilliant out of his ass. "That's a great idea. I'll give money to her agency. What do you think? Five grand? Ten grand?"

"Whoa. Not her agency. We've been through this. It's time to call the feds on Beechwood, not donate to them."

"No, it has to be her agency. It's a show of faith. Then maybe she'll let me root out the guy who's day trading."

"Bad idea."

Jack moved around him, patting his pocket for his wallet and keys. "No, it's not."

"It's called complicity—accessory to a crime. You have knowledge of illegal activity and you're not reporting it."

"It's not that black-and-white." Jack gave Steve a wave and went out to beg and plead if necessary.

To coax and cajole.

To kiss and lick until Jamie saw that they were meant to be together.

That was the problem with having too much time on his hands. With no job, no apartment, and lazy summer days stretching out long and hot, he couldn't help but find himself in front of Jamie's office again.

Lunchtime. She liked to bring her lunch outside and eat in the little garden next to the social services building. There were vegetables growing in uneven rows, and Jamie always spread her lunch out on the picnic table and flipped through a magazine while she ate.

She was pretty, sweet and innocent. She smiled for everyone, including him when she'd met his eye on the sidewalk, which had made him feel good.

He should leave her alone.

But he couldn't help himself. The need to see her was overwhelming, the only bright spot in long, restless days.

He leaned on the bus stop pole and watched Jamie unwrap her sandwich.

Sooner or later he was going to have to do something. Either leave her alone or tell her the truth.

Jack's cell phone rang as he was brushing his teeth in the private rest room he shared with Steve outside their offices. Spitting out the toothpaste quickly, he pulled his phone out of his pocket. He didn't recognize the number.

"Hello?"

"Hi, Jonathon, how are you?"

Wiping his mouth with a paper towel, Jack tried to place the woman's voice, but he was way too preoccupied with quickly securing fresh breath and getting over to Jamie's office.

"I'm fine. How are you?" He used a cautious, polite tone.

The woman laughed, and he suddenly realized who it was. "It's Meredith, Jonathon. How quickly they forget."

Rolling his eyes, he put his toothbrush and paste back in his travel case and left the rest room. Just who he wanted to talk to. The woman who'd loved his money way more than she'd ever loved him.

"Is there something I can do for you, Meredith?"

"Yes. Come back to the firm. Your old job is available again and we want you back."

That gave him pause outside his office. "Really? Tim left?"

"Yes. Forcibly, I might add. He was no Jonathon Davidson. Look, we've got a mess on our hands here and we need you to clean it up. You were the best analyst the company ever had."

Well, that was true. Jack felt a little smug as he tossed his travel case back into his desk drawer. "I have other commitments now, Meredith." Not that it wasn't incredibly satisfying that they wanted him back. It was. And then some. And it was intriguing, the little familiar jump of excitement he felt at going back to Wall Street, needed. He knew he could fix whatever the situation was, knew that he would enjoy the challenge of untangling the numbers.

"Look, I know we have our differences . . . but I'm mature enough to put the past behind us for the good of the company. Even if you dumped me under humiliating circumstances."

That was a joke. It was such a skewed version of reality that Jack actually laughed. "Meredith, I broke up with you after you bragged that my best attribute was my money. The only one who was humiliated was me."

"What are you talking about? I never said anything of the kind."

God, he didn't want to do this right this very second. Jack could picture Meredith, cool and blond, impeccably dressed, intelligent as hell, her wit as sharp as her fingernails. There had been a time when he'd been very attracted to her appearance of perfection.

But it was only that—an appearance. Their entire relationship had been false, a coup for Meredith, an embarrassing lesson for him. He didn't want to wind up one of those fifty-year-old men with no hair and a thick paunch dangling a gorgeous twenty-five-year-old on his arm, denying to himself that money was his sole attraction.

"I loved you, Jonathon."

Oh, God. No, this wasn't where he wanted to go. "Meredith. I don't know what to say, except that I'm sorry things ended the way they did." Sorry that both of them had been hurt. Sorry that the doubts Meredith had given him had made him stumble in this new relationship with Jamie.

"Come back to the firm. We need you."

Jack hesitated in the doorway of his office. Six months earlier he would have thought he couldn't go back, could never go back to the way he was before, an obsessive workaholic. But that life, the job, called him again, the hook firmly in his back, ready to reel him back in.

"Let me think about it, Meredith. I'll be in touch."

Chapter 11

Jamie wondered why in the name of cruel irony had she packed tuna for lunch that day. Now Jack was walking across the street toward the building, and she must smell like the New York Aquarium. She could probably turn every cat in the neighborhood on, but Jack was going to recoil if he got within three feet of her.

Not that she should care. After all, it was over between them. She had only allowed him to stop by in the first place because she was a fair person, and he was entitled to explain himself.

Before she told him to take a hike.

She just could not, would not, allow herself to be talked into forgiving all his lies. If having a long-term relationship meant she had to put up with dishonesty, she'd happily stay single for the rest of her life.

Apparently her nipples didn't understand her firm resolve on this matter. Because they perked up enthusiastically as she watched Jack approach, thumb drumming his thigh. He was wearing a suit. A power suit. Dark charcoal gray with a crisp white shirt that showed off his tan, and a red tie. The kind that screamed for onlookers to take its owner seriously.

He looked intelligent. Powerful. Rich. Hot. Especially

hot. Really hot. Like she was having a little trouble sitting comfortably with this kind of heat in her skirt.

Never once in her adult life had she looked at a man wearing a suit as a sexy thing, and yet here she was drooling over Jack. Imagining yanking that jacket off and ripping his shirt apart again. Picturing running her tongue over his chest, down his navel, taking his thick, firm erection in her mouth and making him groan with naked pleasure.

"Hi." He smiled at her.

"Hi," she said, her voice sounding like she'd been hitting some helium on her lunch break.

He put his foot up on the seat and leaned over, in that guy stance of not sitting, but not standing either. Casual. Confident.

And she was staring at his crotch.

Jamie caught herself and glanced away, feeling heat streak across her cheeks. What was the matter with her? Focusing on the tomato plants she'd planted with some of the program participants' children, she reminded herself that Jack was a liar.

Liar, liar.

Yet Jamie's skirt was on fire.

She sighed.

"You look beautiful," Jack said.

He was staring at her intently, the way he had when they had talked all night, the way he had when he had been deep inside her body.

"Don't do that. Just tell me the truth. Did you know I was Caroline's roommate?"

The temperature was in the eighties, but she didn't think it was humidity that had her shirt sticking to her chest, sweat trickling down her back. It was nerves. It was fear that she wouldn't be able to stand firm against his smile, his persuasiveness.

"Yes. I knew."

She knew that. Had known it all along. But damn, it hurt

to hear him admit it. "Why didn't you tell me?" Jamie stared at his knee, because she couldn't bring herself to look at his face.

"Because when Beechwood requested funding and I investigated the agency's financials, I found some money shifting that didn't add up. Someone is using the agency's funds to trade, and then moving the money earned out of the account."

That wasn't what she had expected him to say. "What? That's impossible. Who would be able to do that? There are only a handful of us who have access to the computer system."

"And one of you is making money borrowing Beechwood's money to trade with. Not stealing, since the money is always put back, but borrowing. Shifting lines from one column to another, you know what I mean?"

Not really. Her financial savvy was less than zero. "I can't imagine who would possibly do that." Not her boss. Janine had dedicated her life to the agency and lived in a dinky little apartment in Queens to prove it.

"I need to poke around a little, see if I can find out who. Otherwise, I'm obligated to call in the FBI."

"The FBI?" Jamie glanced up at Jack. He couldn't be serious. But he looked serious. "You can't do that!"

"I have to. I've seen the crime, Jamie. But if you let me look into it, I'm sure I can figure out who it is. You can just quietly fire them and forget this ever happened so your operations don't have to be shut down."

"So what did this have to do with me meeting you on the subway? Did you know who I was then?" That's what didn't make sense to her. If Jonathon Davidson of the Hathaway Foundation had known who she was, how did Jack on the subway?

His jaw clenched, but he gave a sharp nod. "Yes. I had been to your office here . . ." He gestured toward the building. "And given what Caroline had told me about you in the past, I didn't think that you were involved in any criminal activity. So I wanted to make sure you weren't in any danger. Everything that happened after that . . . well, I didn't set out for any of that to happen."

Everything that happened. Like dinner, hours and hours of conversation, the most romantic and sexual experience of her life? Relegated to an accident of opportunity.

"I'm sorry," he said, looking appropriately contrite. "Really, truly sorry."

Feeling a little sick, Jamie started packing up her lunch, desperate to get away from him, needing to maintain a little dignity. If she cried in front of him, she would just die, shrivel up like a puddle in the heat.

"You're just sorry that I found out." She balled up her sandwich baggie and stuffed it in her soft-side purple lunch box. "And you can leave now. I've heard all I want to."

His leg dropped to the ground, and he was moving around to her side of the table. Jamie scooted down the bench, reaching for her soft drink can. This was much, much worse than lying about being rich. This had required cunning, and more than withholding a few facts. He had set out to meet her. A sob ripped out of her mouth before she could stop it.

Jack reached for her. "Jamie, don't, baby . . . please. I'm sorry, I should have been honest with you. But I was worried if I told you the truth, you'd confront the perpetrator on your own and get hurt. And then, later, well, shit, I was just selfish. I liked the way you saw me as a man, not a millionaire, and I wanted that. I knew the minute you collided with me on the subway that there was something between us, something that had potential . . . and God, I meant every word I said Saturday."

"Except for the times when you were lying." Jamie stood up and pulled her lunch box to her chest, knowing she only had about five seconds before she lost it. "Do your little investigating into Beechwood's computers. But stay the hell away from me."

She whirled around, wanting to run, determined not to, when he caught her by the elbow.

"Don't do this . . ."

"Let me go." Or she was going to shove her sandwich baggie up his nose.

"No," he said stubbornly, looking frustrated and way too cute for someone who was a jerk.

"I'll scream."

"No, you won't." He actually looked amused by the idea.

And damn it, he was right. She wouldn't scream. She didn't like to make a fuss or draw attention to herself. "If you have a single shred of decency, you'll just leave me alone." She tried to pull back again.

"Jamie." He wasn't exactly pulling on her, but he wasn't letting go of her arm either, so she kind of jerked to a halt when she tried to leave.

"I'll make a donation to Beechwood. How does five thousand dollars sound? Could you do something with that?"

That made her stop all on her own. She whirled around to face him, horrified. Outraged. "Excuse me? Are you trying to *buy* my forgiveness?"

"Uh . . . no."

He looked slapped, bewildered, but she wasn't about to let him off the hook. That was exactly what he was doing whether he realized it or not. And it was why rich people boiled her blood. They thought they could have whatever they wanted if they just flashed enough cash around.

"Of course you were. But I can't be bribed, and I don't fall in love with liars."

Oh, God, why had she used the *L* word? Confused and flustered, hot and indignant, she tried to stumble back a step.

"It was meant to be a gesture of apology, yes, but to show you that I understand your job means the world to you."

She was about to mention that he was the one threatening to call the FBI on Beechwood, but movement to her right drew her attention away from him.

"Is everything okay?" a man asked cautiously. "Is this guy bothering you?"

Giving one last jerk on her arm, she broke free, her soft drink sloshing up and out of the top of the can, splashing Jack's shoes. Served him right. She'd be damned if she'd worry about ruining his four-hundred-dollar shoes.

"He's not bothering me, he's leaving." She gave a brittle smile to the man, who looked a little down on his luck. His shirt was faded to a soft gray, and his jeans were threadbare. There were myriad tattoos decorating his arms, and he looked pale for July, his brown hair stark against his skin. But he had a kind look of concern in his dark eyes, attractive bone structure, and a firm, proud jaw. "But thank you."

"Don't I know you from somewhere?" Jack asked, frowning at the man.

"Can't imagine that would be possible." The man gave a wry grin. "Don't look like we run in the same circles."

But Jamie felt it, too, an odd tug of familiarity. It wasn't his face, but his voice. It tripped around the edges of her brain, teasing her, reminding her of something, someone, but she couldn't quite grasp what it was. The sensation was already sliding away, making her doubt it had even existed.

"I know I've seen you before," Jack repeated.

Good to see he wasn't just stubborn with her.

The man just shrugged and turned to her, his hands in his pockets. "Sure you're alright?"

"Yes, thank you. Jack's stubborn, and a liar, but he's also decent. Most of the time. He'll leave if I really want him to." She directed those last words to Jack, mentally pleading with him to let it go, to leave her to repair her broken trust, her broken heart, damn it.

"Shit," Jack swore, looking out across the street. "Alright, Jamie. I'll leave. But I'm not giving up on us. I'll call you."

She really wished he wouldn't, but since he was backing up slowly, she wasn't going to argue.

"You're going back into work?" he asked, nodding toward the building.

She realized he probably wouldn't leave until he saw her safely in, away from the guy who was still hovering by her side. She glanced at him now as she took a step toward Beechwood's front door, her smelly lunch still bundled in her hand.

"Thanks again," she told the stranger.

He nodded. "Take care of yourself, Jamie Lynn." And he turned swiftly on one foot and started down the street, his footsteps pounding on the concrete sidewalk.

Jamie frowned, that teasing memory dancing in front of her again. Puzzled, she backed up until she was next to the big sand-filled ashtray/garbage can that stood in front of the building. Stuffing her trash through the hole, she watched Jack wave, turn, and head toward his car, clearly the fancy blue one wedged in between a Camaro and a rusted-out Chevy Cavalier.

The man was headed in the opposite direction of Jack, walking quickly, head down, the back of his dingy T-shirt darkened with sweat between the shoulder blades. He started jogging when the bus pulled up to the corner.

Jamie Lynn.

Suddenly it was there, and she couldn't understand why she hadn't seen it, felt it, right away. "Wait!" she shrieked, lurching forward.

Jack stopped, turned around, but Jamie barely spared him a glance. Running for all she was worth, wishing she weren't so fond of ice cream, both heart and lungs full to bursting, she headed south down the street, headed for the bus stop.

"Daddy!" she screamed, tears blurring her eyes as he disappeared into the bowels of the bus, and it moved forward with a choke of exhaust before the doors were even finished closing.

She followed for ten feet, screaming for the bus driver to stop, before stumbling to a halt in shock, a stitch in her side. For the first time in twenty years she had seen her father, and just like that last time, he had just walked away without a word.

It was that voice. She could hear it in her mind, locked deep in her memory. *Jamie Lynn, my girl. Jamie Lynn, my angel from heaven. Jamie Lynn can ride her horse without the leash, Myra, don't fuss so. She's a big girl now, ain't ya, honey bun?*

He'd never talked as much as her mother, who was prone to chatter like Jamie did now as a woman, but when Jim Peters had spoken, it was steady, calm, loving. The big hands that held her safe and strong against barking dogs, thunder and lightning, and the big boom of fireworks, and the voice that whispered, *'night, firefly*, when she was warm and sleepy in bed.

But it wasn't his hand that touched her now, not his voice. But Jack's. Jonathon Davidson's. He slipped an arm around her shoulder, turned her to him.

"Hey." His voice was gentle, concern in his eyes. "What's the matter? What's going on?"

She wanted to repel him, this other man who had lied to her, betrayed her trust, but she needed Jack's arm more than her pride. Tears leaked out of each eye, fat and unchecked, as pitiful as she felt.

"That was my father," she whispered, emotion roiling up her throat, making her want to gag.

"Your father?" He brushed her hair back, wiped her tears with the pad of his thumb. "I thought you hadn't seen your father since you were little."

"I haven't. Not until today. It was him, Jack. The way he said my name. He called me Jamie Lynn, and I just knew." Then suddenly, embarrassingly, she was sobbing, her shoulders shaking, her voice shattering. "He left again . . . he just left."

Jack gathered her in his arms. Her face pressed into the crisp white shirt, her eye on his tie, her fingers gripping his suit jacket. Steady hands smoothed over her back as he made little sounds of comfort. Pressed kisses to her forehead, the top of her hair.

"I'm so sorry, baby. Maybe he didn't want to upset you. But he obviously stepped forward to protect you when we were arguing. I don't know why he left, but maybe there's more going on than you know about. He obviously didn't know you knew."

Jamie was grateful he didn't try to tell her she was cracked. That it couldn't possibly be her father, or that she wouldn't know him after twenty years. And she thought he was right, that maybe it was time to call her mother. It seemed odd that her father knew who she was, was standing right outside her building.

Pulling slightly out of his embrace, suddenly realizing that it felt really damn good to be against his chest, Jamie sniffled and tried to stem her tears. "I need to go call my mom. Did you see how he was dressed, Jack? He looks . . . poor." She'd certainly seen the signs of poverty often enough to recognize it. "Maybe not destitute, but lean. Down on his luck. What if he's homeless?"

Jack led her over to the picnic table. He sat on the bench and pulled her onto his lap, and she didn't even try to resist. She was always the one who comforted, who cosseted, who cared. It was nice to have someone to lean on just once, for a quick minute.

"We can find him, Jamie, if that's what you want. It shouldn't be that hard, even if he's living in a shelter. The question more is, do you want to see him again?"

Perched on Jack's thigh, she went to wipe her tears off with her finger, but he shoved his tie in front of her.

"Use this." He dabbed at her with it.

"To dry my eyes?" She gave a startled laugh and tried to pull back. "That's probably like a hundred-dollar tie."

"You already ruined my three-hundred-dollar shoes by spilling Coke on them, and a hundred-dollar T-shirt with spaghetti sauce. What's a measly eighty-dollar tie?" And with a great deal of tenderness, he used the tip of the tie to wipe her cheeks.

She felt the corner of her mouth turn up. "Is that all your shoes are worth? I would have thought they were more."

"Sale at Steve Madden."

A giggle bubbled up. "You know, what you paid for those clothes could probably buy a goat for a family in Africa, providing them with milk and dairy products for years."

His mouth twitched. "Thanks, Sally Struthers. But instead of a goat, what I paid for these clothes provided wages for cattle ranchers, truck drivers, multiple garment workers, button and zipper manufacturers, and retail salesclerks. Not to mention my dry cleaner. I'm driving the US economy, babe. And looking good doing it."

Jamie laughed, part amusement, part relief that he was here with her, distracting her, steadying her. "An alternate perspective I hadn't considered."

Jack was quiet for a minute, his hand stroking her back, wondering if he should just keep his mouth shut and enjoy the moment before she regained her sense and told him to fuck off. But he had seen the hurt, the torment on her face, and it had torn at his own heart. When she had turned, tears streaming down her face, he would have done anything to take that pain away.

Including blow his chances with her. So he ventured, "Maybe your father has a different viewpoint."

"Maybe."

"Maybe he's afraid you'll reject him." Like Jack himself was.

"Maybe."

She wasn't rejecting him yet. She was snuggled cozily into his chest, and his thoughts were shifting into dark, dangerous areas. Ones that involved this same position but without clothes. Of course, he was intelligent enough to know the odds of her appreciating his carnal thoughts right at that moment were about ten thousand to one, so he clamped down on his lust, his desire, his love.

And truthfully, he was enjoying cuddling her, comforting her in a way that wasn't sexual but tender.

A random thought popped into his head. He gripped her more firmly, straightening up. "You know what? I know where I saw him now," he said, positive he was right. "It was on the subway the day we met. When you got on and stumbled, you almost collided with a guy wearing grungy clothes, lots of tattoos, older than you, but not old, old. And I stepped in between so you wouldn't touch him. So you would touch me."

"What?" She jerked back from him. Stared up at him in amazement.

"Yeah, so maybe he's been following you or something." Not that Jack liked the sound of that, father or not. That was a little weird. Of course, he had no freaking room to talk.

"That doesn't make sense . . ." Her words trailed off as she looked out across the street.

She wound his tie around her finger, pulling tighter with each turn, until he felt discomfort at the back of his neck.

"It may not make sense, but you don't need to choke me," he said lightly.

Absently, she refocused her gaze on him and unfurled her finger. "Sorry."

Her lips were cherry red from sitting out in the afternoon sun, her cheeks a pale, sharp contrast to her freckles and dewy hairline. Her skirt spread over his legs in a colorful maze of purple and olive green, and her flowing white shirt hid all her curves.

If she didn't forgive him, he wasn't sure he'd be able to accept that.

But she stared up at him, breath short and raw, eyes wide and awed, nail flicking across the button on his shirt. "Jack, do you believe in destiny?"

He opened his mouth, not sure what the answer was going to be. He had always been a by-the-numbers kind of guy, a make-your-own-destiny purveyor. But could he accept that it was fate that forced him to take a look at Jamie? Absolutely. Could he believe that destiny had pulled him off of Wall Street? Maybe.

But before he could answer, she continued.

"My friend, Beckwith, he tells fortunes. Months ago, he told me I was going to meet a man during an accident with food. On something moving. That this man would make me happy."

That sent a cold rush of awareness tripping up his spine. That sounded like the day they'd met. Which just made it a coincidence.

"I didn't believe him, but then that day, in the station, Beckwith called me to tell me it was about to happen, and then I hung up, ran forward and . . . right into you."

Jack's throat felt tight. His shoulders stiff. This was starting to make him uncomfortable.

"I thought it was you . . . I thought Beckwith meant you. But if you stepped in between us, maybe he really meant my father. Maybe I'm supposed to make things right with my dad."

No, he did not like where this was going. Because he was pretty damn sure it left him out in the cold. "Maybe it's all a coincidence."

She shook her head. "Or maybe we interfered with destiny."

"Maybe this *was* our destiny. You were supposed to meet me. I can make you happy," he said, running his lips across the top of her head.

"Or maybe I can never succeed at a relationship until I fix things with my father. Maybe the timing for us is all wrong."

Nothing had felt wrong between them, until he'd screwed up and failed to tell her the truth. "Maybe knowing your destiny is a mistake, because in searching for it, you manufacture it."

Leaning back, Jamie cocked her head, thought that through, her lips parted. "Maybe you're right," she whispered. "Maybe I imagined things because I wanted to believe destiny was at hand."

Abruptly, she stood up. "Maybe we need to leave well enough alone."

Too late, he realized where she was headed with her line of thinking. "No, Jamie, that's not what I meant."

But she merely smiled at him, a soft, serene smile, her cheeks still streaked from dried tears. She kissed the tip of her fingertip and brought it to his lips. "Maybe it's time to be friends. Just friends."

Jack kissed her flesh, lingering over the plump pad of her index finger, tracing her salty skin with his tongue, not wanting to give her up. "We're more than friends." Jesus, way more than friends.

She pulled her hand back. "You can look into Beechwood's money problem or you can call the FBI. It's up to you. Thanks for the shoulder to cry on and . . . everything."

"Jamie . . ." This couldn't be all there was. It couldn't be the end.

But she just gave him a wave and a sad smile and went into the building, the door snicking shut behind her.

And he took his sticky shoes and his wet tie and he went home.

Chapter 12

Jack Davidson knew when to buy and when to sell. He knew when a risk was too great, when it was a sure thing. He played put-options to his favor, and almost always won.

Money he could do. Dollars talked to him, gave him a direction in which to go. He had a fancy college degree stuck in his desk drawer, and he had a nice wad of cash rapidly making more cash for him while he sat back and watched it toil on his behalf.

That was all fine and good. But he was utterly clueless when it came to women. No instincts. Lousy success rate. And a volatile market.

Steve's advice had exploded like shrapnel, nailing both him and Jamie. Jack didn't know what strategy should be implemented at this point, so he did what any sane man would do.

He called his sister. A woman's opinion was required if he had any chance of being successful with Jamie.

After the usual greetings, he paced across his living room Monday night and went straight to what was bothering him. "Listen, Caro, what would you do if a guy you slept with lied to you?" He added, "For a good reason."

"I'd tell him to have a nice life and never see him again."

Shit. "Why? What if he was trying to protect you? What if he apologized?" Jack bundled up the red cashmere blanket that he and Jamie had abandoned on the sofa, prepared to fling it into his closet.

"I'd figure once a liar, always a liar. If he can lie about the little stuff, he can lie about the big stuff."

One small mistake and a guy has to pay for it for the rest of his life.

"Not necessarily. And what if he wanted to make amends? Show it wasn't going to happen again."

"Actions speak louder than words, Jonathon."

And right now he was burying his nose in the blanket and trying to catch a stray trace of Jamie's scent. My God, he was pathetic.

"True. Hey, Caro, do you believe in destiny?" He shoved the blanket behind a throw pillow.

She snorted. "No."

That shouldn't surprise him. Caroline was a true Davidson. She was aggressive, determined, and when she wanted something, she went after it. He had always been the same way. Was still that way. But somehow, he was wondering if there was more to the concept of fate. He'd have sworn everything that had happened between him and Jamie was meant to be.

"Why do you think certain things happen, then?"

"Randomness. Coincidence. Human choices. Take your pick. I believe in controlling my own destiny."

That was it, wasn't it? Destiny might play a part, but choices and actions drove your future.

Jack believed in controlling his own destiny. And that's what he was going to do.

Jamie sat down in the big overstuffed chair in her apartment, a pint of mint chocolate chip next to her for emergency bites. This was not a conversation she wanted to have, but it was unavoidable. Taking a deep breath, she dialed her mom on her cell phone.

"Hey, honey," her mother answered after two rings.

"Hi, Mama. How are you?" Jamie closed her eyes and sighed. Her mother was a wonderful woman, resourceful and loving. Yet she was going to be upset to hear about her ex-husband, Jamie was sure of it.

"Great, though hot. It's been over ninety all week."

There was the sound of chopping in the background, and Jamie imagined her mother was fixing herself a salad for dinner. "Listen, Mom, when my father left . . . did you know where he went?"

There was a startled silence; then her mother gave a little laugh. "Shoot, where did that come from? I thought you got over all that wondering about your father during your teen years."

Maybe that's what her mother had wanted to believe, but Jamie had never really stopped wondering. She had gotten over it, for the most part, she had thought. But she'd never stopped wanting to know *why*.

Rubbing her hands over her skirt, she stared out the window at the building across the street. A big fat pigeon was doing reconnaissance on the ledge. "I'm asking because I think I saw him today. He was hanging around outside my work, and he called me Jamie Lynn. It wasn't until he walked away that I recognized his voice."

The gasp from her mother was pure shock and horror. "Oh, my God, baby, you stay away from him, ya hear me? Call the cops if you see him again."

"What? Why?" She had expected her mother to be upset, uncomfortable, maybe even a little bitter. She hadn't expected fear.

Her mother hesitated, but finally she sighed. "I never wanted to tell you. I didn't think it mattered. I figured gone was gone and that's all you needed to know."

"Mama, you're scaring me. What are you talking about?" Jamie gripped the pint of ice cream, but had no thought to eat it.

"Your father left because he figured out the FBI was closing in on him. He decided to run and leave us to fend for ourselves."

"Why was the FBI after him?" She didn't like the sound of this. It almost sounded as if her mother was saying . . .

"During the late sixties and early seventies your father was a very vocal antiwar, anti-nuclear weapons demonstrator. He did some breaking and entering, too, to burn draft cards. I imagine they would have let him go after a few years in hiding if he hadn't accidentally burned down a whole building, killing the night janitor."

"Oh, dear God." Jamie covered her mouth. She could not reconcile the man who'd held her as a child, loved her, with a violent activist.

"He didn't tell me any of that when we met and married. It was only later, when he thought his time was running out, that he bothered to mention any of it. I knew he was in the antiwar movement, and I believed him when he said it was all nonviolent, nonconfrontational. I do believe it was an accident, that he never meant to hurt anyone, but I can't forgive him for dragging me, then you, into the mess he'd made. A responsible man would have admitted his mistake and accepted the consequences."

"So he's been in jail all these years?" Jamie closed her eyes again, her throat tight. Destiny propelled people along, but choices could change an entire life. Lives. How would all three of their lives been different if her father hadn't lit that match?

But that was neither here nor there.

"I know he ran for the first few years after he left because the FBI watched our house randomly, checking to see if he had contacted us. As you know, he never did. Then in the late eighties I heard he was arrested and sent back to New York, where he was convicted of manslaughter. It was my understanding he got twenty years."

"Apparently he's been paroled." Jamie pressed her fingers to her temples. When the heck had the FBI been watching their house? The very idea made her shiver. While she'd been riding her horse? Sunbathing with her girlfriends? It wasn't a pleasant path to stroll down.

"Well, you stay the hell away from him, Jamie Lynn. He can't bring you anything but trouble and heartache. He doesn't deserve to call us family, not after the way he lied, not after the way he left me alone to deal with the consequences of his actions. I can't even get remarried if I wanted to, because for the first few years I didn't know where he was, then I didn't want you to know he was sitting in prison, so we were never divorced."

"Well, at the very least, maybe now is the time to finally file for divorce, Mama." She let out a laugh before she could stop herself. It was so completely unbelievable, so ridiculous, so *screwed up*.

She'd known her parents' marriage had ended badly. That had been obvious. But she had never dreamt the extent of the dysfunction in her family. No wonder the man hadn't spoken to her. He had no way of knowing what she knew or didn't know. He was probably terrified of an ugly confrontation.

Her mom choked back a sob. "I wasn't expecting this. God, it's been twenty years and it hurts just as much as the day he left. I don't know if I could handle speaking to him about a divorce."

"Mama, it's okay." Jamie forgot about her own worries, feelings. It was awful to hear her mother, who had been a rock for all those years, sound so emotional. So hurt. Myra Peters had defined strength as a single mother. Her whole life Jamie had never once seen her mom cry, and here there was a sniffle and a tremble in her voice.

Maybe she'd spent so much time staying strong for her daughter, she'd never dealt with her own grief and hurt.

"You do whatever you think you need to do, Mama.

There's no hurry, no worry. I can find him or I can let it go. I don't think he wanted anything. I think he just wanted to . . . see me. That's all."

"I'm sorry I didn't tell you the truth, baby girl. I was trying to protect you. And maybe protect myself, too."

"That's okay, Mom. It's not like I could have seen him anyway." She took a deep breath, fingered the lid of the ice cream. "I had a good life. I have a good life, thanks to you."

"You always were such a good girl, Jamie Lynn. I've always been proud of you."

"I know." Crossing her legs, she wondered why it had been a whole year since she'd seen her mother. She'd give just about anything to have her soft arms around her right then. "Listen, I just need a bit of time to think. How about I call you again tomorrow?"

"Sounds like a good idea. I love you."

"Love you, too, Mama. Bye."

"Bye now."

Jamie cradled the phone in her hand and marveled that while her entire childhood had just shifted and altered in meaning, she felt exactly the same as she always had. In fact, she felt better. Her father hadn't gotten tired of his wife and daughter and gone on to a second family. He hadn't stopped loving his wife, and by default stopped loving the daughter she'd given him.

Jim Peters had been a desperate man, running from his past, and looking to protect his family.

Jamie stopped feeling for herself and shifted that emotion over to him. What a lonely, empty life he'd had.

She'd been loved and cherished, surrounded by her mother's family and good friends. What had he had?

The phone in her hand rang. She glanced at the caller ID, worried it was her mother.

Davidson, Jonathon.

Sighing, she answered. "Hi Davidson, Jonathon."

He gave a soft laugh. "Hey, Peters, Jamie Lynn. How are you?"

It was more than a casual platitude. He was asking if she was *okay*. Which she was. She was sad, terribly sad, but she was okay. And it was nice to know that he cared enough to call, even if he was a liar.

Who had thought he was protecting her. That seemed to be an echoing theme in her life lately.

She sighed again, figuring she was getting good at it now. "I'm fine. I talked to my mom, and I just need some time to think."

"Okay. I just wanted to check on you, give you another shoulder to cry on and . . . everything. If you needed it."

Those were the words she had spoken to him, and she realized how it must have sounded. As if their whole night together could be summed up as *everything*. It had certainly meant more to her than that one word, but she didn't have the energy to get into it with him.

"Thanks, Jack, I appreciate it."

"Hey, what are friends for?" he asked lightly.

Not for getting naked and having sweaty, giggly, therapeutic sex, which was what she really wanted to do with Jack.

"Yeah." Jamie closed her eyes and fought the wave of longing that threatened to tsunami her. "Bye, Jack."

She needed to hang up before she could do or say something she would regret when she wasn't feeling so vulnerable.

"Bye, Jamie Lynn. Call me if you need anything."

When she clicked the off button on her phone, Jamie sat still in her chair.

And let the tears finally come.

In five minutes on the interior of the Beechwood Social Services agency, Jack had figured out who the day trader was.

Jamie, who had a tired smile on Tuesday morning, hadn't looked all that surprised to see him. Not thrilled, exactly, but neither did she toss him out on his ear. Instead, she had showed him around the office. In the third cubicle to the left, he found his man.

"This is Austin," Jamie said, pointing to a teenage boy working at a computer. "He's a computer whiz, so he does a lot of our data entry."

Austin, who looked like he was in the middle of a personal experiment to see how long he could go without brushing his hair or washing his clothes, gave them a brief glance. It wasn't poverty Jack saw in Austin's slouchy, grubby look. It was some kind of fashion statement, from the hair that went down in black-tipped spikes over his eyes to the metal studs sticking out just about everywhere there was skin.

All that piercing and tattooing and purchasing of clothes meant to look well worn could get pricey. And before Austin minimized his screen, Jack saw exactly what he was doing.

Shopping stocks.

Jack could recognize that from across the room.

Jamie didn't seem to notice anything unusual. She put her hand on Austin's shoulder, getting his attention. "What's new, Austin?"

Jack expected a sullen grunt, but instead Austin turned, looked up at her, and gave her a real smile. "Not much, Jamie. Just doing boring shit. I mean stuff."

"Jamie says you know a lot about computers," Jack said, hands in his pockets. He had worn jeans today because he wanted to talk to Jamie's boss about the situation, but he didn't want to come across as official or intimidating. Now he was grateful he didn't look like a Suit, because he needed to talk to Austin without Jamie around.

"Yeah, so?" Austin gave him a suspicious look.

"I was a broker for a Wall Street firm for ten years, and now I run a charitable trust foundation. I could use an intern for the rest of the summer."

Austin looked interested for just a split second, then his features settled into blasé nonchalance. "Yeah, well, I've been convicted for hacking and financial fraud. No place decent will hire me to do anything but clean their fucking toilets. And I don't want to clean your john."

Jack couldn't believe that Jamie and her boss let a convicted financial felon have access to all their computer files, data, and funding. He felt his eyes bugging out in horror. What anyone with half a brain could do with that kind of knowledge was astounding.

While the urge to shove past Austin and throw his arms across the PC was overwhelming, he controlled himself. "As a juvenile or an adult?" he asked, curious if this kid had actually done time.

Austin looked him over, hard. "Juvenile," he finally answered. "I'm fourteen now. Thirteen at the time of the crime." This was accompanied by a smirk, like he wasn't the least bit remorseful for what he'd done.

Most people who committed financial crimes were sorry they got caught, not that they'd done it. It was hard to find remorse when actions were perpetuated by greed. Jack's world was full of good old-fashioned greed, the desire to get more for less, to ride the wave of this stock or that market, to be on the inside of the next big thing.

"Is working here part of your parole?" Jack had thought Beechwood served primarily adults and families, not juvenile offenders, but he didn't really know.

"Yeah."

"How about we go grab a drink on me in the lunchroom I saw and we can talk about a job that won't conflict with your work here. Nothing volunteer. Real money."

"Go ahead, Austin," Jamie said, looking just as suspicious as Austin.

It occurred to Jack maybe she thought he was trying to buy her affection again.

"You can take a ten-minute break."

Austin looked like he'd just as soon join the ballet, but he stood up, pushing his MP3 earpiece off and letting it dangle around his neck.

There was a lunchroom with vending machines Jack had noticed two doors down the hall, and he led Austin there now. He bought two soft drinks and handed Austin one.

Austin didn't take it. He narrowed his eyes and said, "Are you one of those rich guys who's looking for a boy toy? 'Cuz I don't do that shit."

Jack nearly broke his jaw on the floor it dropped so low. Then he laughed, part embarrassment, part amusement. Yeah, he really did suck at this whole spy/intrigue thing. "No. Definitely not." He gestured with his hand toward the door. "My interests lie more with redheaded women, you know what I'm saying?"

Austin nodded in understanding, accepting the soft drink. "I got ya. You're looking to score points with Jamie, huh? Take the loser kid she feels sorry for and clean him up." He pointed his finger at Jack. "Pretty slick, man."

Jack took a seat at the plastic picnic table next to the vending machines. "Maybe that's part of the plan, yeah. But it has also come to my attention that someone has been using Beechwood's funds—nearly a hundred grand through ten different transactions—to trade, making money for themselves. Would you happen to know anything about that?"

Austin shook his head slowly. "No idea."

"It's smart, done well. Pretty hidden, if you're not looking for it, and you're not experienced. And it's one of those things that you figure, hey, you're not hurting anyone, right? You don't *steal* the money. You don't keep it, you just borrow it. Make yourself a little quick cash, put it back, and no one gets hurt. But what if one time you mess up? You don't make money, but lose it? What happens then?"

Jack was trying to sound casual, matter of fact. He had his legs out in front of him, ankles crossed. Austin wasn't looking at him, but studying his Coke can as if the secrets to the universe were scrolled across it.

Finally, when the silence stretched out, Austin locked eyes with him. "What do ya want, man?"

"I want you to knock it off. I haven't said anything to anyone. Jamie knows what's going on, but she doesn't know I think it's you. But if you don't quit, I'm going to have to tell her it's you, and she'll tell her boss. Or maybe I should do what I should have done in the first place and call the feds in."

"You can't prove shit."

"Oh, give me a break, kid. You know how this works. A handful of people had access to these computers and that financial information. You've got a record for fraud. And you've probably got a few grand squirreled away somewhere. They'll pin it on you and you know it."

Austin popped the tab on his soft drink can and took a long drink. "So what, if all activity stops, you're just going to let it go? I don't believe that for a fucking minute."

"Sure, I'll let it go." Jack might be insane, but he had the feeling Austin wasn't a bad kid. He was just smart as hell and bored. "I'll give you that internship I mentioned."

"Whatever," Austin scoffed.

But Jack figured they had just struck a deal.

The cell phone in his pocket rang, and when he answered it, Austin used the opportunity to slip back down the hall before Jack could stop him.

"Hello?" It was his sister's number on caller ID.

"Oh, my God, Jonathon you have got to get here." Caroline's voice was dripping with exasperation.

"Where is *here*, dear?" Lately Caro had been morphing into a mini Bridezilla, and he hoped this wasn't some kind of tuxedo crisis.

"The nursing home. Pops had some kind of tantrum, and the director of the home called Mom, who can't get out of

Darien because she's in the middle of a color treatment. Foil wraps everywhere. And so I had to come down here because the nurses have refused to deal with Pops anymore, and I can see why. He's being totally unreasonable."

Jack could hear Pops yelling in the background, "Don't talk about me like I'm not here! You always were too much your mother's daughter, Caroline."

"See what I mean?" she said.

"And I don't need any damn nurses," Pops yelled.

Jack rubbed his forehead. "Let me talk to him. I'm at Beechwood. It will take me an hour to get there with traffic, but I want to talk to him first."

"Fine."

"What?" Pops barked into the phone a minute later.

"Okay, what gives, Pops? You can tell me the real story."

"I want out. I can't live here, Jack. These people treat me like I'm a two-year-old and a dimwitted one at that. I have assets worth over a hundred million bucks and they won't let me use a fork! This afternoon I had a cigar, and that nurse I hate, the one with the cauliflower legs and the voice like a band saw, she just grabbed it out of my mouth. Didn't ask me to put it out, didn't say it was against the rules. Just grabbed it, like I was a goddamn baby. So I grabbed her ass. See how she likes people getting grabby on her."

Okay, that was funny. Jack fought a grin. "Guess she didn't like it, huh?"

"Nope. Which probably explains why she's so uptight. Doesn't know how to appreciate a little slap and tickle."

Even over the phone Jack could hear his sister gasp in horror.

But Jack suspected at this point, Pops was going for shock. He was tired of the nursing home and wanted to get his point across loud and clear. For a man who'd spent his whole life wheeling and dealing in the fast lane, Jack couldn't imagine how hard of a fall this was for his grandfather. And he couldn't just sit back and do nothing.

"Pops, you know you can't go home yet."

Pops just grunted.

"So why don't you move in with me for a while? We can have a nurse drop in once every couple of days, and the therapist to do your physical therapy. The rest of the time you and I should be able to handle it." Jack figured Pops couldn't live on his own just yet, but he wasn't senile, and he was well on the way to recovery. Being in a more comfortable atmosphere might actually facilitate his progress, and Jack had a fairly light work schedule. And apparently no social life now that Jamie was through with him.

Pops wasn't saying anything, so Jack said, "What do you think?"

"So you'd do that for me?" Pops's voice was tight.

Jack thought about the man who had showed up at all his ball games when he was a kid, the man who had taken him under his wing in the business world, and the man who had always been free with a hug to make up for Jack's parents, who were stingy with affection.

"Yeah, I'd do that for you."

"Don't want to cramp your style when hard-on girl comes around."

Jack laughed, even as his gut gave a little twist, like indigestion. "She gave me the 'just friends' speech, Pops. She's not going to be coming around my apartment."

"Well, shit. What the hell's the matter with her?" Pops was indignant. "You're a damn good catch."

"Thanks. So okay, I'll come down there and get things settled, and we can move you as soon as possible. Let me talk to Caroline again."

"Sure. And thanks, kiddo."

Now it was Jack who felt his throat tighten, but his grandfather passed the phone off before he could respond.

"Are you dating someone?" Caroline asked without a hello.

Jack could practically hear her nostrils flaring in anticipation of gossip.

"No." He knew for a fact if Jamie had told Caroline about them, his sister would have been all over him. Clearly Jamie didn't want Caroline to know they had slept together, so he wasn't going to be the one to mention it. Especially since he'd been dumped.

"Oh. That's too bad." Caroline sounded gravely sympathetic, as though it were a national tragedy that he couldn't find a date.

Time for a diversion. "Pops is moving in with me."

It worked.

"Oh, dear, God. Mom's going to burst a blood vessel."

Chapter 13

"So what do you get paid to do this?" Mike, one of her reentry students, asked Jamie Friday afternoon.

She could see he'd drawn some incredibly detailed sketches on his paper. He was supposed to be writing a résumé, but as far as she could tell he had nothing more than his name on the paper and several well-endowed dragons.

"I don't get paid enough," she told him, truthfully. She smiled and tapped her pen on his paper, distracted. "Now put something down there so we can move on to your housing application."

She'd seen Jack go down the hall past the open doorway. He'd given her a wave and a smile. Nice and friendly. Just like she'd suggested. Just friends.

Only why did it feel so lousy to get exactly what she wanted?

Jack had come in to the agency every day since Monday, laboring over something on the computer with Austin. He had told her that Austin was the one who had been doing whatever complicated thing Jack had thought someone was doing. Jamie didn't understand any of it, nor was she sure how Jack was handling it, though he had assured her he and Austin had worked out a deal.

It irritated her that in typical businessman manner, he had just strolled in and taken over. It was her job to monitor Austin, not Jack's. But since she didn't understand the crime, and wasn't willing to take it to the attention of the authorities, she was stuck letting Jack handle it. None of it thrilled her. She was disappointed in Austin. And a strange, weird, unpleasant part of her felt . . . cut off. Jack wasn't seeking her out. Wasn't trying to apologize or convince her to forgive him. It was like he'd given up, taken her at her word, and was okay with the label of friends even after the amazing night they'd spent together.

She wasn't. Which meant she was nuts.

Another student, Luis, glanced up from the paper he was laboring over. "This is wack. I don't understand why I have to fill all this stuff out. I never got any of this shit for free before . . . Who's going to give me a job, an apartment, free day care now? I thought the government had budget cuts, man."

"These are all private nonprofit organizations who sponsor programs to ensure your successful reentry into society. We work together with them to get you back on track. If you have a decent job, a nice apartment, a safe place for your kids, you won't be tempted to do anything illegal, right?" Jamie put a warning in her voice.

Luis stared at her. "Right."

"Because if you screw up and commit a crime, all these things will be taken away, you'll be back in jail faster than you can say 'this is wack,' and your three daughters will be out on the street, ripe for the picking. They're pretty girls, Luis, and your wife can't watch them if she has to work two jobs to put food on the table."

It wasn't a threat, just the facts.

Luis got it. His jaw twitched. "You're a real bitch, you know that?" he asked, going back to his paper. "That's why I like you."

"So, to get a break in life, all you have to do is commit a crime?" Richard, a physician convicted of insurance fraud, shook his head. "We live in a rather twisted state of emergency, don't you think?"

"Shut up, Doc, and take your free shit," Mike recommended.

"It costs more to maintain the judicial process and the incarcerated care of sixty-five thousand male prisoners in the state of New York than it does to provide services like these. The entire six-month heating and air-conditioning course that we're enrolling Mike in costs less than it did to house him in prison for one week."

"No shit?" Mike shook his head. "And the food wasn't even all that great."

That made Jamie laugh, even as part of her couldn't focus entirely on her class. Her mind was on her father, her mother. And Jack.

She wasn't sleeping well at night, and she wasn't sure what to do, if anything. Jamie was a glass-half-full girl, and she knew she was okay, but she had no sense of direction.

What she should do. If anything. About anything. It made her feel helpless and lonely and frustrated.

Lucky for her, Beckwith had a plan.

Jack was headed out to his car after lunch to drive over to Hathaway for the rest of the day when he spotted Jamie's father sitting on a bench across the street from the agency. He hesitated for a second.

The man wasn't watching him, but was staring down at his feet.

Jack looked back at the Beechwood building. This wasn't any of his business. Dealing with Austin wasn't even really of his business, and yet he was up to his eyeballs trying to straighten that out, convinced that the kid showed promise and potential and shouldn't be thrown away.

And here he was again, standing there knowing he should walk away, but completely unable to.

He and Jamie were friends, he'd like to think, as much as that label made him want to groan in agony and beat his head against the wall in frustrating despair. But that sort of move was a little dramatic for him.

Instead, he'd gotten drunk at Brad's bachelor party and was spending all his free time with a teenage boy and an old man. It wasn't a great form of therapy, but it beat wailing in the middle of Forty-fourth Street.

Jamie's father glanced over at him, narrowed his eyes in recognition. Jack started across the street. He figured Jamie had invited him into the situation by crying on his shoulder. That had nearly killed him, and he didn't want to see her hurt further.

Jack stopped in front of the man, who was now sitting straight up, looking suspicious and tense. Ready to fight, if necessary. Even with some hard years on him, Jack could see the resemblance to Jamie. Same eyes. Same freckles.

"I just wanted to tell you that Jamie knows who you are."

"Excuse me? What the hell is that supposed to mean?"

But Jack could tell he knew. The guy's face went white, his eyes ran scared.

"You know what I mean, Mr. Peters. And if you don't want to talk to Jamie, maybe you'd better quit hanging around."

Jamie's father's head fell into his hands, and he rubbed his scratchy unshaven chin. "I just wanted to see her . . ." he said, his voice breaking a little. "Just wanted to make sure she's okay. I don't mean her any harm."

With a sigh, Jack sat down on the bench next to him. "Look, I don't claim to know anything about relationships. My own family thinks communicating is critiquing each other's clothing. And as you noticed, given the argument we had the other day, I'm not exactly Jamie's favorite guy these days. But I think that you're hurting her more by not talking to her. She wants to know where you've been, man."

"I've been in prison."

"Oh." Well, shit, that explained a lot. Jack cleared his throat, embarrassed to have trod into something so personal. "Well, fortunately, Jamie understands that men make mistakes."

He shut up, not sure what else to say.

"Listen, do you have a few minutes? I need someone to talk to, and you obviously care about Jamie."

"I do." More than he could express without sounding like a cream puff. "And sure, I have time."

"Thanks. Name's Jim, by the way." He stuck his hand out.

"Jack."

They shook.

And by the time they were done talking quite a while later, Jack had another new roommate, and a pretty good idea that Jamie was going to kill him.

By the end of the day Jamie had seven new voice mail messages on her cell phone. Walking to the subway, feeling sluggish and slow, her peasant skirt trailing on the sidewalk, she curiously listened to her messages. She couldn't imagine there were seven people trying to get ahold of her in one afternoon.

First message. Sent at one-twenty-two P.M., the robotic female voice said in her ear. Then, "Sugar, I had another vision. I saw ice, I saw coffee, I saw anger. Call me."

Jamie played with the amber beads on her necklace. That prediction meant nothing to her, so she waited for the next message.

Next message. Sent at two-twelve P.M. "Why haven't you called me back? You need to give me your new work number. There are times when I have to talk to you and I don't like being put off with this cell voice mail bullshit."

Jamie would have to be insane to give Beckwith her new

work number. As it was, she was lucky he hadn't just shown up at her office.

Next message. Sent at two-seventeen P.M. "You know, you're lucky I'm getting my nails done or I'd just come down there. There's a great disturbance in the force," Beckwith said in his deep yet somehow feminine voice. "There's like a Darth Vader moment right around the corner for you."

That made Jamie grin. Darth Vader? Geez, Beckwith certainly had a flare for the dramatic.

Next message. Sent at three twenty-one P.M.

Jamie didn't need psychic powers of her own to guess it was going to be Beckwith again.

"My crew keeps saying, *"They're here . . ."* like that freaky little girl in *Poltergeist*. Why the hell am I seeing your future in movies? And who are *they*? Jams, you've got to call me before I have an aneurysm."

If he'd stop leaving voice mails, maybe she would have time to call him back.

Next message. Sent at three forty-seven P.M. "Whatever you do, do not go to Jack's apartment, do you understand me? I sense criminal feelings . . . like death, prison. Maybe the doorman has a violent past or something, but do not go over there, do you hear me? I repeat, do not go to Jack's apartment."

The frightened tone in Beckwith's voice made Jamie shiver a little, even as the sun beat down on her bare arms. He was great at drama, but he wasn't usually prone to hysteria. Yet she couldn't believe she'd ever come to harm in Jack's presence. Despite his lying, she felt in her heart that she could trust him not to ever hurt her physically. He could shred her heart like mozzarella if she let him, but physically she'd be fine.

Next message. Sent at four-oh-one P.M. "Jamie, this is Jack. I was wondering if you could come over to my apartment tonight after you get off work? I need to talk to you . . ." Jack hesitated. "It's about your father."

Jamie sucked in her breath. That must have been the feeling Beckwith was getting. He was mixing sensations about her father with Jack. Prison, a crime . . . dark shadows of the past like Darth Vader.

"You can come over any time. I'll be here." There was another pause like he was going to say something else. But he only ended with a soft, "Thanks, Jamie."

"Damn," Jamie whispered out loud, heading down the steps into the subway. She wanted to blow Jack off. To hold on to her anger over the lies, and her irritation with the way he'd taken over handling the situation with Austin. But she couldn't. She had a heck of a time saying no to anyone, and Jack had been comforting to her when she'd seen her father.

And no matter how far apart their lives were, or how many issues lay between them, part of her would always remember the night they had shared, when everything was simple and it had just been amazing between them.

She hesitated on the platform. Maybe she should run home and change into a fresh outfit. Maybe her yellow sundress.

Next message. Sent at four-twelve P.M. "Okay, sugar, fine, don't listen to me. Go over there and get murdered. But at the very least, have pity on me and do not wear that yellow dress. It makes you look like a banana."

Okay, apparently she wasn't changing. Jamie stepped on the train and glanced down at her green skirt, and smoothed her red hair.

Watermelon. Banana. Same difference.

"Okay, just hear me out," Jack said when he met Jamie in the lobby.

Met her in the lobby. That was not a good beginning to the evening. Like there was something so utterly horrible and depraved about to blurt from his lips he needed to say it to her in a public space.

"What?" she asked cautiously, sliding her camel-colored hobo bag in front of her. Not that she intended to beat him with her purse or anything, but it felt safer to have a barrier between her and those pleading, pretty eyes.

"Sit down," he suggested, his hands in his jean pockets as he nodded toward the red chairs.

"No, thank you."

One, she wasn't going to be staying that long. Two, those chairs reminded her of *that* night, which she'd rather not be reminded of, thank you very much. Too much contemplation on that morning's particular activities and she would either start crying or spontaneously orgasm.

"Okay, then I'll just get right to the point."

Please do, God, he was going to drive her to drink.

"Your father is upstairs in my apartment and he wants to talk to you."

Maybe she should have sat down. Jamie's cheeks went hot, and her legs turned to rubber. "I'm sorry?"

Jack reached out like he was going to touch her, but he hesitated. "He was outside Beechwood, and I talked to him, told him you knew who he was, and that maybe it was time for him to speak to you. He told me he'd just wanted to make sure you were okay, but didn't want to bother you. I convinced him that it would be no bother. That his daughter would like to speak to him. Was I wrong?"

He looked anxiously at her, and Jamie felt tears well up. She shook her head rapidly. "No, no, you weren't wrong. Thank you."

Suddenly terrified, she glanced at the elevators. "Should I go upstairs or is he coming down?"

"He's waiting upstairs."

When Jack took her hand and squeezed, leading her toward the elevator, Jamie didn't shake him off. And when he said, "I know about the whole prison sentence," Jamie found that she was grateful for the compassion in Jack's voice. Glad that her father had felt comfortable enough to confide in Jack.

Stepping into Jack's apartment, bracing herself to come face-to-face with her father for the first time in twenty-some years, Jamie found herself leaning closer to Jack. It wasn't such a bad feeling to have a man like Jack at her back.

Especially when she saw Austin and an older man, not her father.

"Austin? What in the world are you doing here?"

"I live here," he called from the sofa, looking mighty comfortable with his feet on Jack's coffee table.

She swiveled to level a gaze at Jack, waiting for some kind of explanation for why a teen criminal was channel surfing on his plasma TV.

He shrugged, looking sheepish. "He's such a bright kid and he's living on the streets, Jamie. This is temporary, until I find the right boarding school for him."

"Boarding school? Who on earth is going to pay for that?" That was sure in the heck not in Beechwood's budget. Private school tuition was probably more than Jamie's entire annual salary.

Jack didn't answer, but Austin did, flipping his hair out of his eyes as he glanced over his shoulder. "Dude's crazy, Jamie. He's going to shell out money for me to go to some fancy-ass school. You should stick around, he'll probably throw some cash your way, too."

Her mouth stopped working. Shock made her lips numb. It took several seconds for her to regain control enough to form words. "Do you want to go to boarding school, Austin?" she asked, amazed. It was a little hard to visualize him in a blazer, or with his pants actually around his waist instead of his knees.

"Hell, yeah. It was either that or prison. And I'm kind of

looking forward to showing up those preppy pimps." He cracked his knuckles. "I can get straight A's with my fucking eyes closed."

"Well, everyone does have their own unique talents," she said carefully, feeling floored. Flummoxed. Freaked out. All kinds of *f* words.

The older gentleman in the wheelchair spun himself around. "Aren't you going to introduce me, Jack-o?"

"Of course, Pops. Jamie, this is my grandfather, Will Hathaway. Pops, this is Jamie Peters."

She managed a smile at Jack's grandfather, remembering all the wonderful things Jack had said about him. "It's so nice to meet you. Jack's told me how much he admires you and all your accomplishments."

His grandfather cracked a laugh. "I can only imagine. It's a pleasure to meet you, too, young lady. Jack's been gushing like a faucet about how beautiful you are, and for once I have to agree with him."

Jack made a coughing sound, and Jamie felt a blush rising over her neck and cheeks.

"So, where's Jim?" Jack asked.

Jim. Her father. Jamie stiffened, heart thumping painfully.

Austin's eyes darted back to the TV, but Jack's grandfather set his mouth in a tight line and shook his head.

The silence drew out for a long, awful moment.

"He stepped out for a minute," Pops said.

Jamie felt her throat close off.

"Is he coming back?" Jack asked, loud and demanding.

"He just bugged out," Austin said. "He didn't say shit to us."

The room blurred as tears came swiftly, cementing her mortification. It was just disappointment, really, but still she was ashamed of the emotion.

"Hey, uh, Austin, why don't you and Pops run across the street and get some dinner?" Jack pulled out his wallet and handed Austin forty bucks.

That was all the incentive Austin needed to leap off the couch and grab hold of Pops's wheelchair. "Come on, old man."

Pops swiped the money out of Austin's hand. "Got to be quicker than that, punk."

They paused right beside her. "Sorry," Austin said, solemn and uncomfortable.

Pops reached out and patted her hand with his strong, wrinkled one. "He'll come around."

She just nodded, not trusting herself to speak, their compassion nearly shattering her. When they were gone, she shook her head, pulled her hand out of Jack's. "Please don't say anything. Thank you for trying, but please don't say anything."

If he tried to apologize, she was going to cry. Jamie took a deep breath and called on all her strength. This was not a big deal. Nothing was different about today than yesterday. She was a strong, independent woman who could wrestle a pig to the ground and fend off barbs from ex-cons with equal success.

Her father's rejection was nothing new, and she wasn't going to let it crumple her. The only thing that had been known to bring her to her knees thus far was ice cream, and aside from a slight heaviness in the thighs—some of it genetic anyway—that wasn't a crisis.

"Jamie . . ."

"I'm fine, Jack." Or she would be once she got out of his expensive apartment and went home to collapse on her purple bedspread. Took a breather and meditated to regain her equilibrium.

"No, you're not." He tried to reach for her, tried to pull her into his arms.

Those arms looked all too appealing. Knowing if she let him, she'd be helpless, defenseless against his kindness, she stepped back in a panic.

"Don't."

She expected him to protest.

What she didn't expect was him to drop his hands, stare her straight in the eye and say, "I love you."

Where the heck was Beckwith's helpful second sight right now? She could have used a little warning on that one.

Chapter 14

Why the hell he had chosen that particular moment to confess his feelings, Jack couldn't possibly fathom. As he stood there waiting for Jamie to stop gaping at him and actually say something, he remembered a *Maxim* article he had read out of desperation in LaGuardia when his flight had been delayed and he'd been dying of boredom.

It was the ten most humiliating responses a woman can give when you tell her you love her for the first time.

He had the horrible feeling he was about to get served one of them.

"Thank you," she said.

Ouch. She slammed number three over the net right into his face. It felt just about as good as a real tennis ball to the nose would. He felt smacked, stung, stupid.

"That's sweet of you, and I appreciate your concern, but I'll be fine. Honestly."

Did she think he was professing love to make her feel better? Jesus. He'd told her for purely selfish reasons because he wanted her to smile, say she felt the same way, and agree to move in with him. If he had just wanted to make her feel better, he'd have sent her flowers and gotten her drunk. And it had never occurred to him that anyone would think his love was some sort of balm to any wound.

Take my heart, it's like Neosporin.

At times in life there were no words. Or at least not any that Jack could think of.

So he just went with instinct. Moving in front of the door where they were still hovering, Jack shook his head. "No thanks necessary."

Then when her mouth opened to protest, he closed the space between them at the speed of sound and took her lips in a demanding kiss.

The plan was to catch her off guard and stun her into forgetting she wanted to leave. The stunned part seemed to be working, but that was all. Jamie's lips were slack beneath his, and he had the feeling her eyes were wide open, though he wasn't going to look for confirmation.

This required a step two. Wrapping his arms around her, Jack molded her lush body to his, chest to chest, thigh to thigh, letting his thumbs brush across her lower back as he eased up on her lips. Kissed her softly, gently, his mouth caressing hers.

Better response. She gave a small sigh and kissed him back. Her hands didn't go so far as to encircle his neck, but she made it to his shoulders, which was good enough for him. He had missed her. One night, or one morning, actually, and he'd ached every day since for her.

After worshipping her mouth for a few minutes, he felt the shift in her response, felt her leaning closer to him, felt her kisses change from accepting to questing.

He buried his hands in her hair, his body tight, her mouth soft and giving as they moved from tentative to lustful.

"I love you," he murmured against her mouth, wanting her to understand, to acknowledge he meant the words. And maybe it would inspire some more gratitude, this time in the form of her hand on his fly.

She tried to break away from him.

He wasn't having any of that. He bent half over and scooped her up into his arms, one arm firmly under her backside.

Jamie let out a startled shriek. "What are you doing?"

"I'm being Rhett Butler, but without the moustache. You know, from your favorite movie."

"I'm no Scarlett," she said, though she did crack a smile. "And you said that movie is overdramatic and displays male-female relations in a negative light."

"Han Solo and Princess Leia?"

She shook her head, and tried to put her feet on the ground. "I'm more like Luke than Leia."

Jack let her get down, but he nudged her up against the wall and trapped her with his arms. "You're a man?"

Laughing, she shoved against his chest. "No. I'm whiny."

Jack couldn't believe that. He took a risk, knowing it was a big one. "Maybe in the beginning Luke was whiny with that whole *Uncle Owen, I want to fly* thing, but there has never been anything whiny about you. And in the end, Luke thought more about other people than himself. You're like that, Jamie. And your father is not Darth Vader."

Her eyes widened. "Darth Vader . . . God, that's ironic."

"What do you mean?" He was just using a movie reference to dance lightly around a sensitive issue.

"Nothing. And please don't say you love me . . . you can't. You don't know me, I don't know you. I don't even understand you."

"I do know you." Jack let his hands drop away from her. He was no longer feeling like Rhett. "Being with you, talking to you, getting to know you, you've changed the very foundation of my life, Jamie Peters. You showed me what's important. That when I concentrate on other people and their happiness, instead of myself, my life makes sense."

She skirted out past him, careful not to brush against him. "I'm glad if you feel like I've had a positive effect on your life. But truthfully, I'm sure generosity was there in you the whole time."

"Maybe it was, but I certainly wasn't using it." When he reached for her again she moved right up to his front door.

Why the hell was he always reaching for her and she was always pulling away? That was starting to irritate him. "Why won't you let me love you?"

"I don't trust you," she said.

Well. That pissed him off. "Don't trust me? Or don't trust yourself? Look, you said you have a bad track record with men. But all those losers, and whatever went down between you and your father, it has nothing to do with me. Nothing."

Her face leeched of all its color. "Maybe Beckwith's prediction was right. I was destined to meet you."

That sounded about right to him. So why did she look as if she'd eaten bad fish?

"You found a new career direction. I found my father and my conviction that I am happy with my life the way it is."

"Uhh . . ." Shit, he had nothing left to throw out there. He was a pitcher about to be yanked from the game.

"I'm not interested in a relationship right now."

Whoa. Dude. The ultimate brush-off. This was almost worse than the thank-you after his love confession.

No. Nothing was as bad as that.

But nonetheless, this pretty much sucked, too.

Jamie closed her eyes and took a deep breath, trying to relax so she could survive this ordeal.

"You look like hell," Allison whispered to her from the chair next to her.

She knew that without Allison pointing it out to her. "Thanks a lot."

Her eyes remained closed as she swished her feet around in the warm tub of water. They were lined up all in a row, all three roommates, soaking their feet in a midtown salon, the morning before Caroline's wedding.

"Maybe you should call him or something," Allison whispered.

Jamie nearly groaned with confusion and longing. How could she explain to Allison that she wanted nothing more than to call Jack and accept his offer of love, his promise of a future. But she couldn't do that. Jack wasn't who she had thought he was.

He was Jonathon.

And he had lied to her about several things, starting with being unemployed and ending with his chichi apartment. Which meant she couldn't trust him, no matter how much her heart wanted to believe otherwise.

But Jack wasn't the only liar. Jamie was lying to herself. She wasn't staying away from Jack because he had money, or because he had lied to her the day they met. She was staying away because she was in love with him. Because when she looked at him, and talked to him, and watched him with his grandfather and Austin, her heart melted to mush, about the consistency of goetta or grits. She was that much in love with him. And terrified that if she told him that, he'd have the power to hurt her as much as her father had hurt her.

"I'm not calling him." She was happy with her life the way it was, or she would be as soon as she got over being miserable.

"Well, you know you're going to see him tonight at the rehearsal dinner."

As if she hadn't thought about that every second for the last six days. And regretted that she'd been so abrupt in her dismissal of him at his apartment. She'd never been so cruel in her life—he professed love and she said *thank you?*—but she had been desperate to get out of there with her panties still intact. "I know."

Mrs. Davidson swept into the room, bringing a tray of fruit with her. "Here, girls, I brought you some goodies while you're getting your pedicures." She set the tray down on a table and smiled at them, beaming with maternal pride.

Jamie couldn't look her in the eye for fear Mrs. Davidson

would immediately know that Jamie had seen her son naked. The knowledge felt fairly burned all over her. Slept With Jack. In neon flashing lights across her breasts.

Caroline looked up from her own seat across from Jamie, her long, tanned legs showing under the feminine floral dress she wore. "Thanks, Mom. That looks great."

They shared a smile, which made Jamie feel even worse. This was Caro's big day, and she had done the utterly distasteful by sleeping with the brother of the bride.

Mrs. Davidson was an attractive woman of fifty-something with blond hair shot with silver. She was wearing a sleeveless dress in turquoise, showing well-defined arms that made Jamie feel like a soft down pillow. Caroline and her mother were long and slender, with firm everything, while Jamie was soft and squishy. Jack had called her lush, which had sounded wonderful in the moment.

Now it sounded fat.

Her lip trembled. She felt the signs of a serious pity party descending on her.

"Jamie, honey, are you all right?" Mrs. Davidson asked, picking up one of her hands and rubbing it maternally. "You look a little tired."

Jamie wiggled her toes in the bubbly water and attempted a smile. "I am tired. I think I'm getting a cold."

Allison made a coughing sound behind her hand.

Mrs. Davidson patted her again. "Oh, summer colds are the worst, aren't they? Get lots of rest this afternoon and take some echinacea. Here, have a strawberry."

She accepted the fruit Mrs. Davidson was pressing on her.

"Thank you." A tight smile was all she could manage, but fortunately Mrs. Davidson moved on.

"Mandy, you look absolutely adorable. Motherhood agrees with you, and wherever did you get those cute maternity capri pants?"

Her mother might have accepted her lame excuse, but

Caroline frowned at her. "Are you sure you're okay, Jams? You haven't looked good all week. Maybe it's the flu. I'd feel terrible if you were sick for the wedding."

"I think it's just a cold. The flu would have me knocked out flat. I'm sure I'll be fine." Jamie held the strawberry with one hand and rubbed down the front of her loose, long skirt with the other. She didn't have so much as a sniffle, but she couldn't exactly tell the truth.

Caroline leaned forward, cupping her hand so her mother wouldn't hear. "You're not . . . pregnant or anything, are you?"

Oh, Lord.

The strawberry fell out of her hand, tumbled down her skirt, and landed with a plop in her feet water.

"No!" She wasn't, she knew that for a fact. Jack had used protection every time, and it had been the wrong time. Of course, Caroline knew none of that.

Caroline grinned. "Just checking. You'd be a great mom, of course, but I can't imagine you raising a baby Scratch."

Not that she had ever actually slept with Scratch. "I haven't seen Scratch in months." The implication, of course, was that she hadn't had sex since then, which made Jamie feel like a Big Fat Liar.

This was awful. The very second Caro stepped off the plane after her honeymoon, Jamie was going to come clean.

Time to change the subject. She fished the strawberry out of her water. "So, everything's all set, Caro? No last minute things we can help you with?"

Caroline smiled in satisfaction. "Everything is set for the rehearsal tonight and the whole day tomorrow. Oh, I forgot to tell you. You know I've packed up all my stuff in the apartment, and I thought Brad would just get it when we got back from Paris. But Jonathon offered to move everything to the new apartment for me while we're gone."

Allison gave that horrid fake cough again, her brown eyes dancing with amusement.

Jamie saw nothing funny about it. "Oh, great. Have him call ahead so we can let him in." And so she could be on the other side of Manhattan when he showed up. Maybe even in Queens just to be safe.

Mrs. Davidson leaned against Caroline's chair. "I don't see why you just can't hire a mover, Caroline. It's not like Jonathon knows a thing about moving furniture. Unless that's something else he kept from his family."

Jamie couldn't imagine why anyone would keep the ability to lift wardrobe boxes a secret from their family, but Mrs. Davidson looked serious.

Caroline pursed her lips. "Jonathon actually has hired a mover. He's going to let them in and oversee the loading and unloading so we don't have to deal with it when we get back. It's a wedding gift."

"I'm surprised he has the money since he lost his mind and quit his job."

And Jamie thought she had issues. Clearly, Mrs. Davidson hadn't been thrilled when Jack left Wall Street.

"Mom, please, don't start like this . . ." Caroline started to rub at her temples.

"I think that's awfully nice of Jack," Jamie blurted out, darting an urgent "Help Me" look to Allison. She didn't want Caroline and her mother getting into a fight in a salon the day before her wedding.

Mrs. Davidson tilted her head and looked at her in surprise. "How did you know Jonathon's nickname was Jack? No one really calls him that anymore."

Jamie froze. Oh, help. She was busted. "I . . ."

"Jamie works for an agency that requests funding from Hathaway, Mom. I'm sure *she* understands why he quit his job."

Okay, uncomfortable family undercurrents. Would Caro's contempt shift to her if she found out Jamie had slept with Jack? But this was her opportunity to at least partially come clean. "Yes, and this week I actually met Jack in person. He's working with one of my teenagers."

Caro looked smug, Mrs. Davidson looked appalled. "He's doing *what*?" she said.

"Oh, yeah, Jack and Jamie have been working very closely on this project," Allison said, humor in her voice.

Turning, she shot Allison a warning look. Allison was the one who had gotten her started on this whole secret sex thing, and now she was about to force questions Jamie didn't want to answer while her feet were soaking in a salon. Or actually, she did not want to answer them ever.

Saved by the pedicurists. As four technicians stepped into the room, Mandy asked, "Why aren't you having a pedicure, Mrs. Davidson?"

Jamie could have kissed Mandy for taking the conversation off of Jack/Jonathon.

"Oh, I had a spa day yesterday. I knew I would be too nervous to relax today."

A woman dressed all in black sat on a little stool in front of Jamie and pulled her right foot out of the water and dried it with a fluffy white towel.

She tried to relax, forcing herself to take deep breaths and listen to the classical music playing softly above her head. Okay, that was better.

This was not a big deal. So she was lying. No biggie. So she had bolted out of Jack's place like a redheaded chicken. So she was in love with him. Not a problem.

All she had to do was spend an entire weekend in a wedding party with him and pretend they were platonic acquaintances. Of course, that was no mean feat, considering she had touched every inch of his glorious body and had begged him to make her come.

She had been certain he'd been exaggerating when he'd said he loved her. Sure she'd been doing the right thing. She had thought it wasn't a good idea for them to get involved, but now she couldn't really remember why. The only thing she did know was that she wasn't handling this whole thing very well.

Jamie had always prided herself on being a clear-headed person. Sitting in that chair she felt about as thick as Derby pie.

She had sort of run out on Jack twice.

A flush raced through her.

Maybe she wasn't as mature as she liked to think.

Mrs. Davidson started across the room. "My cell phone is ringing. Excuse me, girls, I'll take this in the lobby."

Caroline closed her eyes as a pedicurist started massaging her feet. "She's driving me crazy." Then her eyes reopened, fists relaxed, and Caroline looked determined to ignore her mother. Her tone was brisk, efficient, purposefully pleasant. "Mandy, you're partners with my cousin, Steve."

"Is he cute?" Mandy joked, flipping her wispy hair back. "Damien will be jealous if he is."

"I do think he's cute, yes, even though he's my cousin. He's something of a flirt, too. I don't want to cause problems, Mandy. I can partner you with Finn, Brad's awful cousin from Ireland."

"No, no, leave me with Steve." Mandy grinned, her hands resting on the baby bump below her waistband. "It practically guarantees that Damien will want to shag me when we get home that night. Branding, you know. And reminding me that I made the right choice in picking him."

Jamie was appalled. Torturing your husband all night just sounded so cruel.

Allison just laughed. "You're too cute to be so manipulative, Mandy. I love it." Then she turned to Caroline. "So, who do I get? The awful cousin or your brother?"

"The awful cousin." Caroline winced. "I'm sorry, Allison, but the thing is I trust you to control him. Jamie, well, sweetie, you're just too nice."

Nice. Sure. That's what she was. Lying and running out on men. She felt just sweet as sugar.

Why had she bolted like that? She might have ruined her new friendship with Jack, except that she knew despite their best intentions, neither one of them could claim they were purely friends.

Allison rubbed her hands together. "Controlling a man sounds like it could be fun, actually. So what do I have to do? Keep him from draining the Cristal, or from trying to look up skirts of fifteen-year-old girls?"

Eew. Jamie wasn't too nice to handle a guy like that, but she sure in the heck didn't want to.

"Allison, he's not *that* bad. He's not a pervert, just a jerk." Caroline's mouth drew down in a frown, and a hand went back up to rub at her right temple.

"So what's so terribly wrong with him?" Mandy asked.

There was no hesitation. "He's rude, he turns everything into a joke, he's underdressed in scrubby clothes at every occasion, and he's an artist, of all things. A broke, mooching artist, and for some reason Brad thinks he's the coolest thing since MP3s."

"I can handle that type, no problem." Allison waved her hand in the air. "I'll prevent him from making an embarrassing toast at the reception, I promise."

Wait a minute. It suddenly occurred to Jamie exactly what that meant.

It meant . . .

"So, that means Jamie is with Jonathon."

Gak. She'd thought that's what it meant. Her heart slammed into her gut. No, no, no. She could not spend the next twenty-four hours being forced to walk with, sit next to, dance with, and pose in pictures alongside Jack.

It had been hard enough to resist him the first week, when he'd just been friendly and pleasant at Beechwood. It had been damn near impossible to say no to the silent plea he'd had in his eyes after he had kissed her, told her he loved her.

Put him in a tux, with champagne swimming through her system, and she might as well throw her skirt over her head and let him at it.

A gurgling sound came out of her mouth. The pedicurist glanced up at her, her eyebrow lifting.

"Are you sure that's such a good idea, Caro? It might make Jack uncomfortable since we know each other in a . . . professional capacity."

Allison gave another hideous cough. "Maybe Jamie has a point, Caroline. I can partner up with Jonathon. It will be fun, since I've known him for years, and he'll feel comfortable."

Bless Allison's heart. She was trying to save her.

"No." Caroline shook her head. "Jonathon will be fine with Jamie. I seriously need you to baby-sit Finn. God, why do we even have relatives?"

Jamie was dead. That's all there was to it. Unless she invoked the three *R*'s. Reduce, reuse, recycle? No, that wasn't right. Resist, reject, retreat. That was it.

Clearly, she had been right in saying she wasn't ready for a relationship. She was a total emotional mess, and it wouldn't be fair to either of them to race down a relationship course that would leave them both bruised and bleeding when they crashed at the bottom.

Sinking back in the chair, she resigned herself to her fate— a really uncomfortable, sexually frustrating weekend.

Jack huddled in the backseat of his cousin Steve's SUV and tried not to grimace. He, Steve, and Pops were on their way to the wedding rehearsal, then dinner, and Steve's driving was making him sick.

Or maybe his life was making him sick.

His empty, lonely, meaningless life.

How could Jamie have left him like that? After he'd handed her his bleeding heart on a bloody stick.

It was the question that had been repeated a thousand times in a thousand different ways.

And he had yet to come up with an answer.

Steve took the corner at forty miles an hour, nearly annihilating a group of tourists trying to cross the street to see the Rockefeller Center.

"Slow down," he growled, pushing his sunglasses firmly back up his nose.

Steve glanced at him. "What's the matter with you? You don't look so good."

"I think I ate bad chicken." It was a total lie, but was better than blurting out the truth, that he was mooning over Jamie. Steve would spend the whole damn night telling him *I told you so.*

"Uh, bad timing, Jack. You can't be puking at your sister's wedding. It won't look good on the video."

No, he didn't imagine it would. "I'll be okay if you slow the damn car down."

"Fine, fine." Steve shot him a grin. "I saw enough of you tossing your lunch last week at the bachelor party."

Jack groaned. "Don't even bring that up again."

The memory made his head pound. After spending a lonely night wondering why the heck Jamie had left him, he had gone to the bachelor party and had proceeded to drink himself under the table. Literally.

He hadn't done anything that stupid since he was twenty-one.

Steve wasn't finished razzing him, though. Shifting gears, he said, "I've never seen anybody throw up down the front of a stripper before."

"It was an accident." One that held no comedic value for him, despite the laughter in Steve's voice. He didn't imagine the stripper had found it all that funny either. It had taken a profuse apology and a five-hundred-dollar tip to keep the whole bachelor party from being thrown out of the club.

But he hadn't meant to do it. He hadn't been interested in the stripper at all, in fact, had waved her away. She had persisted, shaking herself and her red-tasseled breasts in his face. His perception had already gone the way of the whiskey, and she had made him dizzy with all that wobbling. And then an image of Jamie wiggling out of her jeans topless had risen in his mind, and before he even knew what was happening, he had thrown up, splashing those tassels and her red high-heeled shoes.

Not one of his finer moments.

"It was disgusting," Steve said with relish.

Jack wasn't going to argue.

Nor did he feel like discussing it any further.

Pops, who had been making his way through a bag of peanut M&Ms in the front seat, added his two cents. "Bad chicken? Bah. Looks like girl trouble to me."

"Are you supposed to be eating those?" Jack asked, grabbing for a subject change.

"Do I give a shit?" Pops threw a green one in his mouth and chewed defiantly. "I don't have a peanut allergy. And stop changing the subject. If you're pissed that Jamie dumped you, you should do something about it. A hard-on girl doesn't come along every day."

Steve let out a laugh. "What in the hell is a hard-on girl?"

Jack considered crawling under the seat to avoid this conversation. Pops shared none of his embarrassment.

"A girl who gives you a hard-on just by thinking about her. Jamie does that to Jack."

He swore under his breath while Steve nearly ran them off the road from laughing so hard. "He's pitiful, isn't he?" Steve asked. "You should have seen him begging her to meet for coffee. It was sad to see how far the mighty have fallen."

"Fuck off."

Steve only laughed harder. "Come on, Jack, even you have to admit your strategy didn't exactly work."

"So what do you suggest I do, since you're such an expert?"

"You can stop being so dramatic for one thing. No chick is going to like a puppy dog following her around with hopeful eyes."

Pops nodded. "Kid's got a point. And I read that metrosexuals are on their way out of favor. Women want manly men, who take charge."

Oh, good God.

"So stop acting like a crybaby and seduce her," was Pops's conclusion.

"Seriously," Steve added. "And drop the whining about being rich. Makes you sound like a spoiled brat."

Wow, the sympathy pouring forth from his family was just overwhelming.

The evening stretched ahead of him, long and unpleasant.

And he couldn't even seek solace in the wine.

With his luck, he'd throw up on the entire bridal party.

But maybe Steve and Pops had a point, when you waded through the useless crap they had spouted. Maybe he needed to stop moping like a bad cliché and do what had always come naturally to him—take action. Meet the challenge head-on and emerge triumphant.

As he hit the button for the car window to go down, he pictured life without Jamie in it. Desolate, empty. Siberia of the heart. Nope, that just wasn't going to happen.

He would love her, damn it, and she'd learn to like it.

Chapter 15

"Oh, my God, what is he doing here?" Allison said as she opened the door of a cab. "Quick, get in before he sees us."

"Who?" Jamie turned around and spotted Beckwith. He was kind of hard to miss, wearing that floral dress and Charro earrings. "Maybe he was just in the neighborhood." She waved at him.

Allison grabbed her hand and yanked it down. "Stop that! He'll see you, and we're on the verge of being late to the rehearsal. Caroline will have a cow if we're late."

"Jamie!" Beckwith spotted her and waved both hands. "Don't leave, I have to talk to you."

"Who cares?" Allison got in the cab. "Come on, Jamie. Tell him to call you later. Like next year."

But Jamie didn't like the look of concern on Beckwith's face. Even his lip liner couldn't keep his mouth from turning down in a pinched frown. "What's wrong, Beckwith?"

The cab driver yelled out the window, "You going to stand there, lady, or get in the car? I don't have all day."

"We can get another cab," Jamie said to Allison, feeling a little guilty, but needing to see what Beckwith wanted. She couldn't just blow him off without spending the whole night worrying about him.

Allison sighed and opened her purse. She handed the driver a ten. "Here. Give her five minutes."

"Five minutes. No more," came the gruff, staccato reply.

Allison rolled her eyes. "Listen to this guy, Jamie," she said out the window. "He sounds just like a Speak-N-Spell. It's amazing."

But Beckwith was now in front of her, thick hand resting on his heaving chest. "Girlfriend, I ran three blocks in these heels. Nearly broke my fucking ankle six times. And now I have sweat stains. Do you know when sweat dries on rayon you can still see the circle? This is a new dress, too."

"Did you need something, Beckwith? I'm on my way to Caroline's rehearsal dinner."

"You need to stop this wedding."

"What? Why? I can't do that."

"He's going to hurt her, sugar. I mean, rip her heart out and feed it to the fishies." Beckwith wiped the dew off his upper lip.

Jamie believed him, and was sorry for it. It made her ache for Caroline, but she also knew Caro was not the type to believe a cross-dresser's vague warning, even if his predictions for Mandy and herself had come true. Well, hers had been only partially accurate. Man of her dreams might have been a stretch.

"I can't stop the wedding. Caroline has to want to stop it, and trust me, that's not going to happen."

Beckwith grabbed her arms, shook her just a little. "Then you have to be there for her when the ax falls."

"Okay. Okay. Of course." Jamie bit her lip. "Are you sure?"

"Yes." He let go of her. "Oh, and sweetie, I was right about Darth Vader, wasn't I? But this isn't about your father, remember that."

"What is it about?" she asked, frustrated. "Knowing my destiny is a bad idea, Beck, because I just feel like I'm spinning in circles trying to decide what it is."

"Well, stop it!" Beckwith said, squinting against the sun. "Stop thinking! Just listen to your heart." He grabbed at his chest, clasping his faux breast.

If he broke out into a love song, she suspected she was going to be embarrassed.

"Just trust me, sweetie."

Jamie jumped when the cabbie blared his horn. "Your time is up. Get out of the car."

"I will not," Allison declared, but she did lean out the door and call to Jamie. "Come on, we're going to be late."

"I have to go . . ."

Beckwith squeezed her hand. "Don't let him drive at first. He'll take wrong turns." He dropped a kiss on her forehead. "Be happy, precious."

Then he turned and walked down the street, limping as if his open-toe sandals were pinching his feet.

Jamie slid into the cab. She didn't even have the door half closed before the car ripped away from the curb and merged into traffic.

Beckwith's words rang through her head. How could Beckwith be so sure when she was so confused?

The cards were wrong. They had to be.

Jack was from a different world than she was. She had only scratched the surface of knowing and understanding him.

"We are going to be so late."

"I never told you this . . . but Beckwith said Jack is the one he saw in the cards." Jamie turned to Allison, wanting to accept her destiny, terrified she'd make a false move and get hurt.

"You have a big red lip print on your forehead." Allison reached out and rubbed it off. Then her brown eyes softened. "Maybe Beckwith isn't so crazy after all. I've never seen you like this over a guy."

"It could never work, Allison, you know that."

"I don't know that." Allison was wearing a plum-colored sheath dress, her dark hair pulled back from her face, chandelier earrings swinging as she shook her head. "It can work if you want it to. Jonathon doesn't need fixing like your other guys. He's in move-in condition."

"He's attracted to me because I'm different than his usual type."

That was her real fear. That he would dump her when the novelty wore off and go on with the rest of his life. Just the thought of it had fear clawing up into her throat. She wasn't afraid of a lot of things, not even spiders or dogs over seventy pounds, but the thought of giving Jack her heart and having him reject it made her feel downright sick.

Part of why she dated the men she did was because she knew there was no permanency there. She knew the relationships wouldn't work, and when they split, and he went off to a better life, like Scratch had, she'd felt happy, not sad.

But it wouldn't be that way with Jack. It would be like losing her father all over again.

"What makes you think he would walk away?"

Plucking at her skirt, she shrugged. "When you strip away the lust and the fascination, what is there? What do we have in common? Nothing." She stared out at the piles of garbage lining Bleecker Street. "I wish you hadn't talked me into wearing this dress. I feel ridiculous."

Jamie rolled her shoulders in the floral dress in agitation. Instead of being long and loose like the dresses she normally wore, it was short, with a high waist. It was a fun, flirty, summer look, and now she just knew it would send the wrong message to Jack.

Like, *Look at me, I'm a silly goofball.*

Black would have been better.

"My legs look like cracker barrels in this dress."

Allison's eyebrows rose. "What is a cracker barrel? Never mind. I don't want to know. And stop pulling on the neckline. The dress looks great. You look great. You look so-phisticated. Tall."

It was easy for Allison to look sophisticated at five-foot-ten with long, straight, dark hair. Jamie had to work at it.

Gripping a crystal worry stone she'd pulled out of her purse, she tried to think serene, calming thoughts. Waterfalls, dolphins, daisies. Nothing helped. She was hysterical.

"You were right, Allison. We should have never gotten our fortunes read. Now I have all this horrible knowledge weighing down on me. I feel *burdened*."

What would she have done differently if she'd never known anything about her destiny? How could she possibly face Jack knowing that she'd been acting like a fool?

And in this stupid, clingy, short, short dress?

"I feel late," Allison said, grabbing her purse. "Check your boobs and get a grip. You have to walk down the aisle with Jack, and I have to spank an Irish cousin if he gets out of line."

Jamie glanced down at her cleavage, saw too much of it, and yanked her dress up. "Can we switch places? You walk the aisle with Jack, and I'll spank the Irish cousin?"

"No way. Spanking is more my style than yours."

An image of Jack behind her, giving her a playful swat, rose in her mind, and she flushed. That was not what Allison meant, and here her mind went right in that direction. Dang. Her dress was too clingy, and her willpower too shaky to be having thoughts like that.

"You're right. No spanking for me."

Jack busied himself chatting with Pops and ignoring his mother.

It was a bit of a challenge since she kept approaching them to fuss over Pops and criticize both of them, but he was making an effort. This was his sister's wedding re-hearsal, and he was in church. He'd be charitable, no matter how difficult it was.

"Jonathon, I'm so glad to see you got a haircut. You were looking absolutely slovenly." His mother reached out as though she wanted to straighten his tie, then thought better of it. His mother led the family in questioning his sanity.

"I'm thinking of growing it out, Mom. Going for a retro beach look. Taking up seashell collecting and opening a hot dog stand."

She darted a quick look around before whispering fiercely, "I'm sending my therapist to you. He can fix your little crisis." Her hand went up to pat her hair, check her earrings. She was perfection as usual in an ivory dress, minus the suit jacket that accompanied it. It was sleeveless, to show off the biceps her personal trainer, Rafe, was carefully sculpting.

"I'm not having a crisis. I've made a lifestyle change." It was probably cruel to push his mother's buttons like that, but he was feeling downright put upon. No matter what he did, it was wrong.

His mother wanted him rich. Jamie wanted him to be broke. Meredith wanted him back at the firm.

And he wanted what he couldn't have.

"Margaret, lay off the kid. This is your daughter's wedding . . . can't you just pull the stick out of your ass for twenty-four hours and enjoy yourself?" Pops looked disgusted, and his words were firm, despite the slight slur that was still present in them.

Jack's mother clamped her jaw shut. "You should have brought a nurse with you, Dad. Who is going to keep an eye on you?"

"I don't need a goddamn nurse. I can even wheel this chair around by myself."

"I'll stay with him," Jack said, so they wouldn't cause a scene. Not to mention that it was still something of a secret that Pops had moved in with him the week before.

"Oh, wonderful. The blind leading the blind. I'm so reassured." With that, his mother turned on her heel and left them.

Pops smacked Jack's thigh with his right, stronger arm. "Don't let her get to you, Jack-o. She's just trying to get a rise out of you."

But Jack only half heard his grandfather because Jamie had just walked into the church and was coming down the aisle. Wearing a dress that clung to her impressive breasts and sort of shifted and floated all around her. It reminded him of lingerie, soft and delicate, sexy as hell. Her hair was loose around her shoulders, spilling over her peaches-and-cream skin.

He'd never seen her wear shoes with stiletto heels, but these were some serious Barbie sandals. They sent her two inches higher and showed off every bit of her legs from the knee down.

"Wow," he said, gripping the back of Pops's wheelchair.

He'd seen Jamie naked, touched every inch of her, and watching her walk down that aisle brought it all back to him in excruciating detail. What he'd had. What could never be his.

"What?" Pops followed his gaze. "I still can't believe you're actually interested in the con's daughter. She's a little porky for your tastes, don't you think?"

Porky? The very word offended him. Jamie was gorgeous. "No, I don't think that! Watch your mouth, Pops."

The old man just laughed. "There's nothing like a hard-on girl, is there?"

"She's much more than that." Though he did have a hard-on, right as he was speaking. Fortunately, the back of Pops's head was blocking his crotch from general view.

Jamie looked stunning.

"Well, roll me over there and let me chat with her. Barely had time to talk last week, what with her all upset over her father. And I've always liked girls with curves. More to squeeze."

"Pops . . ." Jack was not in the mood to joke about Jamie. "Seriously, don't, okay? This isn't funny. I have a lot of respect for Jamie." Even if she had brushed him off. Twice. Even if she obviously didn't love him the way he did her, or she would have had more to say than thank you.

He wasn't sure how to fix what was between them. How to show her that there could be a relationship between them.

He'd never wanted anything in his entire life—not a deal, not money—the way he wanted Jamie Peters.

Not to possess, but to please, share his time and life with.

Maybe she wouldn't agree with him, but he had to at least try and plead his case.

Will Davidson sobered up. Tried to glance at his grandson over his shoulder, very interested in the tone of voice Jack was using. "Alright, I'll lay off. I was just joking."

The girl was nothing in a million years like the kind of woman Jack usually would be interested in. She was pretty, very natural, looking a bit shy as she made her way toward them. Curvy. Very Chelsea or the Village, without a drop of Wall Street in her.

Will had met two or three of Jack's previous girlfriends, and they were all cut from the same cloth—skinny blondes with careers in finance. But none of them had put that arrested look on Jack's face. Personally, even after five minutes, Will had thought Jamie was Jack's best pick so far, and given his reaction when Will had yanked his chain about Jamie's weight, Jack thought so, too.

Jamie stopped in front of them, biting her lip and tipping her ankles off her heels. "Hi there, Jack. How are you?"

And damned if she wasn't a southerner on top of it all.

Her gaze shifted to him, and she smiled. "It's a pleasure to see you again, Mr. Hathaway."

"Call me Will, please."

"Alright, Will." Jamie had stuck her hand out to shake, which pleased Will. She was talking to him as though he was an intelligent person, not the senile old coot everyone seemed to think he was lately. He was only seventy-seven, and that damn stroke had jerked with his body parts, not his brain.

Will shook, keeping her hand in his. "Jack and I were just discussing how beautiful you looked strolling down that aisle, Jamie."

Her cheeks pinkened. "Oh," she said, giving a little nervous laugh. "Thank you."

"Beautiful is an understatement," Jack said, in a husky tone that made Will suddenly feel as if he were caught in between a bulldog and a juicy steak bone.

Jamie's gaze dropped to the floor, before she glanced back up. "Caroline would like us to be partners for the ceremony, Jack."

"She always was my favorite sister."

Will was impressed. That was a pretty smooth line. But it was time for him to exit before Jack embarrassed the hell out of the girl. She was shooting him helpless, awkward glances.

"I think I see the minister waving everyone up to the front," Pops lied. "Run along you two, before Caroline flips her wig." That one had a bit more of her mother in her than Will would have liked, but she was a good kid. Just a little uptight at times.

"Will you be at the dinner?"

"Of course." He wasn't leaving until Jack did. And thank God he wasn't going back to that mausoleum. Rest home. Hah. It was so restful it had almost put him into a coma. It was like living with *Dawn of the Dead* zombies wearing bathrobes.

"I look forward to chatting with you, then." Jamie gave him a bright smile and started up the aisle.

Jack swore under his breath. "I'm telling you, Pops, I just look at her and I feel like I'm being electrocuted. Fried from one end to the other. It's insane."

It was called lust, which very possibly could lead to love, if Will wasn't mistaken. And he thought that just maybe, this girl was worthy of his grandson.

Will had been surprised that Jack had chosen to leave his career behind, but he had supported him. Only Jack still wasn't happy, and if Jamie Peters could give him a reason to smile again, then Will would owe her a huge debt.

"Embrace the insanity, Jack-o. You just might enjoy going crazy for a while."

Chapter 16

Jamie heard one out of every ten words the minister spoke.

"Commitment . . . relax . . . fun . . . left . . ."

Jack was standing next to her, thoroughly distracting her. He wasn't doing anything exactly, just breathing. She could hear it. In, out, a little sigh emerging every now and then. Out of her peripheral vision she could see his fingers twitching on his pants leg.

Seeing him in that gray suit had nearly dropped her like a KO'd boxer. He was so darn hot, looking dark and dangerous, yet so vulnerable.

Plus she'd had Beckwith's words ringing in her ears when she laid eyes on Jack, and it had taken all the courage she possessed to speak to him. But she figured better to get it over with than have it looming over her all night.

Having his grandfather there had been a useful diversion, but now it was just she and Jack, standing side by side in front of a minister. Okay, so there were twenty other people sitting in the room, and the entire wedding party standing right up front, but it didn't seem to matter.

The only thing she was aware of was Jack.

He touched her elbow, and she nearly jumped out of her dress.

"You cold?" he murmured in her ear, his breath tickling her flesh. "You have goose bumps. Did you bring a sweater?"

"I should have," she whispered back. "I'm always cold in air-conditioning."

"I remember." He gave her a smile that told her he was thinking of exactly how cold she had been naked on his couch before she'd thrown the blanket over her. Before he'd heated her with his own flesh, his tongue.

Jamie shifted. Those were not good thoughts to be having in a church.

And there was something about Jack tonight. He seemed . . . dangerous. Intense.

Polite and gracious, yes.

Thoughtful of his grandfather's needs, Caroline's needs, and her own, but somehow smoldering under the surface. She had a feeling she was seeing a different side to him, the one who went after a deal, the one who focused on success.

Tonight he was focusing on her, and it was disconcerting.

"Do you want my jacket?" he asked, rubbing the small of her back just ever so lightly.

To the casual observer, he was attentive to his wedding partner, but clearly out of duty only. Jamie knew better. Somehow, Jack was managing to look reserved, but he was not. Far from it.

He was boiling under that polite façade. He was touching her, in a casual way, but with eyes that said clearly he wasn't.

That he remembered.

That he wanted her.

That there most certainly was something between them.

It was just a hand on her elbow here, fingers on the small of her back there. But those fingers shifted down as they waited for their turn to aisle march, lower than was appropriate for the recent acquaintances they were supposed to be. Not so low as to be crass, but low enough to claim possession.

Jack's fingers said she was his, that he had touched her there without a dress between his skin and hers.

Jamie shifted a little, fully aware that Allison and the Irish cousin were standing right behind them. Not to mention Caro and her father just a few feet back.

Jamie glanced around the vestibule, searching for a safe conversational topic, and turned to include Allison and Finn, reaching for sexual safety in numbers. "The stained glass here is beautiful." It was a stone Episcopal church with gothic arches and extensive windows.

Jack glanced down at her, an eyebrow arching.

Allison looked at her like she'd lost her mind. "Very pretty, Jamie."

The Irish cousin Caroline had complained so much about turned to study one of the windows. "Have you been to Ireland, Jamie?" he asked in his lilting brogue, which seemed a bit thicker now than it had when she'd been introduced to him earlier.

"No."

"With your coloring"—he pointed to her head—"I thought you might be a fellow Gaelic."

She didn't really have true red hair, and she was tired of people saying she did. Hers was auburn, heading toward regular old mud brown.

Finn didn't have red hair either. He was the black-hair, blue-eye variety of Irishman, and really attractive. He was also a bit scruffy, like Caroline had described. He was wearing a suit, but it looked a little wrinkled, like he couldn't be bothered to press it, and there was no tie in sight. He needed a haircut, but he didn't seem to be the pig Caroline had suggested he was.

"Oh, I've got Irish somewhere in my blood. I think it was my great-grandmother. She was from Cork. But I've got so many different nationalities in me, I'm just a mutt." Jamie took a peek toward the front of the church. Mandy and Steve were still standing there, waiting for the signal.

"Well, the village churches in Ireland aren't on nearly so grand a scale as this, but they do serve to show that sometimes the most startling beauty can be found in the simplest of things." He reached his hand out and moved it in a half circle back and forth in front of her face. "Like the way the light is playing over your striking cheekbones right now."

Jamie was a little startled, but still felt a bit like sighing. That was awfully flattering. Jack stiffened next to her.

"Have you ever had your portrait painted, Jamie?"

Allison snorted and gave Finn a smack on the arm. "Jamie's with Jonathon, if you know what I mean, so give it up."

Finn just shook his head. "My interest is purely professional, as an artist. I'd love to paint Jamie, capture that shadow as it passes over her face. The Madonna and Child, that's the face you have."

Jamie felt that very face split into a beaming smile. She didn't think anyone had ever compared her to the Mother of God before. "Well, that's awfully sweet of you, Finn."

"What kind of face do I have?" Allison asked.

"Aphrodite," he told her without hesitation. "Helen of Troy. Cleopatra. The kind of woman men would kill to possess."

"Wow." Allison grinned. "I'll buy that for a dollar. How about Mandy?"

"She's Alice in Wonderland—whimsical, dreamy, smart, tender."

That sounded just like Mandy.

"What about Caroline?" Jamie asked, interested despite the fact that Jack made an impolite noise.

Finn turned and glanced back at Caroline, who was standing with her father, fussing with his tie. Her blond hair was pulled back, her ivory dress classic and stunning. Jamie thought Caroline was a beautiful bride, striking in a way she could never hope to achieve.

Hands in his pockets, Finn's head went back and forth

slightly. "Caroline? Caroline is Sleeping Beauty, locked in her ivory tower."

Jack placed her hand on his elbow. "It's our turn."

Jamie cast a glance back at Caroline, wondering what Finn had meant. She would have never thought of Caroline that way. But Allison gave her a push, and she focused forward, staring down that church aisle.

"You don't remind me of the Madonna," Jack murmured in a low voice, his lips tickling her ear.

"No?" She wasn't sure she wanted to hear his answer.

"To me you're Venus, a gorgeous, awe-inspiring goddess. And I'm going to love you, Jamie. I'm going to talk to you, make love to you, be there with a ride when you get caught in a thunderstorm. Do you understand me?"

And before she could blink, he was leading her up the aisle, gripping her hand tightly over his elbow.

Chapter 17

J amie loved weddings. She had been looking forward to Caroline's wedding since the engagement ring had been stuck on her finger nine months before.

Unfortunately, Jamie had gotten zero sleep the night before, worrying about Jack. Wondering how he would react to her today, and what he might pull in the name of loving her.

Regretting that her strategy to resist Jack had failed so miserably at the church the night before. He'd spent the whole night whispering phenomenally inappropriate things in her ear. How was it she'd told him she didn't want a relationship and he'd morphed into Don Juan de Wall Street? Throw in a Spanish accent and he'd have the whole thing down pat.

Yet she was determined to enjoy the wedding day, despite Jack and his roving fingers. If Jamie ignored the fact that Jack was constantly undressing her with his eyes, and the encroaching hands, she could make it through this day without making a fool of herself. Not that she was expecting a repeat of the night before.

Nope. She was expecting much worse. He was going to be coming on to her left and right, and she was going to have to be strong. Which she could do.

Now, if only her bridesmaid's dress would cooperate.

"Allison!" she howled to her roommate as she stood in front of the full-length mirror in her bedroom, newly hers and hers alone, now that both Mandy and Caroline had moved out. The rent was going to kill her, but Mandy and Caro had both paid for several more months, until the lease was up. Then she and Allison were probably going to have to take on new roommates, which wasn't at all appealing, or find a cheaper place.

As she surveyed herself in the mirror with dismay, she yanked on the dress hard. She honestly did not remember the dress looking the way it currently did when she had gone to her last fitting.

It was ice blue, which complemented her auburn coloring, but sleeveless, which Jamie was always a little leery of given her healthy chest. Yet if sleeveless was paired with a high neck, it wasn't usually a problem.

This wasn't a high neck. It was straight across the top of her chest, forming a band over her breasts. Strapless. In theory it was an attractive dress, with a straight full-length skirt.

On Jamie the bodice appeared to be suspended in midair a foot from her body due to the thrust of her D cup breasts. Which meant anyone looking over her shoulder could see all the way to the promised land. And it wasn't manna they were going to find.

She yanked harder, trying to move it up. The force of gravity contained within her fifteen-pound chest dragged it back down again.

"What's the matter?" Allison called down the hall from the bathroom.

"Something's wrong with my dress!"

"Hold on, I'm putting mascara on."

Mandy appeared in the doorway, having come to the apartment to get ready with them. "What's wrong with it?"

Jamie looked at her friend. On Mandy, the dress looked stunning, complementing her fair skin and light brown hair swept up on top of her head. Since she was neither short nor tall, the straight cut of the dress served to visually lengthen Mandy's legs. It attractively hugged the small bump of her belly.

And her bodice fit snug against her skin.

She looked cute, damn it, pregnant and all.

"Look at my chest." Jamie pointed a finger to herself, wondering what exactly she had done to deserve such bad karma.

Mandy's eyes widened. But she said, "It looks a bit . . . low, but it's fine."

Jamie didn't believe her for one second. Mandy, bless her heart, was trying to spare her feelings, knowing perfectly well there wasn't a single thing Jamie could do about the dress two hours before the ceremony.

Allison wasn't quite as diplomatic when she walked in behind Mandy. "Whoa. Where's the stripper pole?"

Jamie didn't know whether to laugh or cry.

Mandy said, "Allison! That's a hideous thing to say."

"I can't help it. I'm jealous." Allison looked down at her flat chest and shook her head. "I don't have enough, Jamie's got too much. So unfair."

Jamie yanked the dress again and threw her arms up in despair. "If I could share them I would, believe me. That's it! I'm getting a breast reduction."

"Today? I don't think there's time, sweetie." Allison smiled as she patted a hair back into place that wasn't even out of place, that Jamie could tell.

She laughed, in spite of her dress. "Very funny. I meant later, but soon. As soon as I save up some money."

Mandy said, "But you know if you do that you can't breastfeed."

Jamie hadn't thought about that, but she was doubtful she would be able to, even though she usually advocated anything natural. "Mandy, can you see me breastfeeding? I'd have enough to feed a small village."

Allison snorted. "There's a mental image. It takes a village . . . or Jamie."

The buzzer at their front door rang as Jamie wished her breasts to perdition.

Allison rushed to the door and hit the button. "What?"

"It's us. Come on down, the limo is parked in the fire lane."

Jamie knew that voice belonged to Jack because of the way her breath disappeared and her legs started to spontaneously wobble like one of her mother's Jell–o molds.

"Oh, God!" She dug her hands into her bodice and pulled up as hard as she could. Her hand slipped on the satin, and her fist ricocheted back and whacked her nose.

"Ow." She rubbed her throbbing nose, eyes watering.

Allison ran across the apartment, her skirt lifted up in her hands. "I can't find my purse, and I told Jonathon we'd be right down. He said we're late for pictures." Allison started throwing the sage green couch cushions on the floor in her frantic search.

Mandy had already padded back down the hall, calling, "I don't even have my shoes on yet."

The buzzer rang again.

Allison went into the kitchen, eyes darting left and right for her purse. "Jamie, go on down and appease them. We'll be right down in a sec."

Great. Just what she wanted to do. Appease Jack.

Grabbing her own clutch and giving her hair, pulled back in a knot, a final smoothing, she took a deep breath and headed for the door.

Walking down past the third floor she reminded herself that Jack was Caroline's brother and wouldn't misbehave at her wedding.

Past the second floor she reaffirmed that ending their relationship, such as it was, was the smart, intelligent thing to do.

As she gulped and stepped up to the front door, she told

herself that grimacing from desperate lust most definitely would not look good in the wedding pictures.

She pushed the door open, and there he was, his hand in his pocket, rattling change.

If Jack had looked good in a suit, he looked like sexy sin in a tuxedo. Jamie felt longing blaze up in her like a five-alarm fire.

Her mouth went dry.

She might have squeaked.

And she started to wonder if maybe she should just accept what Beckwith and Jack and even Allison were telling her.

That fate wanted her to get naked with Jack.

Jack turned from hitting the buzzer for the third time and stopped cold. Or rather, hot. *Holy shit.*

Jamie had opened the door and was standing there, a vision in pale blue with her hair tamed and wound up on her head. A picture of passion. His every fantasy called up and brought to life in breathtaking beauty.

She was the most intriguing combination of shy and sensual, naïve, yet knowledgeable. She licked her lips with a little sigh, the wetness of her tongue making a small smacking sound as she rolled it around her mouth.

Blood was rushing in his head, and other obvious places, as he lowered his eyes to her chest.

The sight that greeted him was awe-inspiring. In defiance of the laws of physics, somehow her dress wasn't in a pile around her waist, but was just hanging there in front of her. Barely covering her considerable assets, and leaving a whole expanse of creamy white flesh exposed.

He came close to passing out, a garbled moan forcing out of his mouth.

"You look . . . amazing," he managed to say.

Her cheeks tinted pink. "Allison and Mandy will be down in a minute. Allison lost her purse."

He didn't care one flipping bit about Allison and her purse. "This is nice," he murmured, reaching out and brushing his thumb against the smoothness of her hair, so different from her normal tumble of curls.

A tendril had escaped and spiraled defiantly, and Jack twirled it around his finger. "I love your hair down, but this lets me see your long, luscious neck."

Before he even knew what he was doing, he had leaned forward and placed his mouth below her ear.

She jerked back and crashed into the door of her apartment building. "Stop that. Steve and Finn are sitting right in the limo."

He didn't care about them any more than he cared about Allison's purse. "So, it would be okay if we were alone, then?"

"Yes." She clapped a hand over her mouth. "I mean no! Of course not."

She was flustered, and that was a good thing.

He smiled and started forward, intent on claiming another kiss. He'd thought a lot the night before, wondering what it was about Jamie that he admired so much. After mentally listing about nine hundred things, he had decided the bottom line was that Jamie was totally unselfish and knew herself.

That was very sexy. Except she was completely wrong about what they should do now. She wanted to end whatever was growing between them. He wanted to nourish it, explore it, enjoy it.

"I meant what I said last night, Jamie. I'm not going anywhere. Every time you turn around, I'm going to be there, waiting until you're ready."

Jamie's eyes went wide, and she pressed herself back against the glass door. "You can't," she whispered.

"I can." Jack was almost there, anticipating her mouth under his, her breasts dancing across his chest, when the door was propelled forward and Jamie tumbled into his arms.

Her breasts weren't dancing across his chest now. They were crushed against him, virtually spilling up out of the top of her dress as she struggled to regain her balance.

Allison gave a blithe, "Sorry," as she came through the door and stopped on the sidewalk.

Though Allison didn't look at him as she put on gigantic white-rimmed sunglasses, he thought he detected a slight smile.

Which meant he owed Allison a hearty thanks, if she supported his quest for Jamie.

Who was squirming in his arms, causing a good amount of her to wiggle against a lot of him.

"Are you alright?" he asked.

"Fine." Her gaze dropped to his lips, then back up to his eyes. She gulped. "Really, you can let me go now . . ."

He pressed against her, taking care to meld himself to her body in a particularly intimate spot with his very obvious erection.

"Oh, gracious!" she said, her head falling back, as her eyes drifted half shut.

His sentiments exactly.

He went in for the kiss he was determined to take this time.

And met with air.

Jamie had maneuvered out of his arms and was walking in a zigzag drunken manner toward the limo, wiping her hands on her dress.

He stared in disbelief for a minute until Mandy came through the door and said, "Sorry I'm late. Are we all ready?"

Then her gaze landed on the tent his tuxedo pants were making. Her mouth fell open.

First Pops, now Mandy. He hadn't been caught with this many public hard-ons since junior high. Then he had simply stopped wearing sweatpants and watching *Baywatch*.

There was nothing he could do now about being with Jamie. Or that taunting dress.

Mandy hid a laugh behind her hand. "That answers my question. You are absolutely ready."

Jesus, was he *blushing?*

Mandy shot him a backward grin as she bent over to climb into the limo. "If I didn't have such a delicious husband, I think I might be jealous of Jamie."

He frowned. "She told you about . . . us?" Did that mean his sister knew? He would have thought Caroline would have mentioned it to him. It wasn't as if it were a secret or anything, but he hadn't found it necessary to tell his sister either. Especially since Jamie had dumped him.

"Normally, Jamie cannot keep a secret. But this time, she hasn't said a word. I've just got eyes in my head and the pre-scient skill of a pregnant woman. Don't worry, Caroline doesn't know." She climbed into the car and left him standing in the sun.

"Know what?" he complained to no one in particular, waving a fat pigeon away from his feet. "That we could have, almost, sort of had something going on, but after one incredibly mind-blowing night, it's dead in the water be-cause of me?"

The pigeon didn't answer him, so he got a grip and joined the bridal party. When he got in the limo, Jamie was having a heated argument with Allison.

"I think the girls should sit on this side, and the guys on the other," Jamie said, her face flushed. She wasn't sitting down, but was doing an odd sort of hovering in the center of the limo, head and back hunched over.

"What is this, eighth grade?" Allison rolled her eyes. "I'm not moving because it doesn't matter." She patted Finn's and Steve's knees on either side of her. "Besides, I like all this muscle around me."

Mandy sat down on the seat by the window, and Jack

slid in next to her, leaving the only seat available for Jamie right next to him by the door.

Amused that Jamie didn't trust herself to even sit next to him, he patted the seat invitingly. "I showered today and remembered my deodorant."

Her lip curled.

Allison told Jamie, "You're screwing up your hair standing there like that. It's scraping against the ceiling."

"Shoot!" Jamie grabbed at her head and took the seat next to him, patting her hairs back into place.

In an attempt to avoid him, she flattened herself against the window and turned a little so her back was to him.

It gave him a nice view of her round little behind outlined in satin.

Which he took the liberty of gawking at for a large portion of the drive, alternating staring at her butt with checking out her cleavage. The one time he managed to pry his gaze away, he caught Steve's eye, who gave him a knowing look.

He shrugged.

Steve grinned.

When they pulled up in front of the church, Jamie bolted out of the door first and ran up the steps. He followed her in time to see her retreat into a little room at the back of the church where the bride was meant to wait until her big entrance.

The photographer was pacing in the vestibule and grabbed him by the arm as he walked through the door.

"Where's the rest of the bridal party?" he asked in exasperation. "We're supposed to take pictures of each of you individually, then together, then the groomsmen together, then the bridesmaids together, then the siblings, then the bride and her father."

Jack blinked at the laundry list of photo shots.

The man yanked on his tie and frowned. "We only have thirty minutes or so before guests start arriving."

Jamie must have forgotten about pictures in her haste to put space between them. He told the photographer, "I'll find them."

Or her.

What a great excuse to go and hunt down Jamie.

He knocked on the door and waited a minute, listening to the string quartet warming up in the balcony above. Loud, chattering voices came through the door, and he suspected they hadn't heard his knock.

With a shrug, he opened the door and stepped inside.

His sister was standing there with their mom, looking absolutely stunning.

Forgetting Jamie momentarily, forgetting his mother's unhappiness with him, he went over to his sister and took her hand. Kissed her cheek. "Caro, you look beautiful."

She was cool and classy, his little sister, her straight blond hair pulled back off of her face. Her dress was long and narrow, and she carried a tiny bouquet of white flowers in her hand. Looking very bridal and serene, she made him proud.

The smile she gave him was warm and excited. "Thanks, Jonathon. How's everything going out there?"

"I came to get Jamie. The photographer wants pictures."

Jamie, who had been hiding in the corner, heard him and started toward the door, obviously planning on leaving without even looking at him.

Caroline called out, "Wait, Jamie, you don't have your necklace on."

Jamie's hand flew to her neck. "Oh! I forgot to put it on, it's in my purse. I need help with the clasp though."

His mother opened her mouth and held out her hand, but he was faster. "I'll help you."

Both his mother and sister were preoccupied with the back of Caroline's dress, which they kept touching and tugging, so neither noticed his near run across the room to reach Jamie.

Everything had become absolutely clear to him. He wanted this woman. As his. Wearing white herself.

Good God, he could actually envision that, and he was just going to explain—coax, seduce, threaten, beg—that to her until she agreed.

Jamie thought about just bolting out of the room, but decided that wasn't good form given the circumstances. She'd been raised better than that. She could practically feel her granny's hand slapping hers.

Instead of taking off, she pulled the sterling silver necklace that had been a bridal gift from Caroline out of her purse and tried to squeeze the clasp. If she got it open in the next two seconds, Jack's help wouldn't be needed.

No such luck.

He was behind her, taking the necklace, leaning over her, breathing into her hair.

"Let me help you," he whispered. "There are times I can help you, too, you know."

His arms came around her, resting the chain against her bare skin, as she fought the urge to lean back and close her eyes.

He was telling her something, only her brain wasn't functioning at full capacity. Jack was too close; she couldn't think with the warm aftershave smell of him clouding her nostrils.

Then he dropped the necklace.

And it slid down, down into the cavernous depths of her cleavage.

She was too stunned to move, and heat suffused her cheeks.

"Sorry," he murmured.

Then his hand came over her shoulder and started toward her chest as he said, "Don't worry, I'll get it."

Oh, God, help her.

If she screamed, Caroline and Mrs. Davidson were going to wonder if she had lost her mind. Or worse, see Jack's hand down her dress.

Right now they weren't looking at all.

But if she just stood here while he . . .

His fingers trailed along her breasts as he descended, and she bit her lip hard to prevent a groan from slipping out. His mouth was right next to her ear as he leaned over her shoulder to see where he was going.

To better torture her.

"I've almost got it," he whispered, fingers sliding up and down against her bare skin.

She sucked in her breath when without warning he dipped his tongue into her ear.

If Caroline turned now, there would be no explaining why half of her brother's arm was down Jamie's bodice and his tongue was cleaning out her inner ear.

But Caro didn't turn, and Jack went farther, until his hand was cupping her breast, squeezing it, and she felt the room tilt in ecstasy. Felt her body respond by hardening, tightening, moistening. Nails digging into her palms, she tried to stop the flood of yearning, the hitch of sexual desire.

It was possible that the entire top of the dress was about to drop off of her in the ultimate wardrobe malfunction, and she didn't care.

All she cared about was Jack, and the feel of his breathing over her hard and urgent, a definite erection pressing into her backside.

When he came up with the necklace, she was shaking and desperately disappointed.

And acutely aware that she was no match for Jack. She didn't have a prayer of resisting him.

She wanted Jack Davidson, and he knew it.

And he was going to torture her until she let him make delicious love to her.

How did she end up with these tragic problems?

When put that way, it sounded so damn silly.

As Jamie smiled and posed her way through approximately seventeen thousand photos, she wondered why she couldn't just have Jack.

Oh, she knew the reasons. They were as long as her arm, and they mattered, but it was so hard to resist Jack. So hard to say that they couldn't at least try.

She was an optimist by nature. She wanted to believe if she just loved Jack, it could work out. But the very part of her that wanted to fix the world at work had seen enough of reality to know that nothing was ever that simple.

And she was afraid. When she'd had the chance to talk to her father the week before, and he had chosen to bolt instead, she had been devastated. Now it occurred to her she was in fact her father's daughter. A coward. She was just as afraid to face an uncertain future as Jim Peters was.

"You with the red hair, move closer to your partner, please."

Jamie frowned at the photographer. She was not a redhead. She moved an eighth of an inch closer to Jack.

"Closer."

They were standing on steps on the side of the stone church, and she was already practically in Jack's arms.

Gritting her teeth, she moved again.

Jack's arm shot out, wrapped around her waist, then yanked her until she was snugly molded to him, her thigh resting against his hard leg.

"Good." The photographer clicked his camera.

Jack's hand had slid to her behind and he gave a little squeeze.

"Stop it," she whispered, her smile feeling more and

more forced. She suspected she looked like Jack Nicholson in *The Shining*.

She expected him to say something slick, or suggestive, or to simply ignore her and cop another feel.

Instead, he disarmed her by saying quietly, "I'll catch you if you fall. I haven't always shown them to you, but I do have good qualities, Jamie, and loyalty is one of them. I'd always be there for you."

"Jack . . ." She didn't know what to say. He had shown her good qualities, particularly when it came to Austin and Jack's grandfather.

She couldn't quite bring herself to look at him. He'd see her heart in her eyes, the longing she felt. Which wasn't good. Longing, that is. But come to think of it, nausea wasn't good either, and she was experiencing that in constant waves. And she was not pregnant, contrary to Caroline's off-the-wall concern.

Jamie was still standing next to Jack, speechless as the photographer clicked, clicked, aware that Jack was waiting for her response.

Fortunately, at that moment, Mrs. Davidson opened the church doors and said, "We're ready. Let's go inside, please, when you're done with that shot. All the guests have arrived."

The next few minutes were a scramble as they assembled at the back of the church as quietly as possible. She and Jack were walking down the aisle after Mandy and Steve, just like at rehearsal. Caroline had opted out of having a maid of honor, not willing to choose between the three of them, and not having a sister or a future sister-in-law to single out.

The church was air-conditioned, and the murmuring of the guests settled down into shuffling silence as the musicians began to play louder. Jamie fought the urge to grip her stomach and took deep breaths to steady herself.

She could do this.

The sea of faces, Brad waiting expectantly at the front of the church, all swam in front of her. Jack offered his arm with a sultry smile, and she took it.

He squeezed her hand and whispered to her, "You look fantastic, Jamie. But I bet you would look even better in white."

Whatever calm she had managed to achieve fled. Was he hinting about *marriage?*

She thought she might have a cow right on the spot.

Because of the insanity of the idea, and the presumptuousness, and the fact that they hadn't even managed a second date yet.

And for a much different reason.

Gazing down that aisle, poised next to Jack, she realized she wanted to believe Beckwith. She wanted Jack to be her forever.

Maybe from the minute she had laid eyes on him she had wanted him. Beckwith had said he would touch her soul, and Lord, she was feeling pretty touched already.

She gripped her bouquet of lilies like it was a winning lottery ticket she didn't want to drop.

"Thank you," she said, for lack of anything better. They certainly could not have a major discussion regarding their relationship right at this moment. But Lord, thanking the man for a compliment like that was downright lame. Next he'd propose, and she'd be giving him a thumbs-up.

Then Allison nudged her. "It's time to walk."

"Just like in practice," Jack whispered to her. "No sweat."

Did he actually remember the practice? She couldn't remember anything except the tidal wave of lust that had been crashing over her at Jack's touch.

But she had been walking since her first birthday, after all. She could handle this.

They walked up the aisle, her fingers lightly on his tuxedo sleeve, and Jack's presence next to her reassuring and masculine. She smiled like a beauty pageant contestant and

sank into her seat at the end of the aisle with significant relief.

Best of all, Jack was sitting across the aisle with the other
groomsmen, so she could actually relax and not have to
worry about his wandering hands.

Everyone stood and watched Caroline walk up the aisle
on the arm of her beaming father. She looked stunning, confident and poised, and Jamie felt tears pricking at her eyes.

It was a wonderful day for Caroline, and from the looks
of Brad, wide-eyed up front, he appreciated the woman he
was getting. Jamie was so happy for her friend, and equally
determined that Beckwith was wrong in Caroline's case. She
didn't look like a woman poised for tragedy, and Brad didn't
look like an uneasy groom.

Beckwith's prediction for her rose up into her mind again
and haunted her as the minister began to speak about the
responsibilities that accompany marriage. Beckwith had
said Jack was going to make her happy, and touch her soul.

Well, he had. For one night.

Beckwith had never said anything about forever or marriage.

So there.

Jack could find himself a nice little properties lawyer in a
red power suit, and they could settle down in TriBeCa during the busy work week and head out to the Hamptons on
the weekends.

That would leave her free to find a wonderful . . . someone. That she didn't want.

She wanted Jack.

How dumb was that?

Chapter 18

Jack stood in the corner, choking on a piece of bruschetta. He had been minding his own business, stalking the door, waiting for Jamie, when he had realized something.

He was going to have to give up all of his money if he wanted Jamie.

The thought had come to him out of nowhere that if he donated every last cent, she would see that he was sincere. That he wanted Jamie for the long haul—for forever. For a marriage that lasted until death did they part.

Pounding his chest with his fist, he dislodged the wayward appetizer and sucked in a startled breath. He must have thrown all common sense out the window to think that he and Jamie . . . that marriage to her . . . that she could . . .

That he could give away the financial rewards of ten years of hard work for something that wasn't a guarantee.

Jack took a huge swallow of wine, dribbling some on his chin.

He had only known Jamie for a couple of weeks. He couldn't possibly love her enough to give up all his worldly possessions and live like a monk. Well, like a monk without the celibacy vow. No, no, he could not even be considering this. Living in a tiny walk-up. Selling his car. Cooking at home and having to fly coach class. My God, he couldn't believe he'd do that for anyone.

Yet that sack of pudding in his chest said otherwise.

He'd do it. He'd shed all vestiges of his wealth for Jamie. He'd join a freaking commune if she wanted. Okay, so he wouldn't go that far. But he would definitely take the subway for her. And tell Meredith a big fat resounding no on the job offer.

Now so he could declare his intentions before he changed his mind and went to visit his mother's therapist, Jamie and the other bridesmaids had to actually show up. The rest of the guests and the bride and groom had been mingling for fifteen minutes now and nibbling food off the trays of tuxedoed waiters moving through the room silently.

The minute the limo had pulled up at the hotel and they had all entered the lobby, Mandy, Allison, and Jamie had disappeared. So Jack was staking out the door for when they walked in, which ought to be any minute now or they were going to risk being noticed as missing by his mother.

He wanted to be nowhere near her if and when that happened.

He hid behind a potted plant and tried to look nonchalant. By all accounts, he should be networking and shaking hands, not stalking the entry, but he was powerless to move away.

Female voices rose in excitement. Jamie. She was coming through the doorway.

"Oh, my God. Look at this place, y'all! It's like a garden tent inside right here in Manhattan." Jamie clapped her hand over her mouth as she came to a standstill in the doorway.

The heightened hitch of southern in her voice made Jack smile. She was so unbelievably sexy.

Her arm in the air was giving a mouth-watering rise to her chest, while her dress stayed in place where it was.

Which was way lower than her chest. The exposed creamy, curving flesh taunted him.

Jamie shook her head. "I sound like a total hick, don't I?" she said.

Allison nodded. "Yes, but that's okay. I'm feeling a little plebian right now, too. This is a cool hotel."

"Oh, please," Jamie replied. "You're from Connecticut, and Mandy's from a swanky British country estate. You may not be filthy rich, but at least y'all know which forks to use. I seriously don't have a clue."

Jack came around the corner, not willing to let her escape him again. "You start from the outside and work your way in. Don't worry. I've got your back, remember?"

Mandy said, "Excuse us," grabbed Allison by the arm and took off into the throng of wedding guests. He really liked that Mandy.

"I didn't know you were standing there," Jamie said, swallowing hard.

"I was." He closed the remaining two feet between them and set his plate down on an end table, feeling as though what he said to Jamie tonight might be some of the most important words he'd ever spoken. He needed to go easy, exercise caution. Not scare the crap out of her by attacking her the way he really wanted to.

"Would you like some wine?"

"Okay. Sure."

"You like red, don't you?"

She nodded, so he handed her his glass. "Here, take this."

Their fingers brushed, her mouth slid open in surprise. He watched her lips as she drank the wine, running her tongue across the bottom to catch the stray drops.

Her eyes darkened.

Desire shot through him.

All it took was a little tug, and they were together behind the potted plant. He obviously needed to work on that caution thing.

She shook her head. "No, Jack, no, not here."

"Where, then?" He nipped that bottom lip, tasting the sweetness of the wine, the warm scent that was uniquely hers.

That little hitch in her breath, the gasp escaping her, made Jack's control start to slip. He tightened his hold on her.

"Nowhere." But she didn't pull away, and she didn't say no to his tongue tracing down to her neck, worshipping that graceful arch.

"I miss you, Jamie. Whenever you're not with me, I miss you." He was aware that he was begging for trouble here. Begging probably being the key word. He felt capable of begging if she said no.

But she wasn't saying no and he had little ability to stop where Jamie was concerned. He groaned and forced himself to take a step back so he wouldn't yank the top of her dress down and sink his teeth into that luscious flesh.

"You miss the sex," she whispered.

"No." He pulled back. "Well, yes, I do." He smiled. "But that's not what I meant. I meant I miss you. Your smile. Your laugh. The sweet, sweet things you say. The conversations we have. I like you, Jamie, is that so wrong?"

She sighed. "No. I like you, too."

Then that was all he needed to know. That was enough for now.

"It's probably time for dinner," Jamie said.

"You're right." He smiled and set the empty wineglass down on the end table as they emerged from behind the plant. "Though I don't think what I want is on the menu."

That's what Jamie was talking about. How was she supposed to resist the man when he was being sweet, intense, tossing out sexual innuendos left and right?

It was bad enough she was seated next to him at the dinner table, but every time she glanced at him, he looked ready to devour her.

Or he came right out and said so.

When he wasn't throwing her off guard by asking her thoughtful and informed questions about her job or her childhood or whether she liked Thai food.

It was getting on her nerves.

Because she was unable to resist. She was talking with him, gushing really, if the truth be told, and enjoying every sappy second just like their night together.

"So what do you miss about Kentucky?" he asked her, his thigh brushing against hers under the table.

Wishing she were wearing a really thick dress, made out of say, upholstery, Jamie moved her leg to remove it from his reach.

Now she could think. Somewhat. "My mother, of course. Green space. Horses, like I told you before." She grinned at him. "And Derby pie."

"What's Derby pie?"

"Nothing but chocolate. Layers and layers of ooey gooey chocolate."

"What makes it Derby pie?" Jack cocked his head to the side, as if he were going to venture a guess, then thought better of it.

"My mom always said because it looks like the track the horses run on at Churchill Downs, but to me it looks more like the infield where we always sat on blankets when I was a kid. Muddy and gross."

He laughed. "Sounds like fun."

Jamie pushed her fork around her plate, aware that she had paid attention only to Jack for the entire meal. She was virtually ignoring Steve on her right, but she couldn't help herself. It was a sickness.

"It was. And in high school we used to go with our boyfriends."

Jack reached over and stabbed the last shrimp on her plate and ate it.

"Hey!"

He smiled again, that slow, crooked, sinful smile that made her feel like she was having a menopausal hot flash.

Then Jack moved so quickly she nearly fell backward out of her chair. He stood up and took her hand.

"Dance with me."

"There's no dance music yet. It's background music." She was forced to stand up as well since he was tugging her arm.

"Well, what are they waiting for? Everyone's done eating."

And as if the band had heard him, they began to announce the first dance, calling the wedding party up to open the floor.

Jamie noticed with mortification that neither Steve and Mandy, nor Finn and Allison, were holding hands the way she and Jack were.

And when they danced, neither of the other two couples was flush up against each other sharing oxygen.

"Back up a little," she said to him, trying to shrug away from him without getting off the music.

She didn't even want to consider the fact that three hundred people were watching them right now, including Caroline and Mrs. Davidson, who would have to be blind and stupid not to notice the sex vibes radiating off of her and Jack.

Unfortunately, Caro and her mother were neither.

In fact, Jamie peered around Jack and saw Caroline's mother, *his* mother, studying them with eyes narrowed. Jamie broke out into a sweat and pictured all of her makeup sliding off of her face and onto her chest.

"Jack, your mother is watching us." Jack was already on the outs with his mother, and Jamie didn't want to further contribute to that antagonism.

"So?" His thumb traced circles on her back with his hand.

What did he mean, so? It was obvious. "We don't want her to think there's anything going on between us."

"Why not? There is something going on between us."

He was not being reasonable about this at all. Jamie felt a little desperate, especially since his thigh was rocking into her, raising her temperature yet another five degrees. "No, there's not."

"Yes, there is." He bent over her, holding her snug against him, his mouth hovering inches above hers.

Lord, he was going to kiss her right on the dance floor, like a groping teenager at a nightclub, while everyone else danced elegantly to this classical kind of music that she couldn't identify. She closed her eyes briefly in anticipation, or mortification, she wasn't sure which.

But he didn't kiss her.

Instead he said hoarsely, "I want you, Jamie. I need you."

Yikes.

But she could have stayed strong. She could have resisted that raw heat in his voice, until he spoke again.

"All I want is a kiss. Just one, please. And a date. Promise me we can try that, see what happens. That's all I'm asking. For now."

It was that erotic pleading that undid her. It left her limp against him, eyes still half closed as she confessed, "My head says this is a mistake. That there are too many negative variables making anything between us a poor risk. But my emotions are disagreeing."

"Listen to your emotions and tell your head to go kiss off," he said coaxingly. "I can't wait another minute. I've been wanting you since I woke up and found you gone."

The evidence was pressing against her. As was the knowledge that she, too, had spent two weeks suffering from Jack withdrawal. Right at the moment she felt like someone had

been setting off pyrotechnics in her pricey bridesmaid's
dress.

So despite the feeling that she had lost all common sense
and decency, she heard herself saying, "There's a room in
the hall, called the retiring room or something like that your
mom said. It's meant for the bride and bridesmaids to use
for their stuff—purses and for make-up checks and everything."

She took a deep breath and studied the tie on his tux.
"Maybe we should go talk, get away from everyone." Have
hot sex.

God, had she really just suggested they head somewhere
private? That had a couch? What the hell was she thinking?

Jack's fingers tightened on her back, and he nodded once,
as if he didn't trust himself to speak.

When the dance ended, he led her off the floor, dodging
his mother, who looked ready to stop them, her mouth open
to say something.

"Jamie's not feeling good, Mom, the room's too hot. I'm
taking her outside for some fresh air."

All Jamie had time to hear was, "Oh, dear," from Mrs.
Davidson before Jack whisked her away.

She was sure even the roots of her hair were blushing. "I
can't believe you lied to your mother!"

But Jack only shrugged, clearly unrepentant. "What am I
supposed to say? That I'm taking Jamie out into the hall to
have hot sex with her?"

Now everything on her body was blushing, with the
focus on parts south. "I said we could go talk! You said all
you wanted was a kiss."

"You cannot convince me you suggested a retiring room
so we could talk about pie and past love affairs."

"Well . . ." She hadn't thought she was suggesting anything more, but it did seem pretty lame now.

"So where's the room?" He stopped in the hall and
looked right and left.

"First door on the right." She let him half drag, half carry her down to the little lounge.

She dug her heels into the carpet, plagued with second thoughts. This was tacky. They could get caught. She wasn't the kind of woman who did things like this, and she wouldn't embarrass Caro for the world.

"I'm not having sex with you in this room."

Jack turned back and stared at her. "Okay. You can have sex with me in my apartment after the reception. Right now I'm just going to take a little taste, that's all."

Well, if he insisted.

Then he pulled her into the room, the door swung shut, and all hope of walking away disappeared.

His mouth was on hers before she could catch a breath, let alone object again. In fact, she was just as aggressive as he was. They were both tasting and teasing and tugging, her arms in the back of his hair ransacking it.

He was right. She had been waiting two weeks for this. For the pleasure of being with Jack again.

For that perfect sense that they were right for each other. They belonged in each other's arms.

Their kisses deepened, wet and anxious, and their bodies crushed against each other, seeking, needing.

Little taste. That's all.

Then they'd stop.

Jamie slid her tongue over his, the red wine they'd both drunk mixing between them, swarming her senses.

His hands gripped her head. Despite the majority of her rational brain cells going to sleep, Jamie was still cognizant enough to pull back and stop Jack from shoving his hands into her hair. "No! I'll never be able to fix it like the hairstylist did."

He dropped his hands to her shoulders and pulled her against him, hard. "Feel what you do to me."

Everything about Jack was hard. And she wanted him. "I feel it. I want you inside me."

Gad, had she just said that out loud?

The groan from him seemed to indicate she had.

His hands were moving around her back, rushing up and down. "How do I get this dress off?"

Aware that they were only two feet in front of the door to the hallway, Jamie said, "No, you can't take it off." Her sense of adventure didn't extend to getting caught naked by some wayward guest.

Besides, tossing satin into a heap on the floor probably wasn't the best idea. "It will wrinkle, and I'll never be able to get it back on right." Wait a minute. She wasn't going to take the dress off anyway, because they were Not Going To Have Sex.

"We're not having sex here."

"I never said we were." He held up his hands, a mock look of innocence playing across his face.

Then he reached out and popped her breasts right out of her bodice with one little flip of his wrists.

"Doesn't mean I can't make you come."

Allison watched Jonathon rush Jamie off the dance floor as if someone had yelled fire, and felt something akin to jealousy. Not over Jonathon. She had been serious when she'd said he wasn't her type. Too restless, too intense.

There couldn't be two divas in a relationship, and she had diva down pat.

But a little sex before she died would be welcome.

"It might be quicker if he just threw her over his shoulder," Finn commented.

"Hmmm?"

"Your friend and Caroline's brother. With him dragging and her digging in her heels, I'm just suggesting it might be easier if he picked her up."

Allison studied Finn. She wasn't sure what Caroline found so objectionable about him. Besides the scraggly hair and the five-o'clock shadow that never seemed to disappear, he was attractive and filled his tux well. He hadn't burped or told any off-color jokes, and Allison hadn't caught him smoking a joint in the coat closet.

Yet. "Is that what you would do? Go all caveman on a woman?" Personally, Allison thought she'd shove a stiletto up the ass of any man who tried to haul her anywhere. But that was just her.

"Nah. I'm the moody, artistic type. I'm more likely to forget we even have a date in the first place. I get absorbed in what I'm painting and forget the real world exists."

Maybe that was what Caroline objected to. She revered punctuality and thought Thou Shalt Not Daydream should be a late addition to the ten commandments.

"Do you sleep with your models?" Allison asked as they glided around to the longest piece of music ever composed. God, she hated dancing. But at least Finn wasn't staring at her chin, the way it usually played out at weddings. She was convinced every man over five-foot-ten was married.

There had to be statistics on it, with the proportion of men married decreasing with every inch under six foot. No woman wanted to look like an Amazon next to her man, and Allison thought it was damn rude that short women ran around snagging men ten inches taller than them, when in all fairness, those guys should have been left alone for the tall girls to pick over.

Finn laughed. "Well, I don't sleep with the men I paint. But of course I sleep with all the women. Wouldn't you?" He winked at her.

Okay, so it had been a stupid question. But she was kind of curious. The idea of having male models strip at her direction had a certain appeal. "Not the women. But the men, sure I would. At least that way you get to check out the goods first."

"You're a mercenary little thing, aren't you?" The corner of his mouth lifted.

Allison didn't like his tone. "So is your cousin, Brad. He worships at the altar of accumulate."

At times, Allison wasn't completely convinced that wasn't why Brad had married Caroline. To gather the prettiest, proper society wife, who would balance a career and a family and leave him free to do whatever he felt like.

"If you have the money, why not?"

But he didn't look like he meant it.

And Allison decided this guy was probably a better match for Jamie than Jonathon. Not that Jonathon looked like he'd be willing to give Jamie up anytime soon.

"So you think Caroline and Brad will live happily ever after in banker's bliss?"

He flicked his hair out of his eyes and gave her a wild spin that was dangerous in a strapless dress. "What do I know? I'm just the artist cousin with his head in the clouds."

"Whatever, brush boy."

Chapter 19

Jack wasn't going to have sex with Jamie in the retiring room. He really meant that.

But he couldn't stop himself from giving her pleasure, a little taste of what he could give her later, if she came home with him.

Her breasts had burst eagerly out of the dress with barely any effort from him, and he was staring at her bare chest, creamy flesh, and dusky apricot nipples.

"Jack!" she said in shock. "You can't do that. We'll never get them back in."

He grabbed her hands before she could stuff her breasts back into her dress. "Maybe they want a little fresh air."

She laughed. "They don't have a brain, they can't think for themselves."

"I don't know. They seem to have a mind of their own . . . you're telling me to stop and they're looking pretty ready to go." Jack plucked at one very tight nipple, his mouth going dry.

Jamie sighed. "Betrayed by my breasts. What can I say? But the breasts don't always know best."

"In this case, I think they're smarter than their owner. They know sometimes you just have to feel." Like he was. He wasn't thinking, he was just feeling. Going with gut instinct. Jack ran his lips over her nipple, the taut pebble gliding over his flesh.

"Their owner?" Jamie said, a hitch in her voice. "That sounds completely bizarre. Like they're pets. Like I could take them for a walk, feed them, play fetch. Though I have to say I've always kind of thought of them as beasts. Big monsters that shouldn't really be there."

"Not a healthy view to take of your own body. You need to make peace with your breasts, embrace them. Learn to love them the way I do. See, wouldn't I make a good social worker?" Jack took her hand and placed it over her bare flesh. "Just feel it. Isn't it just the most sexy thing you've ever touched?" He put his hand over hers, pushed them both forward a little, squeezing and cupping her with both their fingers.

"Touching you is sexier," she said, and her free hand slid across the front of his tux pants.

Holy crap, he hadn't been expecting her to do that. Jack gave a little groan.

"But now we need to get back to the reception before your mother comes looking for us."

Now, there was a scary thought. "Okay, okay, we'll go back. But promise me you'll spend the night with me."

Her eyes were glassy with desire, darkened with something else, an emotion Jack couldn't quite pinpoint. "I'll spend the night with you."

"Thank you." He kissed her softly. Then deeper. Then harder.

Every little taste made him want more. Jack trailed his lips over her warm flesh, down to her breasts, wanting just one last lick to tide him over until they could decently ditch out of the reception and head home.

Only she moaned. Which spurred his own desire. Which led him to give another lick. Then a suck. Which escalated into tugging and nipping and groping.

And somehow his hand found its way up her skirt, where

she was wearing a scrap of nothing for panties. "Oh, Jamie, damn, what kind of panties are these?" He tugged at the spandex material and cupped her.

"Seamless panties. So you can't see lines on my butt." Then she gave a startled yelp as he sank inside her with his thumb.

She groaned, she shuddered, as he started to move in her. Jack held her waist, his mouth still on her breasts, and moved his finger with a desperate sort of urgency. The words weren't there yet, weren't making sense, but he had to show Jamie, had to reach in and grab her and not let go.

Needed her with him.

Nails clawed at him as she squirmed, rocking herself onto his finger in total abandon. There was a long pause, where Jamie went completely still, and her wide eyes locked with his. Then she came, shattering over him with soft desperate pants that were the most beautiful sound Jack had ever heard.

"That's amazing, Jamie. Beautiful." He kissed the side of her neck, her chin, the corner of her mouth, overwhelmed with what he was feeling.

And suddenly the words were there, gushing out of him like an unlocked fire hydrant.

"Jamie, I love you. I want to marry you."

Jamie's mouth fell open. Her jaw moved. But nothing came out.

Jack pulled his hand out from between her thighs. Let her skirt drop. Watched Jamie, this woman who had brought contentment to his life, which had been feeling aimless and dissatisfying.

"I'll give it all up, Jamie, all the money. Donate it wherever you want me to, if it's going to come between us. Just tell me who to give it to, and it's done."

"You really mean that, don't you?" she asked, her voice quiet, awed.

"I do." And it didn't even hurt to say that. He meant it.

He took a small step back, amused at her reaction. He'd never seen Jamie at a total loss for words before, but she was staring at him, mouth so wide he could drive his Beemer on in. "Now let's get you decent and rejoin the party."

"Decent? Oh, God, I must look awful!" Her hand went to her head, patted her hair. She fussed with her skirt, until every inch from the waist down was covered and she looked like a respectable bridesmaid once more.

Except for the high color on her face, and the shine in her eyes. The rumpled state of her skirt, and the swollen bottom lip. The disheveled hair and the crushed top of her dress. Her still very much bare breasts, which didn't seem to want to go back where they had come from, no matter how much she tugged and pushed.

Respectable? Hell, she looked like she had just been thoroughly loved. Which she had. By him.

Jack couldn't help but grin. "Here, let me help you." He palmed her left breast with one hand and tried to lift the dress with the other, and stuff everything back where it was supposed to be.

The door flew open, and a voice called out, "Jamie? Are you in here?"

His sister's voice.

The bride.

Oh, damn.

Jamie tried to step back, but his hand was still in her dress, so he went with her. Jamie let out a whimper.

"My mom said you weren't feeling well, so I wanted to make sure you're okay—" Caroline's words were cut off by her gasp. "Jamie? Jonathon? What are you *doing?*"

The obvious answer would be that he was feeling her up, which was wrong, since he was trying to help her back into the dress. Yet it wasn't entirely a falsehood either, since he had been touching her breasts sexually just a minute ago. But that seemed kind of complicated to explain. There had to be an easier answer.

Jamie wasn't going to answer at all. She was motionless and facing him. Her cheeks were stained red, and her green eyes were huge.

It was up to him to smooth this one over. He said with a shrug, "Jamie's having some problems with her dress. She keeps, uh, falling out."

He dropped his hand, which left the blue fabric askew, only covering half her breasts. It had her looking like Pam Anderson trying to wear a tissue as a blouse. "I was just trying to help," he added lamely.

His sister's face contorted into incredulous disbelief. It wasn't a good look with the veil and the dress. Then she started toward them, shaking her head. "Keep your hands off my bridesmaid, Jonathon. Jamie, didn't you use double-sided tape?"

"No."

For which Jack was very grateful. He'd have never gotten the dress off her if it had been taped to her skin. "That sounds medieval, Caroline."

"It's the best way to keep a strapless dress up." She jerked her thumb toward the door. "Move along, show's over. We're going to have to take Jamie's dress completely off to do this."

"That doesn't bother me," he said, most sincerely. "I can be an extra pair of hands in case they're needed."

Besides, he had just told Jamie he'd toss over ten plus million dollars for her. Big moment, major declaration, all of that. He'd kind of like to stick around and see if she had any other response to that besides open-mouthed shock.

Caroline laughed. "Get out."

"Shouldn't you be out there throwing your bouquet? I can handle this, honestly. You know I've always been a problem solver." But he was already heading for the door, knowing Caroline wouldn't trust either him or Jamie not to make a mess of it.

If there was a job to be done, Caro liked to do it. Besides,

Jamie didn't look as if she'd be speaking anytime soon. Maybe a few minutes with Caroline would unlock her lips.

"Go dance with Brad's mother. I don't want her to feel neglected by our family." Caroline was digging in a travel tote and emerged with a roll of tape and scissors.

Yikes. Jack didn't want to see whatever she was going to do with those. "Alright, I can see you have this under control. I'll go play charming host at your bidding, Caroline Davidson-Black."

Caro stopped and smiled at him. "That sounds so awesome. I'm actually Brad's wife."

"Yeah." Jack felt emotion reach up, choke him. Close off his throat, and prick his eyes. "Times are a changin', aren't they?"

"Only in good ways." Caroline patted his cheek with her smooth, cool hand and smiled. "Now leave us women to the mysteries of double-sided tape."

"Okay. See you in a few." He paused at the door. "Jamie, remember your promise."

She was spending the night with him, one way or the other.

He'd need the comfort after dancing with his sister's mother-in-law.

Jamie clutched the front of her dress and tried to function. But her head was like a hunk of Swiss cheese. There were too many holes in her thoughts for any of them to make sense.

"Sorry, Caroline. I've been having trouble with the dress and it never occurred to me to get tape."

"Turn around." Caroline spun her and unzipped. "So how long have you been sleeping with my brother?"

Just when she thought she couldn't get any more embarrassed. "Um . . . what makes you think we are?"

There was a loud ripping sound as Caroline pulled off a length of tape. Jamie glanced back over her shoulder. At least Caro was smiling. "Jams, he had his hand on your breast. I know you. You are not casual about your breasts. Any man touching them has been granted the key to the kingdom, so to speak."

"Oh." Good to know her friends understood her. She turned back around. "Well, actually it only happened once, a couple of weeks ago. I wanted to tell you, but wasn't sure how you'd feel about it, and with the wedding and all, I didn't want to stress you out."

The dress was pooled around her waist, and she was feeling a bit ridiculous as Caroline held up the tape against her breast, measuring for width.

"You're always so busy worrying about everyone else, sometimes I wish you'd worry about yourself." Caroline tore the backing off the tape.

Jamie winced. "There's nothing to worry about. I'm fine."

"So why only once?" With the precision of a surgeon she cut the tape and stuck it to Jamie's breast.

"Why what?" Jamie tried not to squirm. She knew why it hadn't occurred to her to put tape on her chest. It was really uncomfortable and weird.

"Why did you only have sex with Jonathon once?" Caroline slapped the other piece on the left breast and grabbed the dress.

As Caroline tugged and adjusted and pressed so the tape would stick, Jamie tried to come up with a coherent response. "Because I'm not his type."

That sounded ridiculous, even to her.

"Jamie, that's ridiculous. If you're not interested, that's one thing. But if you are, you should go for it. Jonathon is clearly head over heels for you."

"He said he's in love with me," Jamie whispered as she was spun around again for a rezip. She wanted so desperately to believe that, but it seemed too unbelievable, too fragile, too circumstantial. "That he'd get rid of his money for me."

Caroline paused. "Really? He doesn't throw words around

lightly, you know. Jonathon worked his ass off for years to earn what he has. But if he said it, he means it."

"What if it's an impulse?" And why was she even protesting? She already knew what she was going to do.

"What if it's really love?" Caroline asked, patting her shoulders and turning her back face forward. "You once told me your aunt didn't close the door of her double-wide trailer on love. Maybe you shouldn't either."

It was easy to believe with Caroline standing there in her wedding gown, looking serene and beautiful. "Oh, Caro." Tears rose in her eyes like the sap that she was. "You don't mind that I'm involved with your brother? I wouldn't hurt you for the world."

Caroline wiped the tear that had slipped down her cheek. "Of course you wouldn't, silly. And why would I mind two of my favorite people hooking up? I love both of you and I know you won't hurt him, Jamie." She squeezed her hands. "You wouldn't hurt a fly. You'd let it swim in your soup if you thought it was happy there."

Jamie gave a watery laugh. "Is he a privileged uptown fly or trapped in a cycle of poverty in the ghetto?" She reached out and gave Caroline a hug, watching both their heads so there wasn't a hair entanglement. "Beckwith told me Jack is the one in my fortune, that he's my destiny. I really, really want to believe him."

It made her chest feel tight just thinking about it.

"This has nothing to do with Beckwith and his farfetched predictions. Just do what makes sense to you. Jonathon is a wonderful, intelligent man. You're a smart, thoughtful woman. Why shouldn't it work out?" She hooked her arm in Jamie's and headed for the door. "Now let's get back to the reception before my mother sends a SWAT team after me."

"She would, wouldn't she?"

"In a heartbeat."

Jamie figured like mother, like daughter. Caroline had

just managed to convince her that it was completely in Jamie's best interest to have a relationship with Jack.

Jamie felt taken down by logic.

So she might as well enjoy it.

Except when Caroline stepped back into the hall, Jamie happened to glance left and nearly fainted. Beckwith was strolling down the hall in a hot-pink taffeta bridesmaid's dress, floral bouquet and all.

Oh, good Lord. Jamie followed Caroline in half a step, then exclaimed, "Oh, shoot, I think my bracelet fell off. I'll be right there, Caro."

Then she ran as fast as she could in Beckwith's direction, grabbing his hairy wrist and dragging him into the coat-room alcove. "What are you doing? You have got to leave!"

The last person in the world who would appreciate the presence of a cross-dresser was Mrs. Davidson.

"I'm wedding crashing because I had to talk to you. And I thought if I wore this I might blend in."

Jamie thought maybe that would have been better accomplished by wearing a man's suit, but clearly that hadn't occurred to Beckwith.

"I don't think it's going to work. The bridesmaids are all wearing ice blue."

"Well, poo-poo." He pouted as he sniffed the bouquet of teacup roses.

"Did you need something, sweetie?" Because if he didn't, he needed to get the hell out.

"I can't take it, sugar. I'm just plagued with worry for your friend. Are you sure you can't convince Caroline to throw over her husband?"

"Positive."

"And you're sure you can't work things out with Mr. Tall, Dark, and Touch My Soul?"

Jamie bit her lip. "Well, maybe I can. I want to try. But dang, I'm scared."

"Well, I don't give a shit!" Beckwith vowed, flinging his

arms and bouquet around. "I can't live my own life because I'm so bombarded by images of you screwing up your fate. You have got to trust this guy, for my sake, Jams."

Well, gee, if it was all about him.

She couldn't stop herself from rolling her eyes even as she reached out and squeezed his arm. "I'm trying. I'm seeing Jack tonight, after the wedding."

"His name is Jack?" Beckwith narrowed his eyes.

"Yes." And she was in love with him.

"Jamie."

She about jumped out of her bridesmaid's dress and probably would have if it wasn't for the double-sided tape. Damn, that was Jack's voice, and it was coming from no more than two feet behind her.

"Oh, hi," she said as she turned and offered a weak smile.

"Do you know this . . . person? Everything okay?"

"Uh-huh." She nodded rapidly. "I'll be back in a second; we're just finishing up here."

"I'll wait for you outside the door." Jack pointed ten feet down the hallway. "Right there."

He obviously wasn't going to go back into the reception without her, so Jamie was going to have to work hard to get rid of Beckwith. As Jack started down the hall, she opened her mouth to encourage Beckwith to leave, when she noticed him frowning.

"Who was that?" he asked, leaning around her to watch Jack's retreat.

She raised her eyebrows. Who was the psychic here? "That was Jack. Tall, Dark, and Touch My Soul."

"No, it's not."

"Yes, it is." Was he kidding? Jamie stared at him. "The one you saw in the cards. I met him on the subway when I slammed his spaghetti into him."

Beckwith pulled his lip back. "That is not the man I saw in the cards. This one's sexy and all, but he's not the guy I saw. Your soul mate looked more like Tyler Bond from the rock group The Gris Gris. You know, with the tattoos? Sings that song about not being able to satisfy lust. Anyhoo, that's what your man looks like. I've never seen that guy"— he pointed down the hall at Jack—"in my life."

"Are you serious?" Jamie felt the blood drain from her face.

"Totally." Beckwith twisted the back of his platinum hoop earring.

"But that's the guy I slept with." She stuck her thumb out and jerked it in Jack's direction. And that was the guy she'd fallen in love with.

"Well, why in the name of Liberace would you do that?" he asked, astonished. "Clearly you are not ready for love if you meet the man of your dreams, then sleep around on him."

Jamie laughed so loud she actually produced a snort.

Chapter 20

Jack kissed his sister good-bye. Saw Pops into Steve's SUV. Grabbed an uncorked bottle of champagne from a passing waiter.

Then went in search of Jamie.

Once he found her, he was going to rip that bridesmaid's dress off and crumple the hell out of it when it dropped on the floor and he stepped on it. He was going to tear into Jamie's hair and let all those straining curls loose. He was going to put his lips on every sweet, soft spot on her body.

But first he had to find her.

"You seen Jamie?" he asked Allison, who was lined up at the bar doing shots with Finn.

"She's talking to your mom over by the door."

Oh, great. He was tempted to ask Allison to go get her for him, but then he squared his shoulders and thought the hell with it. He was thirty years old, and his mother was already acting like a child. He shouldn't do the same.

"Thanks." He started to walk away, but Allison grabbed his sleeve.

She looked up at him with dark—heading toward drunk—eyes. Allison always looked as if she could be strutting down the catwalk, exotic and confident. Jack was comfortable with her, because they both mutually understood they liked each other as people, but weren't in any way attracted to each other.

"Jonathon . . . be careful with her. Jamie's always taking care of everyone else, but sometimes she needs someone to take care of her, too, you know what I mean?" Allison jerked on his sleeve so his wrist swung back and forth. "Jamie's, like, gold and the rest of us are copper." As Jack blinked, she started laughing. "God, that was a really sucky metaphor. I'm drunk, aren't I?"

"I think so, darling," Finn said cheerfully, and tossed back another shot.

"Well, don't think you're going to be able to take advantage of that."

"I'd never dream of it."

Jack disengaged his sleeve from Allison's damp grip. "Why don't you head home, Allison, and call it a night? And I know what Jamie's worth. I really do."

She was a grade A bond. A hot commodity. A blue chip company. The real deal.

"Oh, that's so sweet. Look at his face, Finn. You really like her, don't you?" Allison patted his cheeks. "You should tell her how you feel."

"I'm trying to, but you won't let me go."

She let out a laugh. "Good point, lover boy. Fine, go, leave us."

So he did. With a wave and a deep breath when he saw Jamie was still chatting with his mother. But he put on a smile and went up to them. "Sorry to interrupt, but I'd like to offer Jamie a ride home."

Jamie bit her lip. "Well, uh, that's very considerate of you, Jack—"

His mother interrupted. "I thought you were taking your grandfather back to the nursing home."

"Steve did." Took Pops back to Jack's place, that is. But now wasn't the time to confess he'd moved Pops out of the nursing home, or go into detail describing how Pops was still getting his daily physical and occupational therapy, that the apartment was handicap accessible for the wheelchair, and that he had a call button if he needed emergency assistance at any time when his nurse wasn't doing her daily check-in.

No, he wasn't about to get into that, not with Jamie standing there and Caroline and Brad still in the room. And he also didn't want to mention that he had made arrangements with Steve for him to spend the night at Jack's apartment with Austin and Pops. Or tell Jamie that he had booked a hotel room five minutes after she had agreed to spend the night with him, since he'd thought having a wild love fest with an old man and a teenager in the next room might be a little tacky.

"Oh, wonderful. It will be a miracle if they arrive at the nursing home alive. Steve thinks the speed limit is just a suggestion. He offered us a ride back home tonight and of course I refused."

"You're spending the night in the hotel?" Jack asked, horrified. That was something of a mood killer to know his mother was staying in the same building.

"Of course. I can't even imagine driving back to Darien tonight. It always feels like I'm riding on I-95 for hours even though it's only thirty miles, and I'm too exhausted tonight. I wish your sister would have gotten married at the club at home, but no, she had to have a Saturday wedding in Manhattan." His mother laughed. "Our portfolio will never recover."

Ha ha. Jack felt like grimacing. He was suddenly so tired of it all. The money, the games, the ever present push and shove of grasping people onto this financial ladder, that social stool. *Don't ever turn your back, Jack-o.*

He just wanted to rest.

So he gave her a kiss on the cheek. "It was a wonderful wedding, Mom."

"It did turn out, didn't it?" His mother sighed, a tired,

satisfied smile on her face. "Now where are you going with that champagne? Are you into drinking alone these days?"

Jack didn't dare say a word. He just waited. It didn't take her long. His mother looked at him. At Jamie, who was studying the floor.

"Oooohhhh, well, I see. Sorry, it's been a long day. I'm not usually so slow." His mother shook her head, her short hair immovable. "Have a good night, Jamie."

"Good night, Mrs. Davidson." Jamie managed to lift her head long enough to give a shaky smile.

But his mother was already gone.

"I'm so embarrassed." Jamie covered her face. "Your mother thinks I'm a hussy."

"No one thinks you're a hussy, Jamie Lynn." He was tired, and he was aching, and he wanted nothing more in the world than to just lie down next to her. "But I'll drive you home if that's what you want."

Her hands fell away. "What's the matter, Jack?"

"Nothing. Nothing." He brushed her cheek with a fingertip. "I'm just worn out."

It was an out, if she wanted to take it. She could show concern for him, suggest they spend the night together another time. As much as he wanted her, he didn't want to coax or suggest or seduce tonight after all.

He'd offered her his entire fortune, and she hadn't said one word about it.

But she said, "I don't want you to take me to my place. I want to go home with you. I want you to tear this dumb dress off me."

Now that perked him right up. In more ways than one.

"Then let's go upstairs."

"Upstairs?"

"I got us a room about an hour ago."

Her head tilted. "Confident, weren't you?"

"Just hopeful."

*   *   *

Jamie was hopeful, too, as she followed Jack into his hotel room. Something about hearing Beckwith say Jack wasn't in the cards for her had shifted a huge burden off her shoulders.

Destiny was for her to determine.

She couldn't live in fear of a man leaving her, like her father had. She couldn't live anticipating that her future was there for her, set out on an unalterable course.

The future was whatever she wanted it to be.

Jack took off his tux jacket, tossed it on the back of a chair, and turned to her. "Do you think you could ever love me, Jamie? Even . . . just a little bit?"

Oh, there was an understatement.

His shirt was stark white against the dark paneling of the wall behind him, and in his fears, in his love for her, he was vulnerable, this strong, intelligent man with a smart mouth and a smarter mind.

"Oh, yes, I could." Already did. "That's why I told you I couldn't see you anymore. I knew I would fall in love with you. Knew that I could the very first night I met you."

She didn't need Beckwith's predictions to tell her what now seemed so obvious. She and Jack. It was meant to happen, just like this.

"Then when I saw what you did for your grandfather and for Austin . . . yes, I knew I could love you."

"Will you? Love me?" Jack undid the buttons on his shirt, one at a time, eyes locked with hers in the dark room.

It came to her that this was one of the most momentous moments of her life. Jack was The One. And she was about to tell him.

Everything was sharp and hot, frozen yet hurtling forward, and her heart galloped wildly.

"Once I love someone, I can't stop. It sticks." He had to see that if she let it go, let it out of its confinement, it could never be stuffed back in.

Jack yanked off his shirt. "I don't deserve you. But I want

you. I'm burning with love for you, Jamie, and I want some back."

Hovering in front of the closet, she felt moisture in her eyes and blinked hard. Throwing her clutch in the direction of the chair, she moistened her lips.

"You have it. I love you."

Ho, boy, no turning back now.

He grinned. "What's that? I'm not sure I heard you."

"I love you, Jack."

"I really like the sound of that." He tossed his shirt toward the chair. "Would it embarrass you if I made like Tom Cruise and bounced on a chair and pumped my fists? Because I'm really tempted."

That made her laugh. "I have a better idea." Reaching behind her, Jamie unzipped the top of her dress. Pulled the pins out of her hair and shook it loose, massaging her sore scalp.

"I'm all . . . ears." Jack unhooked his belt.

Jamie walked seductively—well, her attempt anyway—and sashayed right past Jack, dodging his reach. She darted into the bathroom with a giggle, hoping to solve her problem quickly so they could explore her idea.

"Where are you going, you cruel, cruel woman?" He followed her, crowding into the tiny bathroom right behind her.

Jamie flipped on the light and stared at her reflection in the mirror. The dress was definitely covering her chest adequately. The tape had done its job. Which was a problem. "I can't get this dress off—the tape is stuck to my skin. I need the light to see how to torture myself." She gave a few preliminary tugs and found it stuck tight. This was going to hurt.

"I'll help."

"No!" Jamie peeled the top half inch back and took a gander down her dress. Her skin was beet red at the edges of the tape. "I have very sensitive skin, and I'm probably going to look really weird and whimper when I pull it off."

"Come on, I'll hold your hand. Or better yet, you close your eyes and I'll get it off."

Jamie gave another tentative pull. Oww. Lily white, paper-thin skin did not appreciate double-sided tape on it. Not to mention that her nipples had never suffered such abuse. Gritting her teeth, she tried again and only succeeded in bouncing up and down on the balls of her feet. "Ow, ow, ow, dang it. I'm trapped in this dress."

"You could get in the shower. The water will loosen it up." Jack put his hands on her waist and looked over her shoulder and on down her bodice.

"That would ruin the dress."

"Are you ever going to wear this dress again?" he asked doubtfully.

"Maybe." Probably not. But it seemed so wasteful to just willfully sacrifice it.

"Then close your eyes. I'll pull it off. Like a Band–Aid. Just one quick jerk."

That sounded about as fun as Chinese water torture. But she didn't have a whole lot of options. She couldn't go to work on Monday wearing a bridesmaid's dress. She'd look like she was making a push for a prison prom.

"Okay, go for it." She screwed her eyes shut, spots dancing behind her eyelids.

She felt Jack peel the back of her dress down and stretch it forward a little to give him more room. Then his one hand held her skin, the other her dress, and he yanked.

"Yowww, holy crap!" she screamed as searing, burning pain ripped through her. Before she could even recover, the pain was doubled when he moved to the other breast and repeated the process.

"Sorry, sorry, sorry," he said, blowing on her stinging skin.

Jamie forced her watering eyes open and sucked in a huge breath. "Oh, my, the room is spinning. Do I have any skin left? Are my nipples gone?"

Because she certainly couldn't feel them.

"Let me check." Jack's mouth closed over her, flicking his tongue across her stinging flesh, cooling it.

He gently kissed her nipple and her eyes rolled back in her head—and not from pain this time.

Yep. Still there.

And doing a cheer.

Jack felt such profound sympathy for the pain Jamie and her breasts were in that he decided to give her an orgasm to distract her. Free of charge.

God, she loved him. It was an amazing sensation of wonder and excitement that was zinging through him, filling him with restless energy and overwhelming pleasure. It was unbelievable how whole that made him feel, how strong, how generous.

He wanted to give her the world. But he'd start with an orgasm.

The way Jamie responded so quickly to him just from a flick of his tongue made him hard. He liked that she didn't have that preoccupation with pacing and appearances and neatness that some women did. Jamie didn't look in the mirror to see if her body was displayed in the most flattering way, and she didn't temper the sound of her moans.

So when he sucked her nipple, Jamie didn't give him one of those lazy, you might be on the right track if you work really hard, kinds of sighs, but a nice, drawn-out, guttural groan.

Her body had tightened against his, tensed.

"Feel better?"

"Much better." She gripped his shoulders and shook her hair back off her face. "I'd be even better if you took my dress *all* the way off."

He could do that. "Good idea."

It was pooled around her waist, and it was easy enough to shove and tug until it went past her hips and dropped to the floor. She stepped out of it, and Jack kicked it into the shower.

"Jack! That's an expensive dress."

"There's no room in here. This bathroom is the size of a mailbox. I need space." He had meant to get on his knees and go down on her, but Jamie seemed to interpret it as claustrophobia.

Her face softened with compassion. "Oh, sweetie, are you claustrophobic? Let's go in the other room. It's too stuffy in here."

It wasn't bothering him at all, and he wasn't some wimp who couldn't handle a hotel bathroom. On the other hand, there was something to be said for having such a compassionate woman as his lover. And he hadn't been called sweetie since he was four. He kind of liked it.

"No, we're fine here. I'll be okay if I just kneel down." Jack held on to Jamie's waist and dropped down.

"Are you sure? It will just take two seconds to move to the bedroom . . . you don't have to be brave for me—oh, my!"

Jack rolled down her panties and kissed her. A nice, long French kiss. Between her thighs.

"I'm fine," he murmured, shifting her legs farther apart with a nudge. "Very fine."

"Alright then," she said with a breathless squeak.

Jack pulled back an inch and studied Jamie. Her head had dropped back, her hands reaching out for the towel rack, the counter. Her stomach rose and fell anxiously. Shifting on his knees to a more comfortable position, Jack spread her with his thumbs and swallowed hard. The ripeness of her body, the curve of her thighs, her breasts, her backside. The way she was gleaming moist for him sent blood rushing south, his mouth hot and dry.

"What are you doing?"

"Looking at you." And getting really turned on. Wow, he could really learn to appreciate her body. She was a work of art. Worth ten million and then some.

Shifting one finger, he dipped it inside her. Jamie gave a startled cry. Jack stroked her long and deep, then pulled back. She sagged forward, her thighs bumping his shoulders.

He put his finger in his mouth. Sucked. Tasted Jamie's musky desire. Heard her gasp.

Then pushed deep inside her again, mixing the slickness of his saliva on his finger with the hot smoothness of her core, enjoying the way she jerked reflexively.

"Oh, it's cool from your mouth . . . it feels different."

He could tell she liked it, could hear the growing excitement in her voice, the relaxing of her body down onto his finger, her thighs trembling. But he wanted to hear it. "Is that bad or good?" he asked as he stroked in and out, avoiding her swollen clitoris.

"Good . . . very good."

So Jack pulled out and licked his finger again. Slid it back into her while she moaned, wiggled, tossed her head side to side. He did it again, and again, until his lips were slick and his finger slippery, until Jamie was whimpering and begging and knocking forward onto him.

Until he was so hard he was in pain, and his head swam, eyes narrowly focused on Jamie, on the pink prettiness of her body, the intimacy of what they were doing, what they shared.

And when he thought they might both break, he abandoned his finger and went in with his mouth. The taste of her exploded over his tongue, the warmth of her thighs surrounded him, and he closed his eyes in pleasure, held her ass tight when she bucked and thrashed.

"Jack! Oh, my, good gracious."

Lifting his tongue up and down in slow movements, Jack

savored the way Jamie felt, the way she opened for him, trusted him. Glancing to his right, he watched them in the mirror, his head buried between her thighs, Jamie's back arching, her cheeks flushed with passion.

It was the sexiest, most beautiful thing he'd ever seen.

Focusing forward, he picked up the pace, gave a little suck on her clitoris, and held her tight when she broke in an explosive climax.

She moaned, she pinched his shoulders, she jerked backward, but Jack held on and drew out her pleasure even after she started pushing him away.

It was amazing. She was amazing. And for the first time, he felt as though he understood. That when you love a woman, your pleasure builds from hers.

Jack pulled back and wiped his mouth. He glanced up at Jamie as she shook her head and blinked. She looked dazed and delirious with pleasure.

Just right.

"Now we can go to the bedroom," he said.

"Oh, mercy," was her response.

Jamie tumbled down onto the bed, body flushed with pleasure, inner thighs still tingling. The all white bed appealed to her in its crispness, its stark contrast against the dark paneled walls.

"It looks like a ship cabin in here," she murmured, pulling a stray hair off her lip as she settled her head on a fluffy down pillow, using a second one to cover her naked body.

Jack was stripping his pants off in front of her, his erection springing up. "Ahoy, matey," he said, making her laugh.

He could look so serious when he said things like that—he was deadpan, subtle, where she was always so obvious. She liked that about him.

She loved him. So, so much.

"Come to bed, Jack."

"In a sec." He leaned over the chair, giving her a good

shot of tight buns. He stood back up, a condom wrapper in his hand. "Do that again."

"What?"

"That look." His voice thickened. "The one that says, *Get over here because I want you and love you.*"

"That one's easy to do." Her heart was thudding, her nipples hardening as new desire sprang to life. For the first time ever in her life, Jamie felt sultry. Powerful in her sexuality. "But I don't want you to get tired of it."

"Never." Jack met her gaze with a hot, hungry one. "Tell me again how you feel about me."

Jamie swallowed back the thick arousal that crowded her mouth, made her tongue swollen. She dragged the pillow off of her body and dropped it to the side. Licking her lips, chest rising and falling rapidly, she dragged in a breath. She was turned on and shocked at herself, but she felt confident. "I love you, Jack."

It was so easy to say that, to mean it.

"I love you, too. God, I can't believe how much."

Hands on the bed, he slid over her, covering her with his hard, warm body. "You feel good."

Jamie sighed, content from her orgasm, from being with Jack like this. "The wedding was very lovely."

"Mm-hmm." He nuzzled in her neck, rubbing his lips over her flesh.

"Caroline seemed so happy." Jamie wrapped her arms around his back, caressing him down toward his waist. His skin was hot, hard, his muscles tightening and relaxing as he moved over her, suckling her breasts. Jack was built, more than she would have expected for his lean frame, but he sported well-defined muscles that rippled when he moved. And it pleased her as she lay there stroking him.

"Yep."

"You looked very handsome in your tux." Jamie crossed her feet at her ankles, feeling warm and cozy and only a minute or two from falling asleep.

Jack bit her nipple.

"Ouch! Dang, that hurts." It did, but it also was arousing. Sleep thoughts fled as Jack reached down and grabbed her ankle.

He uncrossed it. Spread her. "Don't close your legs to me."

Liquid heat pooled between her thighs as cool air swept over her warm skin. He was giving her that intense look again—that teasing, yet I really mean it kind of look. It was dark and a little dangerous, his hand still on her ankle.

"I'm always open to you," she told him. "Unless you give me reason to close myself off."

This was her leaping off into trust, and he had to meet her there, or she wasn't sure she could take the risk.

"I promise to not screw this up." He stroked her ankle, up the back of her calf. "Thank you, Jamie. For everything. For you."

His lips followed his fingers, tracing the outline of her daisy-chain tattoo, then continued in a sensual climb from ankle, to calf, to the back of her knee and beyond. To the tight trembling flesh of her thighs, and the creamy wet center of her body. She shouldn't let him pleasure her again, she shouldn't be so selfish and take another orgasm before he'd had his first, but he was so talented, the way he stroked and plucked at her.

It was like drinking too much wine. Her head swam, her voice was too loud, and her body moved with a languid lurching as she lay there, thoughts scattered. Fingers clutching the pillow she had abandoned earlier, Jamie cried out when the hard thickness of his tongue pushed into her.

"No." She tried to wiggle away, desperately turned on, wanting more than his tongue.

"No?" He looked at her, then gave a flick of his tongue just to torture her. "You don't like it?"

"I like it too much." She pulled back her hips, tried to slide up the bed away from him. She knew those prickling pulsing sensations vibrating around her inner thighs. One more lick and she was going to explode.

"Ah. So you want cock instead, is that it?"

Jamie flushed. Her mouth opened, but nothing came out. She wasn't a prude, she wasn't inexperienced, but she wasn't used to Jack's aggression either. Jamie had always dated men who were solicitous and nonconfrontational. They weren't into discussing what they were doing; they just quietly went about their business, efficiently getting things where they needed to go.

Men who thought she was sweet and a bit dull. Men who loved her and left her, because she would never be exciting. Never be anything more than maternal.

"I can be gentle. I can be loving, Jamie." He covered her with his body, heavy and hard.

With one hand, he spread her folds apart, stroked her with the tip of his erection. She moaned, her legs jerking in reflex as her clitoris spasmed in pleasure.

"But it will always be raw with me. That's something I can't help. Because to me you're Venus, a total goddess." And he shoved inside her.

Oh, dang it. Jamie tensed everywhere, holding on to him, feeling that deep, intense rush of ecstasy as he filled her. He stroked in her, then again, with delicious thoroughness, before pulling completely out.

"Just a little tease," he murmured when she cried out in disappointment.

He kissed her with biting little sucks on her bottom lip, with a hot plunging tongue, with wet urgent presses that had her scrambling to keep up, squirming on the bed. She wiggled her hips, trying to get closer to him, trying to coax him back inside, knowing she was going to die from desperation if he didn't get back in there and finish what he'd started.

But Jack leaned more heavily on her, pinning her beneath him so she couldn't move. Couldn't wiggle, couldn't thrust her hips, couldn't reach her hand down and stroke his erection, maneuver it into her. "I'm not allowed to move?"

"I was just afraid you might flip yourself off the bed." He sucked her neck, pulling her skin out just a smidge, his face arranged in what could only be called a smirk.

"You're so considerate." Jamie tried to move her hips again, bouncing the mattress a little. "But I think I'll be okay. If I start to fall, I'll just grab on to you."

"I would catch you." He eased up on her, bent over to kiss each of her nipples softly.

"I know." Jamie scooted down, found him with her fingers and stroked. He needed to know he wasn't always going to lead the charge. Before he could protest or do more than bite off a curse, she aligned her hips and thrust, pushing him inside her. Her hand, still wrapped around the length of him, kept him from filling her all the way, but it was still more than nothing. It was damn good, and she closed her eyes briefly, her body throbbing and aching.

She didn't think he would pull away, and she was right. He took over the pace, pushing in and out, her gripping hand sliding along the slick, thick length of him.

"Oh, yes, Jamie, shit, that's good."

It was. It was arousing to feel that impact, that wet hardness as it shoved into her, the way her body moistened, opened up for him. She moaned in soft, frantic little jerks, careening toward an orgasm quickly.

When she yanked her hand back suddenly and he slammed into her full force, his pelvis rocking hers, she came with a scream, tearing at the bedsheets. "Oh, oh, oh," she said because no other words would form as she shuddered and jerked and dripped with pleasure.

"I do love you," he said. Then exploded inside her, fierce and silent, jaw clenched, brow furrowed, muscles straining, cheeks sucked in.

"Yes." There was a world of meaning in that one word, and she hoped he understood. That yes, she knew he loved her. Yes, she loved him, too. Yes, he was The One, the one and only man for her.

Ever.

Yes, to the future, and yes to everything.

Jack knew he wasn't dreaming. Never could he have imagined anything this fucking hot.

Jamie sucking him in her mouth, making little slurping sounds.

After catching a power nap, and scarfing down half the food in the minibar, he had woken Jamie up, offered her champagne.

She had taken two sips, licked her pink lips, then set the glass down and gone between his legs.

Where she was driving him crazy.

A steely hold on his thighs, she rocked him forward, into her mouth, over and over, while he dug into her hair and tried not to embarrass himself by whimpering. He did moan though, as he buried himself in that hot hole, eyes half closed as he strained on his knees.

Then she slid down onto her stomach, while still sucking him, her knees going out, feet together. He thought she was getting more comfortable, altering the angle of her neck to take him deeper, which she did. Jack gripped her head harder, knuckles white.

But then her breathing got erratic, her movements jerky, and he suddenly realized that his thrusts were pressing her breasts and clitoris down into the mattress in teasing little brushes. Whether she had known that would happen or not, she clearly liked the end result. She was doing that ex-cited little squirm she had. The floral tattoo around her ankle jerked, blurring in his line of vision, as she wiggled around on the bed.

Which turned him on even more.

He pumped harder, while she pulled him toward her. Her lips were shiny, spread around his cock, and her curls fell forward over her cheeks, nose. It was overwhelming, what he felt for her. It was intense, consuming, amazing, and he had to have her, all of her.

Had to let her know he knew what she was saying with her actions. That she was comfortable showing all of herself to him, that she trusted him. And he had immense gratitude for what she was offering him.

Leaning forward, he ran a shaky hand over the smoothness of her ass, dipping down between her cheeks. She jerked slightly, then her knees spread just a little bit farther in invitation. Jack knew he was pressing her face into his gut, but he didn't care. He wanted to give her some of the ecstasy he was feeling.

So he dipped his middle finger deep down inside her, stretching her sideways before pulling back, trailing her moisture up and over her backside, as goose bumps rose on her flesh.

"I want to be inside you but I don't want you to stop doing this."

"We have all night," she said, pulling back off him with a smacking pop. "We can do both."

"You like that position, don't you?" He bumped his cock against her lips. "The sheets are tickling your nipples and clit, aren't they?"

"Yes." Voice sultry and low, she licked at the tip of his erection. "I could probably come like this, with your finger."

"Oh, really?" The very idea intrigued him. That she could have an orgasm while he was coming in her mouth, it fed his fantasies.

The maneuver was a little awkward for both of them, but it was worth it when she made a mewling, whimpering sound as he buried his finger in her. Buried himself in her mouth, cutting off her groan.

He stroked and she licked and they both lost it, climaxing together, blending their pleasure until Jack wasn't sure where he stopped and she started.

Chapter 21

Jack had to shake his head as he and Jamie left the diner with Pops and Austin. He wasn't sure how he'd wound up with a cranky old man and a crankier fourteen-year-old kid on his hands, but it occurred to him that somehow they had all become a package deal.

If Jamie was going to marry him, which he sincerely hoped, she was going to get stuck with these yahoos, too. Especially since he was in the process of officially making himself Austin's foster parent.

"That lunch sucked," Austin complained. "If you're going to take me out for lunch, you should take me someplace *good*." The wheels of his skateboard squeaked as he rolled up ahead of them.

"I was thinking the same thing, kid," Pops said. "Here I get sprung from the nursing home and I get some weenie piece of fish slapped in front of me."

Jack pushed Pops's wheelchair and rolled his eyes. "Next time I'll leave both of you in lockup, and I'll go to lunch without you. Find myself some better company." Not that he really minded their complaining. It seemed nice and normal to be this way, walking home from a lunch that he had to admit was definitely lacking in taste. "Take Jamie off by myself."

"Jamie wouldn't do that, would you?" Pops glanced at

them over his shoulder. "She has respect for her elders, un-like you."

Jamie laughed. "I would never abandon you, Will."

"See?"

Jack kissed Jamie's temple and whispered in her ear. "We can outrun these two, you know. Just say the word and we'll cross the street and lose them in the park."

She hooked her arm through his and smiled. Beamed, ac-tually. He was hoping it was love and afterglow from the night before. And it would never rub off. He loved seeing that smile directed at him.

"Austin's faster than me," she told him.

"Hey, Austin, go grab me a coffee, will ya? There's a deli right on the left." He handed him a five when Austin shrugged in bored acquiescence.

"You're crazy to give that kid money. He might not come back," Pops said.

"You know, you've got to have trust. If he takes off, so what? But if he doesn't, well, that's a good thing." He should have trusted Jamie in the beginning. Should have given her more reason to trust him.

"You're a good man, Jack-o. But that lunch did suck."

Jack laughed. They were almost to the deli when he sud-denly saw him, Jim Peters, Jamie's father, standing across the street in front of his building. Jamie made a soft sound next to him.

She was wearing an orange-colored tank top and a white floral skirt that fell above her knees, and when he glanced over at her, he saw her face was the same color as her shirt, her freckles stark and vivid on her pale skin. It struck him again how beautiful she was. How much he loved her.

"Sweetheart . . . I didn't know he'd be here. Do you want me to talk to him?"

Jamie shook her head. "It's fine. I want to speak to him myself." She stepped in front of the deli store right as Austin came rolling out, a coffee in one hand, a big cookie in the other.

"Watch—"

Too late. Austin slammed into Jamie, who tripped over Pops's wheelchair. Jack grabbed her arm to steady her and flinched when coffee hit him in the chest. When the commotion died down, he saw they were all covered in coffee splatters except for Austin.

"Shit. Sorry." Austin took a bite of the cookie and stepped back a full foot, like he was thinking of bolting.

Jamie blinked, a big brown wet spot on her breasts. Jack patted his pockets as if napkins were suddenly going to materialize. Pops wiped drippage off his cheek.

Then she started laughing. Jack brushed at his own wet T-shirt and grinned in relief, glad to see Jamie was still Jamie. She didn't sweat the small stuff.

"It's okay, Austin," she said. "Accidents happen." Her gaze was already floating across the street to her father.

Jim had spotted them. When Jamie waved to him, he paused a minute, then raised his hand back.

They all stood around, covered in coffee, waiting expectantly as Jim crossed the street.

It occurred to Jack that maybe the rest of them should leave. But Jamie was gripping his hand and not easing up as Jim stopped in front of them, hands in his pockets.

"Hi," he said. "Do you know who I am?"

Jamie nodded.

Jim nodded, his eyes panicked and raw, as he looked away.

Jack stood helpless, wishing he could do this for Jamie.

But he didn't need to.

She stood tall and proud, compassion in her eyes, and said, "I forgive you, Dad. And I love you."

Jack was so damn proud of her and so scared for her heart, he realized he was holding his breath.

"Well, say something," Pops told Jim after a long second had dragged out. "Girl tells you she loves you, you don't just stand there gawking at her."

Her father swiped at his eyes, blinking hard. "Jesus. I love you, too, Jamie Lynn. I always have. Every damn day I've been without you. God, I can't believe this. I didn't cry when they sent me to prison and here I am crying in the middle of Hudson Street."

"Dude, don't worry about it," Austin said.

"Happens to the best of us," Pops said.

"Can the two of you—" *go to hell* came to mind, but Jack restrained himself. "Go get yourself a better lunch." He pulled out a twenty and handed it to Pops, who waved it smugly in Austin's face.

"I get to hold the money again."

"That's only 'cuz I can't hold the money and push you at the same time." Austin dropped his skateboard in Pops's lap and grabbed the wheelchair handles. "How fast can we get this thing going?"

Jack winced as they hit the door with the footrests on the chair, but they made it into the deli with minimal swearing and more speed than was probably advisable.

But at least they were gone. Now if he could get Jamie to release his hand from her iron grip, he could exit, too, and let her talk to her father.

Jamie was aware that Jack was trying to gently remove his hand from hers, but there was no way in hell she was letting him leave her. Her father was still just kind of staring at her, and she felt like at any given second her legs might give out. She needed Jack's strength, support.

"After all this time I can't believe I'm looking at you," her father said, shaking his head. "That you're this close. You're beautiful. And you look like me. Except you have your mother's eyes. Expressive."

She wasn't sure what to say, so she just smiled. This was his move.

"I'm sorry," he whispered. "I just wanted to protect the both of you. I loved you and your mother more than anything and I was just a damn coward, Jamie Lynn. Do you understand that? That I was weak, not that I didn't care."

"I understand. And trust me, I know a thing or two about being scared." She'd been putting Jack and herself through hell for the past two weeks for that very reason. An image of the night before popped into her head. Well, it hadn't been *all* hell.

"So things are going well for you? You like your job, living in New York?"

"Yes. I love my job and I've been happy here. I have great friends and . . . Jack." His hand squeezed hers.

"You've got a good guy here, that's for sure. Gave me his couch to sleep on when he found out I had nowhere to go. He called shelters all over town, but when no one had room, he just opened his apartment to me." Her father turned to Jack. "And I thank you for that. I'm sorry for leaving the way I did."

"I think if Jamie is forgiving you, maybe it's time you forgive yourself, Jim, and start over."

That choked Jamie up. She felt the tears escape her eyes and start tumbling down her cheeks. Then suddenly she found herself caught up in her father's arms, his callused hands patting her back.

"Don't cry, baby girl. It's alright. We'll make it alright."

He smelled the way she remembered. Like leather and Irish Spring.

That was a good scent. And there were good memories, right there, pulled up out of her childhood memory.

"Thanks. With both of us willing, we'll definitely make it alright." Jamie pulled back and saw Pops and Austin coming out of the deli with a large bag in Pops's lap.

"Did you get some lunch?" Jack was holding her hand, keeping her close to him, and it was a nice, warm, fuzzy-blanket feeling.

She was surrounded by people who cared about her, and she had a darn good life.

"Yeah. We got Reubens," Pops said. "Bring on the cheese, I always say."

"Why don't we go to my place and let Jamie and Jim talk a little more."

Jamie nodded. "There are a ton of things I want to ask you about, Dad."

Her father crossed his arms over his chest. "I can't tell you how good it feels to be called Dad again."

"Hey, there's like a really hairy dude dressed as a lady trying to get your attention," Austin said, gesturing down the sidewalk.

"What?" Jamie looked in the direction he was pointing.

Jack squeezed her hand tighter and asked in puzzlement, "Isn't that the nut job who was talking to you last night in the hall at the reception?"

Of course it was. Beckwith was striding down the street, wearing a white sundress with Donna Reed pearls and waving at her frantically.

"Jamie! Honey baby, we need to talk."

Didn't they always. "What's the matter, Beckwith?" She didn't bother to ask about the dress. There was no telling.

"You know this guy?" Jack asked in disbelief, wrapping his arm tighter around her waist.

"Oh, yeah."

"Allison told me you were probably here," Beckwith called as he jogged the last few feet to her. Suddenly he drew up short. "Oh my gawd," he said as he took in the group collected around her. "Who are all these *men* around you? And why is this one prettier than me?" he asked, pointing to Jack.

Jack blanched. Jamie laughed. "Beckwith, this is Jack Davidson, Will Hathaway, and Austin. Just Austin," she said in a James Bond imitation voice. "And my father, Jim Peters. This is Beckwith Tripp, professional psychic."

"Psychic? Dude, tell my fortune," Austin begged. "But not if it sucks—just make something up if it sucks."

But Beckwith was whipping his hands around in a sort of feminine karate chop as if he were being assaulted. "Whoa, too many sensations. But this makes so much sense, sugar. Oh, oh, oh, this all makes sense. Sadness," he said, pointing to her father. "Darth Vader, and prison." His finger shot over to Austin. "Prison. Prison? Kid, you're too young to be a criminal. You'd better straighten out. But you're past, present, and future in Jamie's karma. These two both have the tattoos, we've got the light hair."

Beckwith touched Pops's shirt, causing the older man to swat at him.

"Coffee. Food. Dang, I am so good."

She had no idea what Beckwith was talking about.

"Too many men, Jamie. They were all blending together, mixing with my mojo." Finally he reached over and patted Jack on the shoulder, almost knocking Jack into the street. "He is the one for you! Shit, that's so sweet. You didn't have sex with him for nothing after all."

While Jack sputtered, Jamie saw what Beckwith was trying to say. He'd seen them all in her destiny. Pops, Austin, her father. And Jack.

"Oh, Beck."

Dang, she was going to cry. She'd chosen her destiny, and it was a good one.

"I know, I know," Beckwith said, looking triumphant. "Okay, people. Everyone." He clapped his hands together loudly. "With the true gift of a psychic, I can tell these two crazy kids need time alone. Everyone but Jamie and Jack needs to scat."

"Can we go into the apartment?" Pops asked. "Or at least the lobby? My cheese is congealing."

"Sure, old man." Austin pushed the wheelchair, and Beckwith walked alongside it, giving a minilecture on karma, and the inappropriateness of giving predictions for old people and kids. Jim had lit up a cigarette and was ambling along beside them, listening attentively.

"What the hell just happened?" Jack asked.

"I think my father and I made some headway."

"That's great. But who was the guy in the dress? And do you think we can duck out and go hide at your place?"

She shook her head and grinned. "Not a chance. They'll find us. Beckwith's psychic, you know."

"You really think he is?"

"I know he is. He told me about you, remember. That you'd make me so happy other people would gag at the look on my face."

"Is it true? I make you happy to the point of causing illness in others?"

"Yes. Very much so."

"Did he predict this?" Jack picked her up, held her right under her ass, enjoying the feel of her tight up against him. He wasn't letting her go, ever again. "Marry me. I don't want to wait, there's no reason to wait when I feel this way."

She sniffled. "No, he didn't."

She hid her head in his shoulder, and Jack felt a little panic rising. She wasn't answering him.

"Marry me, Jamie, and tell me where to give my money. Help me find a new start, a new apartment that we can afford on our pitiful do-gooder salaries."

Then she lifted her head and said, "Yes. I'll marry you."

Jack spun her around, nearly taking out a chihuahua trotting by on his leash. "Yes! That is totally the right answer."

She laughed, her pert little nose lining up with his as she dusted a kiss across his lips. "I think so. And you don't have to give away your money, Jack. I'm not that insecure, nor am I that selfish. You worked hard to earn that money, and you deserve to keep it and do whatever you want with it."

Jack put her on the ground, stunned. "Are you sure? I don't want the money between us, Jamie Lynn. Seriously." But he'd be a liar if he didn't admit he was glad. He kind of liked his cash.

"I know you're a good man, a generous man. You donate a ton of your time and mental resources to other people. I have no problem with you keeping what's yours." Sincerity shone in her eyes.

"You're amazing," he said, kissing the tip of her nose. "And do you know, Jamie Lynn, that I have the feeling I was waiting to meet you?"

She sniffled as he repeated words he'd spoken that first night they'd met. "I couldn't agree more." Then she grinned. "You know what this means, don't you?"

"What?"

"Beckwith's going to want to be a bridesmaid."

Don't miss this sneak peek at
Shannon McKenna's
HOT NIGHT.
Available now from Brava!

Abby was floating. The sensual heft of Zan's black leather jacket felt wonderful on her shoulders, even though it hung halfway down to her thighs.

They'd reached the end of the boardwalk, where the lights began to fade. Beyond the boardwalk, the warehouse district began. They'd walked the whole boardwalk, talking and laughing, and at some point, their hands had swung together and sort of just . . . stuck. Warmth seeking warmth. Her hand tingled joyfully in his grip.

The worst had happened. Aside from his sex appeal, she simply liked him. She liked the way he laughed, his turn of phrase, his ironic sense of humor. He was smart, honest, earthy, funny. Maybe, just maybe, she could trust herself this time.

Their strolling slowed to a stop at the end of the boardwalk.

"Should we, ah, walk back to your van?" she ventured.

"This is where I live," he told her.

She looked around. "Here? But this isn't a residential district."

"Not yet," he said. "It will be soon. See that building, over there? It used to be a factory of some kind, in the twenties, I think. The top floor, with the big arched windows, that's my place."

There was just enough light to make out the silent question in his eyes. She exhaled slowly. "Are you going to invite me up, or what?"

"You know damn well that you're invited," he said. "More than invited. I'll get down on my knees and beg, if you want me to."

The full moon appeared in a window of scudding clouds, then disappeared again. "It wouldn't be smart," she said. "I don't know you."

"I'll teach you," he offered. "Crash course in Zan Duncan. What do you want to know? Hobbies, pet peeves, favorite leisure activities?"

She would put it to the test of her preliminary checklist, and make her decision based on that. "Don't tell me," she said. "Let me guess. You're a martial arts expert, right?"

"Uh, yeah. Aikido is my favorite discipline. I like kung fu, too."

She nodded, stomach clenching. There it was, the first black mark on the no-no's checklist. Though it was hardly fair to disqualify him for that, since he'd saved her butt with those skills the night before.

So that one didn't count. On to the next no-no. "Do you have a motorcycle?"

He looked puzzled. "Several of them. Why? Want to go for a ride?"

Abby's heart sank. "No. One last question. Do you own guns?"

Zan's face stiffened. "Wait. Are these trick questions?"

"You do, don't you?" she persisted.

"My late father was a cop." His voice had gone hard. "I have his service Beretta. And I have a hunting rifle. Why? Are you going to talk yourself out of being with me because of superficial shit like that?"

Abby's laugh felt brittle. "Superficial. That's Abby Maitland."

"No, it is not," he said. "That's not Abby Maitland at all."

"You don't know the first thing about me, Zan."

"Yes, I do." His dimple quivered. "I know first things, second things, third things. You've got piss-poor taste in boyfriends, to start."

Abby was stung. "Those guys were not my boyfriends! I didn't even know them! I've just had a run of bad luck lately!"

"Your luck is about to change, Abby." His voice was low and velvety. "I know a lot about you. I know how to get into your apartment. How to turn your cat into a noodle. The magnets on your fridge, the view from your window. Your perfume. I could find you blindfolded in a room full of strangers." His fingers penetrated the veil of her hair, his forefinger stroking the back of her neck with controlled gentleness. "And I learn fast. Give me ten minutes, and I'd know lots more."

"Oh," she breathed. His hand slid through her hair, settled on her shoulder. The delicious heat burned her, right through his jacket.

"I know you've got at least two of those expensive dresses that drive guys nuts. And I bet you've got more than two. You've got a whole closet full of hot little outfits like that. Right?" He cupped her jaw, turning her head until she was looking into his fathomless eyes.

Her heart hammered. "I've got a . . . a pretty nice wardrobe, yes."

"I'd like to see them." His voice was sensual. "Someday maybe you can model them all for me. In the privacy of your bedroom."

"Zan—"

"I love it when you say my name," he said. "I love your voice. Your accent. Based on your taste in dresses, I'm willing to bet that you like fancy, expensive lingerie, too. Am I right? Tell me I'm right."

"Time out," she said, breathless. "Let's not go there."

"Oh, but we've already arrived." His breath was warm against her throat. "Locksmiths are detail maniacs. Look at the palm of your hand, for instance. Here, let me see." He lifted her hand into the light from the nearest of the street-lamps. "Behold, your destiny."

It was silly and irrational, but it made her self-conscious to have him look at the lines on her hand. As if he actually could look right into her mind. Past, future, fears, mistakes, desires, all laid out for anyone smart and sensitive enough to decode it. "Zan. Give me my hand back."

"Not yet. Oh . . . wow. Check this out," he whispered.

"What?" she demanded.

He shook his head with mock gravity and pressed a kiss to her knuckles. "It's too soon to say what I see. I don't want to scare you off."

"Oh, please," she said unsteadily. "You are so full of it."

"And you're so scared. Why? I'm a righteous dude. Good as gold." He stroked her wrist. "Ever try cracking a safe without drilling it? It's a string of numbers that never ends. Hour after hour, detail after detail. That's concentration." He pressed his lips against her knuckles.

"What does concentration have to do with anything?"

"It has everything to do with everything. That's what I want to do to you, Abby. Concentrate, intensely, minutely. Hour after hour, detail after detail. Until I crack all the codes, find all the keys to all your secret places. Until I'm so deep inside ya . . ." his lips kissed their way up her wrist ". . . . that we're a single being."

She leaned against him, and let him cradle her in his strong arms. His warm lips coaxed her into opening to the gentle, sensual exploration of his tongue. "Come up with me," he whispered. "Please."

She nodded. Zan's arm circled her waist, fitting her body against his. It felt so right. No awkwardness, no stumbling, all smooth. Perfect.

Please turn the page for a preview
of the next book in Jessica Inclán's
marvelous, magical trilogy,
REASON TO BELIEVE,
a Zebra trade paperback available now!

Fabia cut off the communication and opened her door, quickly running down the hall and stairs and then pushing out onto the street. The temperature had dropped even more than the report had predicted, Fabia's cheeks flushed from the slick slap of cold air. Rubbing her gloved hands together, she walked toward the man, slowing as she neared him.

"Hello," she said softly, blinking against the streetlight.

He stared at her—no, past her—his face expressionless. His face was smudged with dirt, a deep, dark red scratch running from temple to jaw, one eye blackened. Blood swelled the skin under his eye and hung in a painful purple moon over his cheek. As Fabia moved closer, she realized that his hair wasn't so much matted from the wet, dank air as from dried blood. There was a clear, perfect circle of reddish, broken skin around his neck, and she noticed now that the dirt she'd seen under his nails this morning was actually blood.

Whatever had happened, he'd fought back. Whoever he'd fought with probably looked as bad as he did.

"Are you all right?"

The man turned to her, tried to look up, and then took a deep breath, his mouth trying to move. He was trembling, his arms tight against his body now, his black eyes filled with fog and sadness. Again, she tried to reach for his mind, but the iron wall was still there, planted solidly.

What do you think? Fabia asked Niall without even meaning to.

All that blood, Niall thought. *Maybe it's not his. Moyenne are messy murderers.*

He hardly looks capable of a right killing, Fabia thought.

True. He didn't do his level best, there. So he might be on the lam. Injured from the barbed wire he crawled under, Niall thought. *Just call the police.*

Fabia stared at the man, ignoring Niall for a moment. Maybe she couldn't read the man's mind, but there was something about him. Something kind even in his quiet, painful desperation.

Bloody bleeding heart, Niall thought. *But just be ready to escape. Be prepared to step into the gray, okay? Hop back to your flat.*

Yes, sir, Fabia thought, shaking her head. But Niall was right. It was easier to extend this kindness knowing that if the man grew strange or crazy or even dangerous, she could disappear in an instant, traveling through matter to the police station where she could report the crime she'd just escaped. The *Moyenne* she worked with at the clinic were always amazed that Fabia would go to flophouses and tenements and dark alleys looking for clients. What she couldn't tell them was that she was protecting them by doing so, keeping them away from danger from which they might not be able to escape.

Fabia bent down, trying to attract his gaze. But he wouldn't look at her, and she could feel the tension radiating from inside him.

"Hi, there," she said. "My name's Fabia Fair. I live at the flat just down a bit."

He didn't move his eyes, but he blinked, once, twice.

"Would you like to come with me?" Fabia said, crouching down farther and looking into the man's desperate, searching eyes. "How about a wee bit to eat?"

He licked his lips, breathing in, scanning the ground as if he'd dropped some change. *Not drunk*, Fabia thought. *Schizophrenic.*

Perfect, Niall thought. *Go from Cadeyrn to just another crazy. Get yourself into another fankle.*

Haver on, man! Would you mind affording me some space here? she thought back. *Go watch your bleeding telly.*

Fabia closed her mind to her brother and moved closer to the man. He was shaking, his knees hitting together. Again, he moved his mouth, but then shook his head, tears streaming from the corners of his eyes.

Fabia watched him, trying everything she knew to get inside his mind, but there was no opening, as if the block was put there on purpose. And not by the man, who clearly was in no shape to create or even maintain a block, even if he were *Croyant*, magic, like her. And there was something about him, even with his quaking gaze and his long, thin, dirty body. Fabia couldn't read his mind, but she could feel . . . kindness.

"All right," Fabia said. "That's it. Please, come with me."

She stood up straight and held out her hand. The man breathed in, looking at her hand and then her face, her hand, her face, and then slowly, he lifted his dirty palm from his knee, studying his movements with surprise as if he'd never moved before. His fingers quivered, shook, and Fabia took them in her small gloved hand, feeling how cold he was even through the leather and wool.

Shit, she thought to herself, hating how *Moyenne* treated their castaways, knowing that in her world, the world of *Les Croyants des Trois*, this man would have food and a bath and a bed, no matter what was wrong with him. Adalbert Baird made sure of that, finding places for the damaged and weak—the only people who escaped his care were the ones who disdained it. Like Caderyn Macara. Like Quain Dalzeil. *And what will happen if Quain wins?* she thought.

We'll end up like this poor sod, Niall thought.

Shut it, Fabia thought and clutched the man's hand more tightly.

"Come on," she said. "Don't be scared."

But the man was scared. More than scared. She felt his fear in the energy coming off his body, in the sizzling whites of his distracted eyes, in his stiff, hesitant walk. Who had done this to him? What had happened?

"It's all right," Fabia said, her hand holding his as they walked slowly to the door of her building. "You'll be fine."

He turned to look at her, his black eyes so dark she couldn't see the irises. His forehead was creased with worry, his face gray with cold and hunger and fear. Despite the filth on his clothing, the blood on his head and body, and his clearly distressed mind, Fabia wanted to stop, pull him to her, and comfort him.

Here's a look at Lori Foster's
"Do You Hear What I Hear?" in
A VERY MERRY CHRISTMAS,
available now from Brava . . .

He was thinking of warm Christmas cookies, songs on the piano, and strings of popcorn, when he spotted the confusion in front of the funeral home. Lights from a police car flashed blue and red and an elderly couple, bundled in coats over pajamas, gestured with excitement.

Ozzie pulled up behind the cruiser and parked. It took him only moments to identify himself to the officer and to find out that someone had stolen a donkey from the Nativity scene erected on the funeral home's lawn.

Marci. Somehow, he just knew she was behind this. She'd probably claim the damned donkey was shy, or that he didn't like the colored lights, or God-knew-what. But Ozzie's instincts screamed and so, with a few more words to the officer, he gave up on the idea of sleep and instead headed to Marci's apartment.

Lucius used to live in the apartment across from Marci but, thankfully, he'd recently moved out—so Ozzie didn't have to worry about Lucius finding him at Marci's door. He and Bethany had purchased a home of their own. Lucius still owned the apartment building, but he left Marci in charge of it.

Not a good idea, in Ozzie's opinion, given that Marci was a kook. But far be it for him to tell Lucius how to run his business.

When he parked in front of the building, Ozzie looked toward Marci's porch window and, sure enough, her inside lights were on. Okay, so it was seven-thirty and she was maybe getting ready for work.

Or hiding a donkey.

Ozzie slammed his truck door, trudged through the crunchy snow and ice, and went up the walk, inside, and up to Marci's door. He knocked twice.

Breathless, Marci yelled, "Just a moment!"

His body twitched. More specifically, his cock sat up and took notice of her proximity. *Damn it.*

A full minute later, Marci opened the door. A look of pleasure replaced her formal politeness. "Osbourne. What a surprise."

He stared down at her and thought, if she'd just not talk about animals, if she'd just smile at him like that, he'd be happy to ravish her for, oh . . . a few hours maybe.

When he said nothing, her smile widened, affecting him like a hot lick. She wore a soft pink chenille robe, belted tight around her tiny waist. Her small feet were bare, crossed one over the other to ward off the chill. Her baby-fine, straight brown hair had the mussed look of a woman fresh out of bed—or fresh inside from the blustery outdoors.

Shaking out of his stupor, Ozzie looked beyond her. He saw nothing out of the ordinary in her tiny apartment, but that didn't clear her.

She took a step closer to him, staring up in what seemed like provocation to him, a heated come-on, a . . .

She tilted her head and said, "Osbourne?"

Lust tied knots in his muscles. He cleared his throat. "Busy?"

Big blue eyes blinked at him, eyes so soft, and with such thick, long lashes she didn't need makeup. "I just got out of the shower, actually." She patted back a delicate yawn. "It's early. Would you like some coffee?"

He'd like her.

And, now a look at Jamie Denton's
romantic suspense novel,
THE MATCHMAKER.
Coming next month from Brava . . .

Travis winked at her and she tossed him a narrowed eye hiss before walking back to the open grave and Manny. "Get rid of that reporter," she said irritably to Travis. "Make sure he knows he's not to print a word until he hears from me."

Travis's smug expression faded into one of confusion. "What reporter?"

She pointed to where she'd last seen the NYT wannabe. "That . . ."

"Hello, Greer."

The husky undertone of *that* voice slammed into her with all the subtlety of a runaway freight train. ". . . reporter," she finished weakly as she turned around and faced her past.

The air between them sizzled. She looked into the breathtakingly handsome face of the one man from whom she had no secrets.

The high-pitched ringing in her ears deafened her. The ground beneath her feet shifted. This simply could not be happening. Why did that damned loose end she'd left dangling for so long have to become a noose tied around her neck today? Why now?

Ash.

Her every dream, her every regret rolled into one painful

reality staring her in the face. Those delicious dark brown eyes once filled with affection were now colder than the granite headstone behind him. She expected or deserved, nothing less.

"What the hell are *you* doing here?" she blurted rudely. The suit. She should've known. Standard FBI blue, she thought, remembering her own closet once filled with the same dull rainbow of subdued hues.

"The report you filed with VICAP. It was brought to my attention."

"Faith." Who else? Faith worked closely with Ash, and had been the only person she'd kept in contact with at the Bureau for a short time after she'd left. Of course Faith would've passed the report on to him. She was Ash's eyes, ears, nose and throat for crying out loud.

Ash nodded. There was an underlying arrogance to the slight curve of his mouth that set her teeth on edge one second, then made her as nervous as a whore trapped in a confessional with a judgmental priest the next.

"And you thought you'd just come on down and take over my investigation, is that it?"

Travis cleared his throat. "I thought you—"

She glared at her boss, warning him to shut up. True, she wanted no part of the investigation, but having Ash breathing down her neck wasn't something she was anywhere close to being able to handle.

Thankfully, Travis wasn't a stupid man. "Never mind," he said, then clamped his teeth around a half smoked, unlit cigar.

A glinting flash of light caught her eye when Ash moved his hands to tuck them into the front pockets of his trousers. Probably just the sun reflecting off his watch, she thought. Anything else was unthinkable.

"You know how the system works, Greer," he said with a slight shrug of his shoulders.

"You're right. I do. And this case doesn't come close to

meeting the criteria for ISU's involvement. I don't recall a section in the manual about steamrolling an investigation, either. You're not wanted here, Ash." She didn't want him anywhere near her. "Go home."

He leaned toward her and she breathed in his scent. Flashbacks of a different kind peppered her conscience. A private celebration. Candlelight. Champagne. Making love until dawn. His hands, his mouth. Never getting enough of each other.

"You develop a sudden understanding of the word?" he said in a low voice with enough of a hint of controlled anger to push her past the edge of reason.

 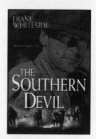